James Campbell was born in Inverness. During the war he flew on thirty-eight bombing operations with No. 158 Halifax Squadron based at Lisset, Yorkshire. His first novel, 'Maximum Effort', is the story of a morale-shattered bomber squadron and includes a chapter on the Nuremberg raid. After the war he returned to journalism, turning down the chance of continuing in the RAF on a short service commission. For the last twenty-two years he has been the Lobby Correspondent of a daily newspaper. In 1962 he was the only journalist to anticipate Selwyn Lloyd's 'lollipop' Budget, and Granada TV's 'What the Papers Say' acclaimed his story as "the scoop of the year".

Also by James Campbell

THE BOMBING OF NUREMBERG

James Campbell

Maximum Effort

Futura Publications Limited

A Futura Book

First published in Great Britain in 1957
by Frederick Muller Limited
First Futura Publications edition 1974
Reprinted 1977
ISBN 0 8600 7065 4
Printed in Great Britain by
C. Nicholls & Company Ltd
The Philips Park Press
Manchester.

Futura Publications Limited
49 Poland Street
LONDON WIA 2LG

To
ELIZABETH, MY MOTHER
and
IRENE, MY WIFE

1

THE pale wash of a January sun filtered into the mahogany
panelled room on the ground floor of the sombre, grey stone
mansion house hidden from the highway by the tall, gaunt
birch trees. It streamed over the wooden frames of the high wide
window to project watery squares of light on the quarter-inch-scale
air map of Western Europe.

The map sprawled across the wall in front of Air Commodore
Charles Dudley Cartingham's carved oak desk. Cartingham half
turned in his swivel chair and rested his great bulk awkwardly into
the green leather cushion of the seat. His mottled grey eyes
alighted on a black pin stuck in the map below Flamborough Head.
From this marker a thin red thread streaked across the blue shading
of the North Sea.

North of Texel Island the red cotton wheeled round another pin
and went off at an obtuse angle to a dead reckoning position south
of Bremen. From Bremen it ran in two zig-zag legs, before
arrowing eastwards. He noted that it skirted dangerously close to
red shaded patches which mushroomed from the German terrain,
before it pierced the big, black square that was Berlin.

A faint creak from the revolving chair lanced through the sparely
furnished room. Group Captain Hendry Frederick Dorton,
D.S.O., D.F.C., surveyed with calm, critical eyes the finely chiselled
profile of the Air Commodore and wondered, again, why Cartingham's face had not run to fat like the rest of his body.

Cartingham glanced from the map and his eyes met and held
those of the Group Captain. He cleared his throat, and his words
came slowly and deliberately.

"186's morale is bad, bloody bad. I find it hard to say this
but the rot has set in."

The Air Commodore paused and his hand stretched mechanically
towards the ebony-handled paper knife on his desk. Sitting back

7

in his chair he idly toyed with its long blunt blade. He was shrewd, he considered, in selecting Dorton—young enough to inspire and interpret the minds of operational aircrews, old enough at thirty-nine to co-ordinate and infuse life back into a squadron badly mauled in the saturation raids on the great cities of the Third Reich. More important, he thought, the man had the calibre to extract the maximum efficiency from aircrews and ground staff alike. Two gruelling tours of operations were behind him.

His tired hooded eyes gazed gently across the desk at the Group Captain. The flecks of iron grey along the sides of the jet black hair had not been there the last time they had met.

But then the Group Captain had not got his D.S.O. up six months ago. The high cheek-bones, the heavy bushy eyebrows and the obstinate set of the jaw gave Dorton a sternness that only his humorous brown eyes belied. He felt satisfied he could have done a lot worse than choose Dorton for the job of whipping 186 into shape.

"Only once in this last six weeks have they been able to put on a maximum effort. Even then it was an abortive one," Cartingham snapped. His fingers clenched on the paper knife, his knuckles showing white. "Their casualties have been shockingly high and their record of target aiming points correspondingly low. Tonight they've reached a new low—only nine aircraft taking part in the raid. Their sister satellite at Nassington, for instance, are operating twenty aircraft tonight."

Cartingham tossed the paper knife lightly on to the desk, and drummed on his blotting pad with a bony finger.

"The Air Marshal," he said firmly, "is determined that they get back to what a front line bomber squadron should be." The voice curt, and uncompromising rose in pitch. "Even hinted that he would disband them otherwise."

Looking speculatively at the ceiling, he said absently, "Group Captain Pittle was a sick man, a very sick man when he took over 186. Now we have had him rested. Frankly, he's on the verge of a nervous breakdown. Kept muttering about abominable luck and that the squadron had some sort of jonah around it. Yet they get the same crews and the same aircraft as every other squadron in the Group. . . ."

His eyes flicked back to Dorton and he laughed shortly but there was no humour in them. "Dammit," he growled, "he almost had me believing in this nonsense about a hoodoo! Of course, we may have overlooked the fact that, in building an operational main force of one thousand bombers with the reserves to keep that force operating two or three times a week, quality has to suffer to some degree."

He sighed and went on, "Still that doesn't solve the trouble at 186. Men who have done well at their operational training units either go missing very early after coming on the squadron's strength or, if they come through their first half-dozen trips, rapidly deteriorate in morale."

He broke off and looked thoughtful. He took a cigarette from a box at his elbow and pushed the box with a mechanical movement across the desk to the Group Captain. He lit his own cigarette, then leaned over to Dorton and gave him a light.

Dorton drew heavily on his cigarette. Before he had arrived at Group headquarters, he had, already had a fairly complete picture of the assignment waiting him. 186's dismal showing had filtered down, through its satellite station, to other squadrons in the Group. The deep furrows on the Air Commodore's brow tightened.

"Losses have been on the high side lately," he said softly. "I'm afraid they'll continue to fluctuate around the four per cent mark, even touch and go over the five per cent economic level. This is disastrous. On this four per cent basis, a squadron can be wiped out in twenty-five raids. Thirty raids a crew have to complete before they're rested. Can't blame them in some ways for working out the odds against coming through."

Dorton stubbed out his cigarette and looked sharply at the Air Commodore. "Thinking is bad, sir," he said brusquely. "They had plenty of time to ruminate on that before they put in for aircrew training. By the time they reach a squadron they should have their minds disciplined not to look too far ahead."

Cartingham sat rigid in his seat, staring vacantly at the wall map, his cigarette held limply in his hand.

Dorton's voice rasped cold and harsh in his ears. "Every now and then a squadron hits a bad spell. Sometimes it takes a while before their loss-rate gets back to normal. In the meanwhile, they start to conjure up all sorts of reasons why their luck has run out."

The Air Commodore nervously tapped the ash from his cigarette and moved restlessly in his chair before replying. "Yes, that's sometimes the case." Then curtly he added: "By the way, I have sent a new Wing Commander to 186. Carter's the name. Understand you were at Halton together?"

Before Dorton could answer, Cartingham went on: "I wasn't too keen about approaching Carter, as he was half-way through his third tour. However, I think the situation at 186 justifies the step I've taken. As you will appreciate, much depends on the Wing Commander in charge of flying."

Dorton stifled the anxiety which came over him. Obviously the Air Commodore was unaware of the private hell Carter was going through at this moment. Cartingham's voice jolted him from his thoughts. "You will take over at Nissindon immediately. I don't expect miracles, but I do expect you to be able to meet a maximum effort signal within a month."

The tone was now crisp and authoritative. Dorton eased himself from his chair as he saw Cartingham lift his spreading shape from behind the desk. "I'll do my best, sir. These things often come in cycles. Perhaps Carter and I may be able to give the wheel a push?"

The Air Commodore picked up his hat and gloves, walked to the wall map and jerked out two black pins. He watched them swing gently on their red cords. Turning to Dorton, he said: "I hope so. I sincerely hope so." Then glancing at his watch he smiled thinly. "We are just about right for some afternoon tea. If any point occurs to you which may need elucidating, please bring it up."

The pale sunshine had given way to a damp cold greyness when Dorton drove down the tree-lined drive from Group. Once on the main road to York, he settled back and watched the wet black macadam surface flash beneath his wheels as his speedometer crept towards seventy.

It was seven days now since he had first known he was to take command at Nissindon, and the prospect aroused no enthusiasm in him. He was glad it was a wartime station with no suitable accommodation for his wife. It would leave him unfettered to concentrate on putting Cartingham's problem squadron back into shape.

A steady drizzle of rain lashed by a gusty wind blurred his vision. He switched on his windscreen wipers and thought of Carter.

Maybe he should have asked Cartingham for someone else. No, he reflected, the affair of a wife who went to live with a Canadian major was not a matter he could have brought up at Group level, even though the picture of the two small children she had deserted was in Carter's mind every time he took off.

Dorton swore lustily. Carter, top bomber pilot that he undoubtedly was, could well be a liability to him at Nissindon. Somehow, he didn't quite know how, he would have to get the Carter business straightened out. Trouble was that both the Wing Commander's and his wife's parents were dead. He recalled his meeting with him, only a fortnight ago since he had met him in that London club, although it seemed months.

Dorton stabbed his horn button. A heavy, mud-splattered transport with the roundels of the R.A.F. on its rear mudguards, lumbered towards the verge of the road. In his driving mirror he caught a glimpse of the airman mouthing something to his co-driver.

A flicker of a smile creased Dorton's lips, but as he remembered his own reactions when Carter had shown him the letter, the smile slipped from his lips. It was from the Wing Commander's aunt, who was temporarily looking after his children, and it told of childish whimpers in the small hours of the morning. His first feelings were of pity, then anger at the woman for writing such a letter. Then the after-thought came to him that Carter's aunt was in her seventies, and this was her way of impressing upon her nephew, that he had a greater responsibility than taking a four-engined bomber far out into the fickle skies.

Carter had reasoned that sooner or later he would have to complete his third tour. Once it was over he could sit back and leave the actual operating side to men whose records were well below his. In the close proximity of the great night bomber aerodromes crammed throughout the flat farm lands of Yorkshire, this reasoning seemed only that of a gambler's last throw to lose or win all.

"Losses fluctuate four per cent mark . . . odds against finishing one tour. . . ." Cartingham's words echoed ominously in his ears. Carter was playing it too close. He was still pondering on telephoning the Air Commodore and requesting someone else to take Carter's place when he pulled into the courtyard of his hotel in York.

Tomorrow, he decided, he would leave early for Nissindon.

The clock on his dashboard showed it was almost 19.00 hours. Dorton suddenly resolved to leave things as they were. Better to have the Wing Commander with him, under his eye; this way he could discreetly watch him, even censor his trips. He slammed the car door shut and walked briskly towards the dim lighted doorway of the hotel.

2

FLIGHT SERGEANT SHERN DOUGLAS leaned against the
taproom bar, contemplating with distaste the watery froth on
the pint pot in his hand. Leisurely he raised his elbow and took a
long calculated draught.

His restless grey eyes, sighting over the rim of the tankard, saw
by the bar clock that it was precisely 1900 hours. Perhaps it would
have been better had he gone with his crew mates for a meal.

Still, the beer was drinkable when it was laced with a little Scotch.
The mellowness melted the tiredness that had come over him
since the tedious train trip from the Halifax conversion unit at
Rufforth.

They had arrived in York two hours before. According to the
pass in his pocket, he was due to report at a place called Nissindon
at 2359 hours. The pass did not reveal the fact, but he knew it
was 186 Heavy Bomber Squadron. The posting had come through
hurriedly and he hadn't much time to find out what they thought
of Nissindon at the Conversion Unit. But his friend was there,
and, after all, there was no hurry any more.

Probably the rest of the crew had arrived at Nissindon. Maybe
he would travel tonight, maybe he wouldn't he reasoned. It
would depend on two factors, he mused, whether he got drunk or
whether he picked up a woman. The prospect of staying over-
night in York held no other appeal to him. For one thing, it was
full of bomber boys. And he was painfully conscious that, unlike
himself, the majority of them had operations to their credit and a
ribbon below their brevets.

He took another pull at his pint and measured the froth mark.
When he was alone he liked drinking his pints in four pulls.

He wondered what had ever happened to his brother since they
had been parted. He had hoped to see him in London while he
was there; but he never had. Maybe he wasn't there at all, it

was so long ago, the last time he'd heard from him. Strange they should be twins, and yet have no feelings for each other. As for himself, it had been a long roundabout route since he had transferred from the Army in 1941. And it had not ended the way he had planned, that day when he had first inserted the white flash of an aircrew cadet in his forage cap. Instead of the full wings of pilot, the mirror behind the bar reflected the silver half-wing of an observer.

The bitterness was still there. Sometimes it welled over him in piercing swells of jealousy. More often it sent searing blasts of frustration through a mind that was seldom tranquil. For two years ago those wings had been within his grasp.

He had passed through the elementary flying training school at Clyffe Pypard with eighty hours to his credit, fifty of them solo. Sixty more hours at a service flying training school and he would have had them up. What was it his instructor had said: 'You either kill yourself at S.F.T.S. or you get through,' were his words.

The Luftwaffe smashed any hopes of going to a S.F.T.S. Their spasmodic raids on training aircraft had spawned the Empire Training Scheme. Empire!—They had got that a bit mixed up, he thought, for he had landed in an American training school. Knew it before he sailed. But it was not until they had arrived at the holding station in New Brunswick that he had learned of the wash-out rate in the U.S. flying schools. Douglas drained his pint, lit a cigarette and slowly inhaled. Two weeks before his wings parade the American instructor had scrubbed him.

He could see the complacent smirk on Lieutenant Kaufner's face even now. They had disliked each other from the start. The chemical mixture bubbled and spluttered and mutual emotion became hate. The taunts he had taken about the fall of Singapore and the sailing of the German pocket battleships up the English Channel. But then, Kaufner was a first generation American-born German. However, patriotic he was, he must still have had a sneaking admiration for his ancestral home. What was the use of trying to explain that to the R.A.F. Re-selection Board in Trenton, Ontario. God, he had begged them hard enough for just one check flight with an R.A.F. or R.C.A.F. instructor. Firmly the grey-haired Wing Commander had shaken his head. The stream of washed-out cadets coming from the American General Arnold training scheme was too great for the Board to do anything but remuster them. All day long, week after week, month after month, they had sat in that red-bricked administrative block in Trenton listening to similar pleas. Pilots were plentiful, they had told him; observers were short.

Then came the new category of straight navigator and straight bomb-aimer to split the duties of the observer. He was too early for that, but not too late for the long dreary, monotonous course which culminated in the observers' wings parade.

He caught the barman's eye and called for a whisky. Letting it hit the back of his throat, he thought of Flight Sergeant Lew Carson, his skipper. Carson had gone through his flight training at one of the few all R.A.F. training schools in the States.

He frankly admitted to himself that Carson's flying scared him, frightened the whole crew for that matter. Five times he had nearly killed them all. There was that night, eight weeks ago at the Oxfordshire O.T.U., when he failed to correct the Wellington swinging on take-off. The thought sent a shiver through him. He downed his whisky and looked round the bar.

It was still not clear to him how they had got out of that one. Only the alertness of the Chief Flying Instructor in cutting the throttles saved them as the bomber swung off the runway at a crazy angle. For a full two minutes after the aircraft had come to a stop on the soggy grass field skirting the runway the Squadron Leader had sat trembling. Whether the predominant emotion was fear, temper or a mixture of both, he was never quite sure for, sitting behind Carson, his view of that ghastly swing was limited.

He would never forget that voice screaming over the inter-com, freezing him to his seat.... "Let go, you bloody fool ... I've got her...." The undercarriage had buckled as the Wellington, shorn of flying speed, lumbered into the ditch. The C.F.I. got out, but before he walked back to the dispersal flight alone, he had said menacingly: "Carson, I'll never fly with you again. You'll kill yourself.... How you got this far I just don't know...." The voice had been plaintive, almost childlike in its whine. Then, as the numbed senses flexed and came to life again, it had snarled: "Christ, I wouldn't trust you to taxi the bloody thing!"

His skipper had said nothing that night. Not that he ever did say much. On the whole he liked the tall, ungainly, raw-boned Yorkshireman with the thick curly brown hair. There was a hidden strength in Carson that was hard to define. He had noticed it more of late.

It was Morphy the wireless operator, who had summed up their feelings when, back in the billet, he made the remark that flying was bad enough, flying on operations was crazy, but flying with a mediocre pilot was suicide. Mostly they refused to think about their skipper's take-offs, but the fear of them was always in their minds.

Douglas ordered another Scotch. It was nearly pay-day and he never believed in having surplus cash on him. He idly recalled Birrell, who had saved £80 at O.T.U. and was killed when his Wellington crashed near St. Abb's Head on a night cross-country— Birrell who never drank, never smoked, and never went with women.

The barman leaned over and said confidentially, "Sorry, Flight, you had the last of our Scotch quota. Can get you a rum if you like?" Diluting the rum with water, Douglas saw that the bar was filling up. Carson should have stayed with them instead of haring off on his own to Nissindon. Most crews, he reflected, went on drinking bouts with their skipper. Yet he had to land with a practically teetotal captain.

"Hello, Tosh!"

The voice was impudent but the Lancashire accent was warm and friendly. He turned round and smiled at the mid-upper gunner. With him was the rear-gunner, Sergeant Jock Callaghan, and Sergeant Ted Morphy, the wireless operator.

Callaghan was slight, wiry, with fair straight hair. His dark blue eyes were set in a long, narrow, mournful face. He had replaced Sergeant Titch Woods in the rear-turret. Grudgingly, the Lancastrian had moved to the mid-upper turret. He was smaller in stature than Callaghan, with a round rugged baby face. Barely nineteen, he had the infectious grin of a small boy. Only his half wing and his three stripes saved him from being hustled out of public houses as a precocious sixteen-year-old. But they seldom came tougher, as they found at O.T.U. when Titch had licked an airman twice his size in a bar-room brawl. Three years younger than Callaghan, he had a trusting, unshakable belief in the tiny white elephant he carried on the metal identity disc on his wrist.

On a tip from the gunner of another crew, Douglas had dropped in to the corrugated iron hut at Conversion Unit which housed the gunnery turret trainer. When he came out, Titch was with him, begging him not to say anything to Carson. "It was an off day. Shern . . . Honest to God, it was . . ." Carson checked for himself. Callaghan moved into the rear-turret and Titch had not spoken to him for two days. How he had ever got through the vision tests was a mystery to them. Probably, Morphy was not so far out when he had said that he must have memorised the charts, for the gunner's memory was almost photographic. Twice he had tried to persuade Carson to get rid of the mid-upper and get one with average eye-sight, but each time Carson smiled and did nothing. Callaghan glanced at his near empty glass and said laconically: "Being in the higher income bracket, Shern can start the round."

Morphy nodded and Callaghan, eyeing him quizzically, said: "Don't be so eager, Ted. Titch and I have nominated you as wine-buyer number two." Douglas grinned, ordered their drinks, and thought again of the unfairness of paying gunners a mere 7s. 6d. a day, when his own rate of 16s. 6d. a day never seemed to last the whole week. He could never see the logic in the Air Ministry's argument that the difference was a matter of skill, stressing that it took two years to turn out a pilot, observer or navigator to the eight weeks required to train a straight air-gunner. Yet the lives of an expensively trained crew and an equally costly aircraft more often than not depended on the split-second reactions of a seven-and-six-a-day gunner.

"That Scotch?" Callaghan asked.

"No," Douglas said, "it went off twenty minutes ago. I've switched to rum."

"We'll have some, too, then. This beer is lousy," Callaghan said airily.

The gloom and the uneasiness slipped from him as he paid for the round. The good-humoured bantering which always criss-crossed the gunners' conversation seldom failed to put him in a better mood.

"By the way, Shern," said Titch, "we can't get to Nissindon

tonight. We dropped in at the station on the way here. The last train went an hour ago."

Morphy stretched for his glass, looked at Douglas and asked: "Think we ought to phone them and let the gate know we're stuck?"

"If we phone they'll probably send a wagon to collect us. That will mess up our night and it will be the last we'll have for a while," Callaghan said.

Titch frowned and looking hopefully at the rear-gunner said: "I haven't got enough cash to stay here tonight—not, that is, if I'm going to do any drinking."

Callaghan snorted. "That's too bad! You'll just have to stop drinking!"

Douglas handed the mid-upper a pound and Callaghan asked: "You rolling or something?"

Before he could reply, Morphy said: "This is lousy beer and I hate spittoon and sawdust bars. Let's move to the Band-box. There's always women there, and besides, they have a music licence."

Callaghan nudged Douglas. "Okay by me, but weren't you meeting Kiwi and his crew tonight? They could 'gen' us up on what this Nissindon place is like. After all, it was your idea that we put in for 186."

Douglas flicked over his wrist and saw it was nearly eight-thirty. "He's almost two hours late. Doubt if he'll come now."

They pushed through the swirling haze of tobacco smoke and went out into the rain-swept street.

It was then they heard the distant drone of the heavy bombers as they circled for height in the starless dome above the broken cloud base.

For a moment they loitered in the street, their necks craned backwards for a glimpse of a twinkling navigation light. Then the noise increased until it became a thunderous rolling wave upon wave of ear-shattering sound.

"Christ!" Morphy said. "It sounds like a thousand bomber do!"

Douglas said nothing. His whole body was tingling with a sensation he had never experienced before. The soft skin round his eyes and forehead tightened. That steadily mounting crescendo of sound had a lulling, hypnotic effect on his mind. But it went as quickly as it had come, leaving in its wake a glow of relaxation which swept away his earlier feeling of fear and foreboding. He wanted to say, "I'd like to be up there tonight. For the first time I really would." Instead, he said: "Let's get that drink."

3

THE damp, marrow chilling wind whistled down from Flamborough Head, whipping the spray from the white caps rearing and plunging in Bridlington Bay. It whined through the village of Nissindon and scythed across the aerodrome. Mournfully it howled over the N.A.A.F.I. roof, rattling the drain-pipes against the corrugated iron walls.

Seating himself on a wooden form near one of the huge, cylindrical stoves opposite the tea counter of the L-shaped room, Corporal Tubby Watson pulled a sweat-rag from the pocket of his greasy boiler suit. Carefully, he wiped the floating rim marks from the rickety table and put down his pot of steaming N.A.A.F.I. tea.

He wasn't quite sure how many mugs he had drunk since he left the Flights two hours before. One thing he was sure of—he was not feeling so good. For that matter, he hadn't been for some time.

The squadron, the thought brought a sardonic smirk to his weather-beaten moonface, had taken off at 2020 hours to rendezvous with the main force bombers. Nine aircraft—sixty-three men. This, he recalled bitterly, was their worst record yet.

"Maximum Effort," 'Chiefy' had told him at lunchtime, casually trying to convey that he knew the target.

Six aircraft were unserviceable. Hopes that at least three of them could be got ready by nightfall had fallen through by mid-afternoon. He could have told them that when the 'stand to' first came through.

No one except the aircrews and the briefing officers knew the target. Unofficially, it was the same as other nights—Berlin. The load was the same, the petrol on board identical. But the load of incendiaries had been increased. He'd been long enough a fitter on Halifaxes to guess shrewdly the target by carefully noting the variations in bomb load and petrol load carried. High load, low petrol, the Ruhr. Low load, high petrol, somewhere deep in Germany.

The technique of obliterating industrial and built-up areas, as he had often expounded to his armourer, required the use of masses of incendiaries. Given a favourable surface wind, they could raze whole sections of cities to gutted shells.

Two thousand pounders, and the four- and eight-thousand pounders carried by the Lancasters, had a more glamorous appeal to the aircrews, but it was the insignificant incendiary, dropped in clusters, which caused the fires that devastated built-up areas.

Watson rolled a cigarette, flicked a black fingernail on a loose match he extracted from his pocket, and inhaled deeply.

He was a regular, and until now had little experience of how men feel when they are temporarily laid off an assembly line. To-night he had no affinity with the men flying the Halifaxes. Not even a perspex nose to polish, let alone 'revving' the engines in a final check.. And no S—Sugar was operating.

The last time he had serviced an S—Sugar was ten days ago. He remembered how they had waited for it on the wind-swept dispersal in the bleak hours of the morning. They were still waiting, long after the last aircraft landed and taxied to its ramp.

Before that they had three Ss—one never came back after a raid on Essen, the second was lost on an attack on Dusseldorf, and the third, which had only done two operations, went down over Stuttgart. The fourth was believed to have crashed in the sea on the way back. Its Mayday signal, weak and faint, had been picked up, but the Air Sea Rescue boys never found even a piece of its wreckage.

They had lost Ss before, but never four in less than a month. Little wonder people were talking about a hoodoo lurking over the Sugar Bay. Worse still, from what he had heard that morning, S was to be scrubbed from the operational rota. Instead, there would be two Rs, an R1 taking the place of S. Nobody had openly said there was a doubt about his team's maintenance work. They were thinking, though! Why else, he asked himself, were they questioned so persistently by the Engineer Officer and Group Captain Pittle? No matter how he looked at it, things were bad. Put it down to a hoodoo or sheer coincidence, it all added up to the same thing. However one interpreted it, the result did not enhance his reputation.

Watson sipped his tea. He took out his tobacco tin and began to roll another cigarette. As he did so, he scanned the big N.A.A.F.I., which was half empty, quiet and subdued; but then, it was always like that when the squadron was out. The high pitch of excitement and feverish activity which heralded an operation tapered off as the last bomber was airborne. There was nothing to do then but settle down and wait. Usually the camp cinema was crowded on such nights. The shows were old, but they allowed his mind to rest and sometimes he could fall asleep. He idly watched a couple of Waafs from the M.T. section flirt with two L.A.C.s from the stores. All right for these duration men. They got it lightly. Here he was, a Halton boy entrant, and still a corporal at thirty, with 1944 just in and no sign of his third stripe coming through. With the way things were going, it looked as if he'd never be made up to sergeant, although the Engineer Officer had told him eight weeks ago that he could bank on it coming through early in January. The increased allowance that went with it would mean a great deal to Mary and the kids. He was so engrossed in figuring out the increase, he barely saw the blond airman with the shoulders of an ox lower himself on to the form in front of him.

Neither man spoke for a while. Watson accepted the Woodbine offered and lit it off the stub of his home-made cigarette. "Thanks, Curly," he grunted. Curly was his armourer, a duration man who had worked before the war with Armstrong-Vickers, and was one of the best armourers on the squadron. He was as eager for that third stripe to come through as himself. When it came he would go up to Corporal. And Curly, he knew could use the little extra which went with it, for he was married with a child of five.

"You heard the buzz about them scrapping S and just having an R and an R1?" asked Curly.

Watson nodded gloomily and the armourer went on, "I hope there's nothing to it. If that happens it's a slap at us. How can we help it if Jerry's partial to the letter S? With no more Ss we won't be able to prove it wasn't our fault. Reckon our team'll be split up? If that's the case, I'd . . .".

Quietly but firmly, Watson interrupted. "Curly, you know

and I know. The whole maintenance crew know. We don't have to prove a thing. We've worked our guts out over every S we ever had. Time and again we stripped them when complete engine overhauls weren't due for weeks. There's not been a nut, screw or wire we haven't personally gone over, checked and re-checked." A great weariness sheathed Watson's voice. His pale brown eyes held an expression the armourer had never seen before. Curly thought the old evangelists must have had that look when a down-pour of heavy rain dispersed their audience.

"Flight knows the work we've put in. Don't forget that, Curly. He's worked with us, and it's as much his responsibility as ours!"

Curly reddened. "Hold on, Tubby! I didn't mean it like that. Only some of the cracks which have been coming our way lately have got under my skin."

"Forget them!" Watson barked. "Some bastards are never happy unless they're taking the Mickey out of folk. At times it's damned-well vicious."

"Take it from me, I'll clock the next bastard I hear making any of these insinuations!"

Watson cursed fluently. "The whole bloody business gets me mad!"

His armourer sat pensively, drawing evenly on his cigarette. "Think it could be the aircrews?" he asked. Watson shrugged. Curly cocked his head, and looked at him sharply. "Some we've been getting lately aren't so wised-up as they used to be," he muttered.

"Take that last crew, Tubby. The skipper was a nice guy. Just made up to Flying Officer. The rest, though, were down-right scruffy!"

Watson sighed, picked up his pot of tea, and took a short draught. "Might be something in that. Smart crews usually dolled themselves up when they went into town. Hawkin's crowd, now you mention it, looked like tramps." His eyes roamed lazily over a group of airmen lounging against the tea counter. They settled speculatively on a stocky, thick-set Corporal, third in the queue, before coming back to the armourer.

"Maybe things will change when we switch over to the new Halifax IIIs?"

"Those Hercules engines make them climb like birds. Drink

23

up the juice, though. Even so, they're a darned sight better than what we have now!"

Watson tugged at his lower lip and pointedly asked. "You don't believe in this hoodoo stuff?"

His armourer hesitated, a trifle awkwardly he thought, before replying. "I don't know. I ain't any more superstitious than the next bloke and I don't take seriously this O'Hara tale of a Banshie being heard around the Bay." He ran his hands through his thick blond hair. "That don't mean, however, that such things don't exist. Some people are born Jonahs. It's the same with some houses. There's some which have an evil atmosphere you can sense. I lived in one once. It fair gave me and the wife the creeps!" A grieved expression came over the armourer's face. "You needn't smirk, Tubby! What about those prayers the Church puts up and all that palaver about exorcising spirits? I reckon it's about time the padre did some of that exorcising stuff around here. Couldn't do any harm, huh?"

Watson was about to retort when he saw Corporal Diston, his counterpart on Y—Yorker, stroll towards him from the tea bar. For a second he considered rising and leaving the N.A.A.F.I. Tonight he was in no mood to listen to Diston's bragging about the engine life of Y—Yorker.

The Corporal stopped in front of him, smiled in a sickly way and winked broadly at Curly.

Turning abruptly, he looked insolently at Watson. "Well Tubby, looks like you and your boys have written off the letter S from this squadron. Reckon they'll give you a Tiger Moth to play with next. . . ."

Diston's clinching taunt choked in his throat. The mocking tone of his voice sent the blood surging in Watson's overwrought brain. He had a vague, rabid sensation of barbed darts jabbing his eardrums. A racking pain darted up his right forearm as his fist smashed into the Corporal's leering mouth. The taut skin veiling his knuckles glistened in tiny, fast swelling beads of bright red as they ripped across the Corporal's nicotine stained teeth.

Diston swayed on his heels, reeled backwards, his arms threshing aimlessly on each side of him. A table crashed to the floor as it folded under his sprawling form. A Waaf screamed shrilly. Watson felt his arms being roughly pinned to his sides.

"Let up, Tubby! For Christ's sake, let up!" a voice bawled in his ear. Two Station policemen seated at the far end of the hut jumped to their feet, and raced across the room. The singing in his ears grew quieter and his heart stopped pounding.

"Ease up, Curly. I'm all right now!"

"It was an unprovoked attack, Corporal. We saw it all."

Turning round, Watson saw it was one of the S.Ps speaking.

4

NISSINDON, a rural hamlet of cobbled-stone cottages, straggled both sides of the secondary road which five miles to the North intersected the trunk highway from Bridlington to Hull.

At one end of the village was the Ostler public house, at the other the Swan. Between them was a general store which also housed a sub-post office. Behind the Swan, on a grassy hillock some two hundred yards from the main street, was an eighteenth-century church of rough hewn sandstone.

Two miles to the east lay the aerodrome. Beyond it stretched the grey waters of the North Sea.

Group Captain Dorton slowed down his M.G. coupé as he passed through the village, only to accelerate suddenly as he climbed the steep gradient on the far side of the Swan. At the top he braked and pulled into the verge. The morning was cold and clear. A thin veil of sea-mist hung low over the coast-line.

Dorton got out of the car. From where he stood he had an unobstructed view of the airfield. The aerodrome proper he saw, was built on a rectangle of raised land. Sheltering in a saucer-shaped hollow were the sleeping quarters. One runway—the main arm he decided—ran directly towards the shore line, to disappear in the mist. The high, wide hangars were carefully camouflaged, their true outline dwarfed and distorted by spotches of dark-brown and green paint.

Half a mile from the main runway an irregular cluster of low-roofed wooden huts skirted the side of a ploughed field. On the near side of the subsidiary runway, which slashed across the secondary road he was travelling on, were a group of larger huts.

The road, he noted, had been broadened and reinforced with concrete where the runway passed over it.

A water tower loomed behind a further group of buildings,

which he guessed by their shape to be the administration blocks. To the side of them were two long L-shaped outlines, obviously, he decided, the officers' and sergeants' messes.

Surveying the airfield, he recalled the stations he had been on since the war began. At the beginning, each had had an individual look. But as the months slipped by and more and more temporary airfields were ripped out of the land to meet the growing expansion of the bomber fleets, their pattern became identical. Seldom deviating from the original blue-print, they saved time, money and materials.

He turned back to his car. Another ten minutes, and he would be having breakfast as Commanding Officer 186 Bomber Squadron.

The R.A.F. policeman in the white blancoed belt and gaiters snapped to attention as he drove through the main entrance. Pulling up sharply outside the smaller of the L-shaped buildings, Dorton eased himself out of the driving seat.

The mess was smaller than he had imagined. On one side of a square hall was the dining-room. Directly opposite, double doors opened on to a long comfortable lounge with a large red brick fireplace. The bar was to the side of the hall. Through the open door, he saw that the imitation oak beams and the brass ornaments on the walls caught something of the atmosphere of a country inn.

There were less than ten officers in the dining-room. A mental picture of the wall map in the Air Commodore's office flickered across his mind. Of course they had been operating last night. He was speculating on how they had fared, when a trim fair-haired Waaf, in a freshly laundered smock slipped from behind a highly polished coffee urn and ushered him to a table.

Half-way through his second cup of coffee, he was interrupted by a slightly built Squadron Leader in his early forties.

The voice was pleasant and friendly. "Excuse me, sir. I'm Farley, the Adjutant. We didn't expect you until noon, otherwise I'd have . . ."

"Quite all right," he interjected. "I didn't expect to get here so early."

Motioning the Adjutant to sit down, he took in the lean intelligent face and the frank brown eyes, and felt instinctively that he liked Farley.

Half an hour later, from behind the scarred mahogany desk, in the room recently vacated by Group Captain Pittle, Dorton asked: "How did they get on last night?"

Farley, he noticed, shifted uncomfortably in his chair and crossed his legs.

"Two are missing and one, A—Able, made an emergency landing at Carnaby. Pilot didn't reckon he'd get in here. They were pretty well shot-up."

Dorton's right eyebrow arched. "Not so good! There was no change in the number?"

"No, sir, nine went out."

Dorton rubbed his chin. "Doesn't make an operation worthwhile as far as this squadron is concerned. Considering how few went out, their loss is well above the percentage expected."

He pulled out his cigarette case and offered a cigarette to Farley. "Things have been rather bad for sometime now. Any personal ideas on what's gone wrong?"

"Well, not exactly, sir. It all seemed to begin—I mean the bad spell—about nine weeks ago. Then we lost six out of eighteen. Before that our losses were well within the number normally expected." The Adjutant shrugged his shoulders. "Since then, a hoodoo seems to have hit us!"

Dorton said sharply, "You surely don't think that? I would say you were much too intelligent to believe in such nonsense."

Farley flushed, and his voice was glacier-smooth and equally cold as he answered: "In a broad manner of speaking, sir, yes. The squadron have been monstrously unlucky. Our aircraft are as well-serviced as any in the Group. The aircrews are as good as any going, yet we can't seem to shake off this . . ." Farley stopped himself from repeating hoodoo. Instead, he substituted: "this bad spell."

Dorton's smile faded. Icily he said: "Morale isn't so good. Is it?" He snapped out the last two words and saw the Adjutant jerk forward in his seat and as suddenly relax. He felt sorry for him. After all, it was not his responsibility, for Farley's job was administration. The aircrews were the responsibility of the Group Captain and his Wing Commander flying. Still, he wanted the Adjutant's opinion badly—wanted, for that matter, a whole lot of opinions. The man opposite him, trying so hard to be calm, was clearly torn between loyalty to the squadron and telling the truth as he saw it.

Flatly and with a strange finality Farley said: "I would like to make it clear that this is purely my personal opinion. Morale, as you say, is not quite so high as it was when I first came here. But then, the raids were not on the same scale in those days. Consequently our losses were much smaller. I think that they've struck subconsciously a despairing attitude of mind. Men worked up to their present pitch can be easily affected by things which seem to other people merely trivial."

"Affected by what things?" Dorton prodded.

"As I said, sir, things which on the face of it seem too trivial to mention. Not one specific factor but a host of pin-pricks. Self-pity spawned out of their bad luck, and now any little grievance, imaginary or otherwise, is magnified out of all proportion. Sort of escapism on which they can vent their wrath."

"Name one," Dorton insisted softly.

"Compulsory physical training! Compulsory church parades! Compulsory inter-flight bombing competitions on stand-downs! I'm not a flyer, as you know, sir, but I can understand; and bluntly, sir, I sympathise with them. They didn't expect such things on an operational squadron. Group Captain Pittle was acting in what he believed was their best interests. Unfortunately, they didn't appreciate this. He also banned all mess socials and dances. Argued that the aircrews had to get plenty of rest. 'Fraid it back-fired though, and they were, still are, pretty sore about it. They used to be allowed sleeping-out passes on week-ends when they were on stand-down. These too were cancelled."

Farley leaned forward. "Then they've been bitterly disappointed about the rumour that they're well down on the list for the new Halifax IIIs. How the rumour got about, we don't know. The story is that A Flight Commander asked Group Captain Pittle about it and was told the squadron were not considered good enough for them."

Dorton made a mental note to telephone Cartingham on the question of the new Halifaxes.

Concealing his intention, he said: "Group Captain Pittle has a fine record and a great deal of experience. You seem to overlook the fact that your sister satellite has nothing like the losses this squadron has had. In fact, they have one of the best aiming-records in the Group."

"Excuse me, sir." Farley's voice was firm. "I don't wish to appear impudent, but the conditions are vastly different there. For one thing, the aircrews are treated as operational flyers, not as cadets under training. . . ."

"That," snapped Dorton, "was uncalled for. I take it you did not get on with your former Commanding Officer."

Farley flushed, and was about to rise, when Dorton said genially: "Look here, Farley, I don't want you to think for a moment that I am holding you or anyone else on this squadron responsible for how things are. Certainly, the flying side is not your business. But you have been here for a considerable period and I was hoping you might have been able to give me a pointer as to what is wrong."

"I'm sorry, sir, but I have tried," he said in a quiet dejected voice.

Dorton shifted sideways in his chair. "Well, you've been very helpful. Now tell me; discipline generally: how is it?"

"On the whole, fairly good. The aircrews are apt at times to be a little high-spirited but they've never been really difficult. . . ." Farley hesitated and looked puzzled. "Perhaps I shouldn't mention it, sir. But we had a small incident last night which might give you a pointer on how some people feel. In the N.A.A.F.I. a Corporal fitter, one of the best—a regular at that—made a rather vicious attack on another Corporal. He has been charged, and according to the man with him, this other Corporal made some disparaging remarks about his efficiency."

"A regular, you said?"

"Yes, sir, fitter on S—Sugar. Was due for his third stripe shortly."

The Adjutant surveyed the toe-cap of his right shoe before looking up.

"Incidentally, everyone looks on S as an unlucky letter. Four aircraft bearing the letter were lost in swift succession. Squadron Leader Roberts, A Flight Commander . . ." Farley lowered his voice . . . "He went missing last night, decided that in future the squadron should substitute R1 for the letter S."

Farley, noticing the surprise on his Group Captain's face, added hastily: "Group Captain Pittle agreed!"

"That," Dorton replied, "practically gives official blessing to the hoodoo you referred to."

"It may. Most people—certainly the aircrews—don't take it lightly," Farley said gravely.

For the next half-hour he acquainted Dorton with the various files stacked in the green metal cabinet along one side of the room, and with the general routine of the station.

As he turned to leave, Dorton asked casually: "Would you be good enough to send in this Corporal who was in trouble? I think I'll deal with him myself."

Farley nodded grimly.

"And by the way, has Wing Commander Carter arrived?"

"Yes, sir. He came three days ago. Shall I tell him you——?"

"No, that's all right," Dorton interjected. "I'll see him later."

Back in his office at the end of the long highly polished corridor, the Adjutant doodled absently on his blotter. His Waaf Corporal came into the room and gave him a breezy "Good morning."

Farley, concentrating on his interview with the Group Captain, drew a series of Ss on the white surface before him. Deftly he transformed them into dollar signs and thought of the American W.A.C. Lieutenant he had met in York. He was oblivious to the greeting of the Waaf.

The Corporal vented her chagrin on her typewriter. It had always been a noisy machine. Now she increased the pressure on the keys. She often wondered about the Adjutant. She didn't have to look in a mirror to know she appealed to men. The pressure against the top button of her tunic reassured her. Yet never once had he so much as noticed her. Perhaps, she mused, he was afraid of an affair with someone on his own station.

She liked the Adjutant. He was better mannered than the aircrews—not, she reflected, that there was any future with them. She had lost three boy friends in two months. It was all rather tedious. She hoped her posting to Group would come through soon. The marriage rate among the girls there was pretty high, she had heard.

A stout dark-haired ACW came into the office, flushed and breathless.

"Makers!" snapped the Corporal. "You're late again!"

Farley, ignorant of the chain reaction he had triggered off, stubbed out his cigarette. Something, he felt, was hatching in the new C.O.'s mind. He wasn't quite sure what it was.

One thing was clear to him. Dorton was of a vastly different calibre from Pittle. On the face of it, his order for that Corporal to be sent in did not augur well for the squadron. He could be another disciplinarian.

Picking up the telephone receiver, Farley asked for the guard-room.

For a full two minutes Sergeant Hoskins inspected his burly form in the guardroom mirror. Two black buttons sunk in a red blotched face blinked back at him. A squat pimply nose poked over a ragged black moustache. He stepped back three paces and the hair line above his mouth, reflected in the mirror, resembled a swarm of blue bottles twitching on a piece of wet liver.

To Hoskins, the picture was that of a Guards R.S.M. dressing down a Colour Party.

The fleshy lips gaped. The striven-for bark was weak, eunuch-like in its shrill high note. "Watson, you've done it this time? Get your best blues on and try and look like an airman! You're up before the C.O. in twenty minutes!"

Twenty minutes later Watson reappeared in a tunic which threatened to burst at the seams.

"You're late! It won't help you any," Hoskins piped.

"To hell with it!" Watson said indifferently.

Hoskins spluttered, quickened his pace, and together the two marched towards the administration block, only Watson conscious of how ridiculous they looked.

"When did he arrive?" Watson asked quietly.

"If you mean the Group Captain," Hoskins tone was haughty, "he came this morning. Reckon I'll get my 'Flight' through him." He looked sharply at the Corporal.

When Watson made no reply, he added quickly: "He complimented me on my appearance. Said he could always tell a man by the way he was turned out." Watson smiled. He had listened before to the Sergeant's flights of fancy. Then the ugly disturbing thought that Hoskins might be for once speaking the truth tugged at his mind. The new C.O. might be a real dyed-in-the-wool disciplinarian who could not think further than the barrack square. Not, Watson reflected, that Pittle had been any better.

Hoskins grunted and slackened his pace. "Bet," he said, "he'll throw a blinking fit when he sees that scruffy aircrew intake of sergeants that have just come in. I'd give a week's pay to have them on the square for an hour!"

"Your pay's safe," Watson said laconically.

His armourer had seen the new C.O. when he was on his way to the Flights. Hoskins, Watson felt sure, had never been near the main gate. He liked his bed too much to be shaved before nine. And the C.O., according to Curly, had driven in shortly before eight o'clock.

Watson looked on the S.P. Sergeant with the same detachment he gave to a beetle about to be crushed under his size eight boots. The S.P. was never happier than when he was booking someone. If that person happened to be an aircrew Sergeant, so much the better.

Aircrews, in Hoskins's view, got their rank too easily. What grated most with him, and made his daily routine a misery, was the cursory attitude which the flying men adopted towards him.

At last it seemed to Hoskins, Watson thought, that a Group Captain had arrived with similar ideas to his on how a station should be run. Pittle, for all his faults, had given up trying to get the aircrews to turn out smartly.

Hoskins knocked loudly on the Adjutant's door and walked in. Saluting sharply, he said: "Corporal Watson, sir!"

Without looking up, Farley said: "Very good! You can go now, Sergeant." The voice was limp and colourless. The Sergeant's jaw dropped on to an invisible chin-strap. Then the mouth opened and the face reddened. "Don't you wish me to escort the . . . ?"

Farley said icily: "That will not be necessary."

Hoskins hesitated, before he turned on his heel, and his salute was much less vigorous than when he had first come into the room.

Farley rapped softly on the Group Captain's door, and turned the knob.

"Corporal Watson, sir."

Stepping back discreetly, he closed the door behind the Corporal and walked back to his office.

Watson, his face set grimly, his forage cap tucked under his left arm, stood rigidly to attention.

His eyes stared intently at the centre pane of the window a foot above the Group Captain's head. Vaguely he wondered why there was no escort with him. He was acutely aware that the Group Captain was sizing him up, tabulating his category.

"At ease, Corporal." The voice was pleasant. .

He had imagined it to be stern and sharp.

"You know why you're here?"

"Yes, sir."

"You're a regular. A Halton entrant, I hear."

"Yes, sir."

There was distinct pause. "I don't like hearing of Halton men in trouble. They usually set the standard the rest follow." The voice was almost too casual.

Bawl me out, thought Watson. .But leave Halton out of it. Public school types had their memories. Halton was his.

"Why did you assault Corporal Diston?"

"I'd rather not say, sir."

The Group Captain could keep up his purring. It was going to be kept a personal matter. He was not stupid enough to draw the new C.O.'s attention to Diston's slanderous jibes. Much better to keep his mouth shut. Otherwise the Group Captain might believe there was something in the taunts after all.

"I had hoped I might have been able to help. You see, I happen to be an old Halton boy myself. Your attitude, however, makes it rather difficult for me."

Dorton noted the widening of the Corporal's eyes, the quiver which rippled along the top lip line.

"The Adjutant tells me you are about due for promotion. You realise, of course, that this might well mean your dropping a rank instead of attaining one? I will not tolerate my Corporals brawling in the N.A.A.F.I. before other ranks. I take it you have considered the consequences of your conduct?"

"I understand, sir."

As the deadness in the voice came to him, Dorton leaned forward intently and his tone was softer.

"I don't think you do! So, as one regular to another, I am telling you not to be such a fool. It so happens I know why you struck this man. He made certain remarks about your ability. Isn't that so?" The voice cracked like a whip.

"Yes, sir."

"Very well. Stop playing the ass and tell me the full story right from the beginning. Start from when things began to go bad with the S aircraft."

For thirty minutes the fitter talked. Now and then Dorton interrupted him to ask specific questions or to request him to expand a point more clearly.

"Then came the big slap, sir! We heard that no more aircraft bearing the letter S would be operating. The crew took it hard. Sort of personal slight, it seemed. Honest to God, sir, we slaved over these aircraft. Diston's remark was the last straw!"

"What do you think, Corporal, of this hoodoo talk?" The question was lazily intoned.

Watson waited for the noise of an M.T. engine to fade away. His eyes rested on the Group Captain, who was watching him through half-closed lids, hypersensitive eyes that found amusement in the question.

Was there anything this man didn't know about the station? Barely three hours since he had arrived, and here he was, prying and probing with searching intimate questions. Of course, the Adjutant must have told him. Watson relaxed. "Not much, sir. We've had a bad spell. People talk, but they don't think enough. It's easier for them to conjure up such things. After a while they start believing them. Soon they'll be seeing ghost aircraft with Ss on their fuselage."

Watson's tone was bitter and his lips parted. They abruptly shut, as if he realised he had already said too much.

"Go on: what was it you were about to add?"

"If I may say so, sir, most aircrew are very superstitious. What with their good luck charms and mascots, well, a hoodoo is a natural step."

The same thought had already occured to Dorton.

"I think you are talking sound common-sense," he said quietly.

Picking up one of his leather gloves, he slapped it lightly against the edge of his desk, before continuing in the same slow measured tone: "We are going to lay this nonsense about the S bay. I expect shortly the first of the new Halifax IIIs. The men who will fly them are already on the way. One of these aircraft will be assigned to the S bay. Look after it and its crew. Stamp on any stupid talk you might hear about so-called hoodoo spells and don't go around hitting people. That clear?"

Watson felt a tremor shoot through his limbs. A warmth of happiness came over him.

"Yes, sir!"

Dorton, watching his broad grin, smiled wryly. "Very good, then. That will be all!"

The ink-well on Dorton's desk rattled loudly as the fitter thumped to attention. His limbs were still tingling as he strode down the corridor and out of the door of the administration building.

Sergeant Hoskins, who had been keeping a lone vigil on the entrance, speculating on what the C.O.'s punishment would be, eyed Watson curiously.

"You all right? To me you look bomb-happy."

Watson ignored the remark and whistled softly.

"What happened in there? No point in trying to be tough about it! I'll know soon enough!"

Watson stopped whistling. "That's where you're wrong," he said quietly; "you won't be knowing much about anything. But I'll tell you this. There's no 'bull' about the new Groupie. Another thing: S aircraft will be flying again."

Sergeant Hoskins watched the tubby figure saunter towards the Flights. He wondered if Watson was trying to work his discharge on a psychiatrist's ticket.

5.

A STRONG gust of wind knifed its way across the perimeter track and slammed the heavy wooden door of dormitory "A" against its flanges. The short, sharp crack echoed down the corridor.

Flight Sergeant Kiwi MacArthur started violently in his sleep. Red and green lights exploded in his brain. Jagged fragments seared through the lights and danced in an endless ragged line of needle-sharp points, to be swept away in a rolling void of blackness. He clawed in a frenzy at the suffocating mask pressing hard against his mouth and nostrils. Deep red flickering flames licked the edge of the dark curtain of unconsciousness. Drifting spirals of dense black smoke slowly and inexorably swelled over him, choking his throat.

He felt himself falling, and wrenched at the mask, to awake, sweating, his breath coming in short sudden gasps. For a long time Kiwi stared at the white-washed ceiling of the room. God, he would stop taking those pep pills they handed out before an operation to banish the tiredness of long flights. The nightmares which came in their wake were terrifying.

Anxiously he glanced at his room-mate. Davis, his navigator, was huddled under the blankets in a deep sleep.

Kiwi stretched lazily. Reaching for a cigarette, he saw by the watch on his locker that it was nearly noon. Dressing hurriedly, he decided to shave in the mess. The stove had gone out and the room was cold, uninviting.

Gently he shook Davis. He shook him three times before the Canadian dragged himself on to an elbow, his eyes bleary and bloodshot.

The wind howled mournfully as he cycled, head bent low over

the handle-bars, along the wide perimeter track on the half-mile journey to the mess.

Shern Douglas, with whom he had gone through the Observers' course in Canada, was due in that morning.

For two years they had somehow always managed to get posted to the same stations. He thought of the seven trips to his credit. They had a long-standing bet as to who would be the first to operate. He'd collect that double Scotch tonight. Hardly likely they would be on operations again so soon.

The wind cut through his battle-dress, penetrating the thick wool of his flying sweater. It came in short powerful blasts and repeatedly threatened to hurl both himself and the bicycle off the perimeter track.

Parking his cycle in one of the wooden racks behind the mess, he strolled round to the front entrance hall and scanned the mail rack.

Seldom had he seen the mess so crowded. But then, the new crews had arrived. Short men, tall men, fat men, broad stocky men, all wearing wings and half-wings.

His eyes roamed over the white blur of faces until they lighted on Douglas, tall, dark and lean, standing among a group crammed against the bar. Suddenly he looked up, smiled broadly, and eased himself through the group.

They shook hands vigorously. Kiwi pointed to a table near the window. "Park yourself over there, Shern, till I get some beer. I've a lot to tell you."

A few minutes later the New Zealander came back, a pint pot in each hand. "Can't help thinking," he said, "how damned lucky we have been in following one another around." His voice was warm, eager and friendly.

They talked steadily, then Douglas, with a trace of anxiousness in his voice, said: "Hear it was Berlin last night? Tell me, Cobber, what's it really like?"

The mess was filling up with crews who had operated the night before. Quickly they were being accosted by men who had arrived that morning, and always the questions were the same: "What was it like?"

They had heard it before from their instructors at O.T.U. Now they were on a front-line bomber squadron and the question took on a new significance. This was January 1944 and the Battle of Berlin was raging. Life suddenly became sweeter, more precious, now that they were on a squadron than it had ever been before. They were going to notice more things, too. Little insignificant details, the way a sparrow pecked at a crust of bread, the way a field was ploughed for the spring sowing, though few, pitifully few, of the men in that mess were ever again to look on the rich yellow of a ripening corn field. Letters home were to be imperceptibly subdued. The flamboyant, flighty strain of elementary flying days was to give way to a restraint not easily discernible to the hasty reader. Letters were to be answered quicker than they had ever been before. Most men realised that the greater burden—that of waiting and wondering—was borne by those dispassionately listed in records as 'next-of-kin'.

Kiwi searched the new faces—already terrified at that thought of death which was nearer to them than at any time in their lives—and remembered his own first day in the bomber mess. "Not as bad as I expected," he said to Douglas, "Bloody terrifying, the stuff they pushed up. We got in fast and out faster. Hope they'll all be like that."

Douglas asked quietly: "You're not soft-pedalling, Cobber?"

"No! Flak was heavy. Always is over the Big City. Gunners saw a few combats, but we were lucky. Nobody bothered us. Weather fortunately was bad. Ten-tenths cloud over most of the route and totally obscuring the target. Kept most of the fighters grounded!"

Kiwi dragged heavily on his cigarette and swallowed the smoke. "Of course, a raid that's easy for one crew might be the chop for another. All depends on how you take it. Make-up of some people differ. Big worry, main one really, are the 88s and 190s. If a fighter gets a burst in, you've more or less had it! For one thing, the gunners are probably looking the other way when it comes. It's so quick, you can't do much about it. Best you can hope for is to grab your 'chute and get the hatch open bloody quick!"

The New Zealander's dark blue eyes changed to mauve as the faded sunlight streamed into the big room.

"Personally, I don't think it will bother you unduly, Shern. You're not exactly the sensitive type! Your imagination always stopped short at a skirt. No, I reckon you'll be O.K. I was going to add, don't think too much, but then, you never did."

Douglas recalled Titch's below-average vision and some of the old uneasiness came back to him.

"Tell me," Kiwi asked, "has Carson cured himself of that hellish swing on take-off?" As an after-thought he added: "And how's the crew?"

"The crews O.K. Not the sort I'd have picked, but you have to take pot-luck, as you know. On the whole, they're not so bad. We picked up our engineer at Conversion Unit. Big, burly fellow by the name of Don Pastone. Seems O.K. But like most engineers, has had only a handful of flying hours."

Kiwi grimaced. "That's the trouble! They don't get enough flying hours to get acclimatised to working in the air. How many hours you got in now?"

Douglas caressed the lobe of his right ear. "Taking in pilot training, about three hundred."

"Engineers get here with around twenty-five," Kiwi said softly.

"Getting back to Carson," Douglas said. "He just can't seem to control a heavy aircraft on take-off. One of these days he's going to pile us up. I'm telling you this because I've long realised it, and been resigned to it."

Kiwi's lips tightened. "You should have switched from that crew at O.T.U. when I told you to," he said sharply.

"I know!" Douglas said irritably. "But it wouldn't have looked so good."

"Christ!" the New Zealander said. "Others have done it. Why, he nearly wrote you all off, including the C.F.I., at O.T.U.!"

Douglas downed his beer. "Too late now. I'm stuck with them. You're damned lucky with the crew you landed with. Martin's a top-class pilot."

"I'm not bragging, Shern, you know me well enough for that. But F—Freddie has the best crew and ground crew on this squadron," Kiwi said proudly.

"Good to hear that. By the way, what's this outfit like?"

Kiwi blinked, as he reached for his pint. "Let's go into town tonight. Been a long time since we had a booze up. Can't see us being on tonight. Anyway, I've a little bet to collect, remember?"

"I remember," Douglas said cuttingly; "but answer the bloody question!"

The New Zealander fingered the tiny green Maori charm attached to the whistle on his tunic collar. He took a long time before speaking. "You'll hear soon enough! So you might as well get it from me, Shern. You've come to about the unluckiest squadron there is. Helluva part of it is that it's through me you got Carson to plug for this posting. Not one crew has finished a tour since we came here. We've also got the highest loss rate in the Group—some say in the Command. Other squadrons send out maybe twenty to twenty-five aircraft and lose perhaps two or three. We despatch eighteen, and about five don't come back!"

Kiwi blinked again, and sipped his drink thoughtfully before adding: "Believe me, Shern, it shook me when I came here. First day in this mess a Sergeant Observer, never saw him before, was standing at the bar. He looked at me strangely and asked me if I was one of the new crews. When I nodded, he flicked my charm"—Kiwi thumbed the talisman to emphasise his point—"and told me I'd come to the original hoodoo squadron, adding that old Wakiti here would be powerless to influence my luck."

The New Zealander emptied his glass. "Two nights later, this guy went missing over Essen. S aircraft are particularly unlucky. He was in one. They seem to be singled out for special treatment. Anyway, they've scratched the letter. Orders of the last Groupie. Maybe you didn't know it, but we got a new C.O. today."

"Any idea what he's like?" Douglas asked.

"None! Fellow by the name of Dorton. Hear he got his D.S.O. on the first Stirlings, and those boys had it rough. Glad the last bastard's gone, though! Proper stuffy type! Always giving pep talks, proper training command type. Something like old Smethison at that Ontario navigation school."

Douglas nodded gloomily. "Fine time! Fine goddam time to tell me all this!" he said bitterly.

The New Zealander jerked a thumb towards the milling crowd round the bar. "Let's eat before that bunch moves in on the dining-room. Maybe the messing officer has slipped up—it's happened before—and the cooks are working on the old ration strength."

Douglas said nothing, but followed the New Zealander through the double swing doors.

6

FOR forty-eight hours the weather kept the bombers from operating. The telegram addressed to Sergeant Callaghan said tersely: "Bringing goods Tuesday. If muck clears."

It was signed by his brother, now ferrying Halifaxes as a rest from operations. It was Wednesday, and a steady breeze from the north-west broke up and hourly thinned the blanket of sea fog enveloping the aerodrome. Callaghan watched it from the Mess and wondered if his brother would be able to spend the night at Nissindon. The last time he had seen him was eight months ago, as the Pilot Officer captain of a Halifax MK II. He had gone up to Flying Officer since, but that, he knew, didn't mean so much to him as the D.F.M. he had won as a Flight Sergeant.

No, Dougal hadn't done so badly. His mother had argued strongly against him following his brother into the Air Force. In the end she had resigned herself to the fact. He smiled faintly when he thought of her. She was so proud of them, bragged about them almost as much as their father did, when he was not pounding rivets into corvettes in that Clydebank shipyard.

"Think it will clear enough, skipper, for them to get in?"

Flight Sergeant Carson, his hands stuck in his battle-dress pockets, moved nearer to the window.

"Should be O.K. in another hour or so. Did your brother say how many they were flying in?"

"No, I merely got a phone call saying he was coming. Then early yesterday his telegram came. Thought he'd be here shortly afterwards, as the weather looked like clearing."

In the Officers' mess Dorton replaced the receiver of the telephone in the bar. "That was Farley. He's just got the signal," and, turning to Wing Commander Carter, he added: "They are coming in after lunch!"

43

Nodding towards Carter's empty glass, he asked: "Sure you won't have another?"

The Wing Commander shook his head. "Thanks all the same, but I'm taking B—Baker up on an air test. Incidentally, it was good of you to arrange for my old crew to be brought over. They didn't at all relish the idea of being taken over by some 'sprog' pilot."

"Least I could do, Bill!" Dorton said. "Oh, I almost forgot. I was speaking to Cartingham this morning. He's pulling some strings so we can expect the first of the new Halifaxes by early next week. General policy is that they are not to be operated until most of the squadrons in the group are fully equipped with them. By the time we get converted, the ban should be raised."

Carter flicked the ash from his cigarette. "Should have all the new crews blooded by then. With the replacements that are coming today, and the repair jobs, we'll be fully operational again."

Dorton nodded, endorsing his Wing Commander's view. In the short time he had been on the squadron Carter had astounded him with his organising ability. From the day he arrived he had worked non-stop, shaping the framework on which the squadron would hereafter operate. He had already allocated crews to the aircraft due in that afternoon. 'Circuits and bumps', to get them familiarised with the Halifaxes, would begin in earnest at dawn. Six-hour cross-country trips had been drawn up. At the same time they would test the Humber air defences. From a dead reckoning position above the North Sea, the new crews would make a mock daylight attack on Hull, dropping 'Window'—the metallic strips of paper used to confuse ground radar stations. Spitfires from Catfoss would be sent aloft to intercept them. That, Dorton thought, would give the air-gunners some dummy practice.

Carter had handled it all. The programme had to be flexible, for they were liable to be called, should a Maximum Effort come through. With this in mind, he asked: "You're quite sure you can have the new aircrew ready for operations, say, by the end of this week? It doesn't leave you much time."

"Of course I'm sure, sir! They already know all there is, at least they think they do! In a sense, they're right! I've impressed on them that the only difference now is that they'll be carrying live bombs instead of practice ones!" His lips parted in a thin smile. "All they lack is operational experience, and that can't be laid on as part of the O.T.U. syllabus . . ." Then, remembering how the bottom of the barrel had been scraped for the thousand-bomber raid on Cologne, he added: "At least, not any more!"

Dorton splashed some soda into his gin, and watched the tiny bubbles float to the surface. "Taking into account crews going on leave, sickness and such like, we will then be able to make our full contribution to any effort the Command may order?"

"Yes." The answer was crisp, firm and confident.

Shooting a sidelong glance at the Wing Commander, Dorton asked lightly: "What type of crew have you given to the S bay? Dominion or R.A.F.?"

Carter eyed him, puzzled. "Can't tell you off-hand. Have to check with my list. . . . No! Wait a moment! There's no S! Evidently Group Captain Pittle. . . ."

"I know all about that," Dorton interrupted, "and I've decided that S shall remain on the rota. It would be, I think, bad psychologically if we altered it."

The Wing Commander shook his head. It would be equally bad, he mused, to bring back the S bay, from what he had heard.

"Don't you think, sir," he queried, "that, mentally, the crew which takes over S will be at a disadvantage? They are bound to hear of the bay's previous ill fortune. I've found that most air-crews are as superstitious as any old gypsy crone."

Dorton frowned. Carter was probably right. He should delete the blasted letter from the Ops board. Obviously the Wing Commander had carefully weighed the chances of losing another S and its after-effect on the hoodoo myth.

But there was that Corporal, the Halton fellow. He should never have committed himself like that.

"We'll give it a trial," he said firmly.

"Very good. It so happens I now recall the crew I assigned to the second R which was to replace S. All sergeants. Fairly mediocre skipper, according to the report of his C.F.I. at O.T.U. I'll inform C Flight that their letter will revert to S."

Dorton found himself in half a mind to ask Carter to put another crew on the S aircraft. God, if any pilot was to fly S he should at least be a good one. He decided the Wing Commander would think it more than strange if, because of some undefinable whim, he began altering what was, after all, his Wing Commander's list.

Deeply regretting that he had ever meddled with the flying list, he said: "Since we are not operating tonight, how about having dinner with me? Maybe you know some place around here?"

Carter smiled. "Your petrol or mine?"

"Mine, Bill!" And for the first time since he came into the mess, the Wing Commander laughed.

At 1400 hours that afternoon a green Very light burst across the secondary runway and the first of the aircraft replacements swept into the circuit. They came in singly, at intervals of a minute. The vibrations set off from their four powerful engines rattled and shook the flimsy wooden buildings of the flights below.

As one landed, another slipped down from the aerial taxi-rank in a wide sweeping circuit, before banking into the funnel of the runway. They were all down now but the seventh. Wing-Commander Carter watched its approach from outside A Flight office.

Four of the landings had been good, one fair and the last a trifle rough. He was speculating with a critical eye on what the next would be like. The Halifax was coming in, the pale sunlight glinting on the transparent nose. With her flaps down, she had the appearance of a monstrous fan-tailed pigeon. Her under-carriage jutted stubbornly from her belly. Nothing soft or weak about that landing gear, he decided. Solid and big, it accentuated the great strength of the airframe.

The Halifax roared over the hawthorn hedge beyond the start of the runway and she was coming in fast—too fast, he thought.

"Bit high and a bit fast," said the tall, lanky Canadian Flight Commander at his side.

"Probably going round again. He's cut his circuit a bit fine and it's messed up his approach," Carter replied.

The bomber was directly over the start of the concrete when they heard the throttles being cut. A good third of the runway flashed beneath the Halifax as the Flight Commander said: "Christ! He'll never get in. Why doesn't the clot open up and go round?"

Carter paled, his eyes hypnotically held by the bomber. God, the fool was going to crash unless he opened up his throttles instantly! The Halifax was losing flying speed but not shredding it fast enough to attempt a safe touch-down.

A cold sensation trickled down his neck, shivering along his spine. The bomber was about to embrace its long grotesque shadow. Carter braced himself for the crash. He'd seen too often how they started not to recognise the end. God, how unnecessary it was! "Open up, man, and go round!" He started at the fury in his voice, as the bomber's wheels skimmed the concrete, touched, bounced and bumped viciously before settling. The Halifax flashed past his line of vision, its tail at a flying angle.

"He'll never brake in time! Never lose that speed . . .!" he shouted.

The bomber plunged over the end of the concrete and lurched crazily, as it hit the rough surface of the ploughed field. It seemed to sink. The tail broke off and hop-scotched across the black uneven earth, in irregular, jerky leaps.

From where he stood, it looked to Carter as if the undercarriage had buckled under the tremendous strain. The bomber reared again and careered violently into a clump of barren trees.

A deep muffled explosion rolled over the airfield. A column of dense black smoke curled lazily from the crumbled, shattered fuselage. Dark red flames seared through the smoke, shrouding the trees. In their wake, darting yellow tongues of liquid fire blazed along the broken wings and scintillated feverishly up the petrol-splashed trunks of the trees.

"This sure is a Jinx squadron . . .!"

"Jinx be damned!" Carter, his face ashen, turned furiously on his Flight Commander.

"That was plain bad atrocious flying! You saw him come in, and should know it!"

The words cracked, stinging with the force of a wet whip. The Flight Lieutenant flinched. Carter's eyes, and the contempt they spat, flicked from his face to the D.F.C. ribbon beneath his brevet.

"I would have expected that a Flight Commander would be able to recognise rank bad flying! You disappoint me, Flight-Lieutenant Ross!" He turned sharply and walked to his car.

A burly Flying Officer in the dark blue battle-dress of the R.A.A.F. said drily, "Some strip he tore off you, Rossie!"

The Flight Commander turned his head slowly towards the speaker. "He was so right. I opened my big mouth, and in a couple of seconds tossed away any reputation and judgement I ever had."

"I cry for you!" said the Australian.

The station fire engine, racing bonnet to bonnet with the crash-tender, hurtled past A Flight. Behind them bumped the two station ambulances. Carter stood on his accelerator and sped after them. At the end of the runway he jumped out of the car and half ran, half stumbled over the furrowed field. When he reached the wreck, the fire was spluttering furiously against the concentrated deluge from the chemical hoses.

Three men in dirty asbestos suits hacked grimly at what remained of the Halifax's cockpit. A squat airman with thick asbestos gloves was half lifting, half dragging a blackened torso from the pilot's seat. Two hundred yards to the right, and behind a derelict plough, lay the smashed tail of the Halifax. Three men were coming from it, carrying a formless bundle. As they passed, he noticed the heavy rubber gloves on their hands.

A gust of wind caught the loosely tucked in end of the grey blanket, whipping it back. Two blobs of glazed pink jelly stared at him from the reddish-white pulp of a face which ten minutes earlier had a bird's eye view of Nissindon.

He bent over and with a deft movement of his hand flipped back the loose flap of the blanket. That would be the rear gunner—human ballast to keep the tail down—must have smashed against the butts of the guns.

There was unlikely to be more than four in the aircraft, which had been on a short delivery flight. A skeleton crew—the phrase was apt, he reflected wryly—of pilot, bomb-aimer, wireless operator and rear-gunner would have been enough. Might not have been the rear-gunner. Could be the W.O.P or a flight engineer riding in the rear turret?

He turned back to the smouldering wreckage. A young L.A.C., his face deathly grey, rested with one hand against the side of the ambulance. Suddenly the airman retched and Carter's eyes moved from him to the Flight Sergeant coming towards him. "How many have you found?" He knew it was a hopeless question, but he added: "I suppose none got out of it?" The Flight Sergeant dabbed his smoke-grimed face with a soiled handkerchief, and shook his head gravely.

"We reckon four, sir, but it could be five. We're making another search!"

Carter looked inside the big ambulance, which was spotlessly clean—and empty. What bodies had been recovered were being put into the smaller vehicle, cynically known to the aircrews as the Meat Cart.

Fifteen minutes later, he knocked on the door of Dorton's office and walked in.

The Group Captain's face was set in hard taut lines. "It's those fellows in his crew that I'm sorry for. Why in the devil didn't he go round again? Either too damned confident or too damned lazy! Whatever it was, it was criminal!"

Carter lit a cigarette before replying. Dorton noticed his hand trembled a little. "I've come from the wreck. They think there were four, possibly five. But it will be for the S.M.O. to say definitely. Don't envy him his job."

The full-throated roar of a Halifax taking off made Carter look up. Dorton said: "I've ordered the circuits to go on. Better to get the new crews up straight away. I've also instructed all aircrew to be in the main briefing room at 1730 hours."

He paced restlessly to the window, turned and added: "I want to ram home the difference between a so-called hoodoo and rotten flying!" he said frigidly.

Carter looked at him steadily. "I've been doing a little of that myself. I don't think you could have picked a better time, sir!"

7

EYE-CATCHING Air Ministry contents bills with bold head-lines screaming 'Have You Done This?' . . . 'This is Important' . . . 'Remember That?' . . . plastered the green painted walls of the main briefing room.

Aircrews sprawled over the rough wooden forms, and leaned inertly across the ink-stained tables. Others, who could not find seats, lounged along the walls in attitudes of complete and utter boredom. Through the blue-white haze of tobacco smoke a hundred-and-sixty voices rose in a noisy babble.

The older crews made pungent remarks, bitterly resenting that the early transport into town had been cancelled until the briefing was over. As Pilot Officer Martin put it to his navigator: "Next thing they'll be giving us homework in our spare time!"

Crews who had not been flying had changed into their best blues. The rest were about to change when the loud speaker system blared the parade. A shuffling of massed feet, punctuated by a few wooden forms crashing to the floor, greeted Group Captain Dorton as he entered with the Wing Commander.

Dorton leapt lightly on to the raised dais in front of the huge wall map constructed from sections of Mercator charts. He searched the rows of white faces in front of him, contemplating for a full half minute the assortment of brevets and uniforms. Ignoring the fact that half the crews were smoking, he said: "Sit down, gentlemen! Smoke, if you wish," he said crisply.

He cleared his throat, but there was no nervousness in his manner.

"First, I want to welcome the new aircrews and introduce myself to the older crews. Before very long I hope to meet you all personally."

Motioning to Carter, he said: "Wing Commander Carter is also a comparative stranger to this squadron. He will see you here at 0930 hours tomorrow. Listen carefully to what he says, for he is one of Bomber Command's most experienced pilots. We are lucky to get him."

Dorton waited expectantly until a restless, inattentive shuffling which had suddenly sprang up faded under his relentless glare. When he spoke there was a challenge in his voice.

"Carter and I have decided that 186 has been slumbering long enough. We are going to wake you up! There are new aircraft coming along. I expect the first of them next week. More important, there's some new equipment, and we want it. You would want it, too, if you knew how easier it will make your job."

A murmur triggered through the long wide room. "First, we have to prove that we're good enough to be trusted with it!"

His voice rasped and the words flew in slivers of ice and men recoiled at their sting.

"At Group they have almost written you off as a bad squadron, not worth the operating costs. They tell me you're sorry for yourselves. You imagine the Hun has a personal vendetta against you. Looking at your aiming points, I consider you flatter yourselves!"

A cathedral silence stifled the room. Someone at the back coughed. The sound reverberated sharply. Dorton waited for the shuffling to start off again.

Still that muteness. They were more apathetic than he had imagined.

"I don't put a great deal on what they think at Group. If you have had higher losses than other squadrons, then you're obviously not as efficient as they are. And conjuring up a hoodoo, as you seem to have done, as a shock-absorber from facing the facts won't help you any!"

Dorton surveyed the room. No one was smiling now. Men who had earlier been doodling on their desks stopped. His words were going home to them. Their very attitude told him that. Some showed open resentment in their eyes, some eyes smouldered with hostility, but most were perplexed and bewildered. A few looked hurt and embarrassed.

"If you go out thinking you won't come back, you give the Hun that psychological advantage which comes from your own inferiority." Dorton thundered. "We are the *elite*! Never forget that! Any man on this squadron who thinks the going is too hard had better get out now!'

A slight tousled-haired R.A.F. Warrant Officer seated in the front row flushed.

Dorton's eyes ranged the room at random. "Don't think for one moment we can't replace you, and replace you damned quickly! So many young men are clamouring for aircrew training that the selection boards can now afford to be a little more choosey. Our shortage is aircraft. So if any of you want to chuck it, you can do so. You always could, you know!"

His voice dropped and he said placidly: "I'd prefer it that way. However, I have a hunch that I've the making of a good squadron here, and from now on we are going to let Group know it. There's just one thing more. A valuable aircraft and a costly trained crew were lost on this station a few hours ago. I have no sympathy for the fool who was flying it, but I have a deep sorrow for the men who died in that crash. Their deaths were quite needless."

The bare electric bulb above the raised platform glared down on the Group Captain, sending flint sharp flickers of light from his eyes.

"Those of you who saw his approach will understand when I term his flying criminal. There was no jinx! No honest-to-God Gremlins about that! He had every opportunity of opening his throttles and making another circuit. That was the first lesson they taught at elementary flying school. Probably he was in too much of a hurry to get down and head the afternoon tea queue! Whatever it was, you had a lesson I hope all pilots here will never forget!".

Dorton stepped back and the Wing Commander barked: "Attention. . . . Dismiss!"

In the coach into town the Group Captain's address was hotly debated. There was unanimity on only one point. The crash had been the result of tremendous 'finger trouble'. The new crews were careful not to express any strong opinion on the C.O.'s remarks. Accepted as part of the squadron, they sensed acutely the invisible barrier between themselves and the men who had operated. After their first trip that barrier would crumble but there was for them still the first Op to be completed.

Flight Lieutenant Chuck Ross, the A Flight Commander, was

speaking in a slow drawl to Flight Sergeant Bowson, his Manitoba rear-gunner.

"Quit shouting me down, Bluey, and try and use your head for once!"

Bluey cursed. "I still say Groupie's got a bloody nerve to bawl us out like that! He's hardly unpacked his bags and knows sweet darn-all about this squadron. Yet he gets up and calls us a bunch of no-good bastards. Instead of nattering, he should come out with us some night!"

The Flight Commander opened his mouth. Bluey waved to him to be quiet.

"Hell!" he snarled. "They're all the same, so why excuse the sonofabitch?"

A gaunt, hatchet-faced Warrant Officer with a Scots burr said: "Shut up, Bluey. The old man didn't get that D.S.O. for hanging around the Flight Office!"

Encouraged by the interruption, the Flight Commander said evenly: "There's no getting away from it, we haven't had very many aiming points lately. On Stuttgart we had the worst record of the lot."

"Go on! Blame the ruddy bomb-aimers!" mocked a voice from the front of the bus. "We can't bomb accurately if the drivers weave all over the ruddy sky. Anyway, we don't get any bouquets for doing dummy runs."

Bluey snorted. "And no gol'-damned wonder! Half the time you bomb-aimers are mucking around so much you don't see the stuff that's coming up."

"Aw, pipe down, Bluey," said an Australian. "You couldn't see an 88 at ten yards, let alone hit it! Wonder why Chuck carries you?"

The coach rounded a bend sharply, flinging its occupants against one another. A couple sprawled on the floor and swore loudly. The Flight Commander picked up his hat and dusted it carefully. "Groupie was right about a lot of things. He was not so far out either when he said we were a sorry crowd. I often wondered what it was. Guess I was too near the wood to see the trees. Reckon we're going to be all right with this Dorton guy and the new Wingco!"

Kiwi said softly. "I think so too."

"We'll see! We'll see!" Bluey snarled.

The coach lurched to a stop in the High Street.

Over a plate of chips, spam and baked beans, Kiwi glanced at Douglas. "Bloody tough on your rear-gunner. I watched his face when the Group Captain made those remarks on his brother's flying. It was ghastly. I thought for a moment he was going to go berserk. Can't understand it. From what Marty heard from the pilots of the other aircraft, Callaghan was pretty good."

Douglas laid down his knife and fork. "He saw it all, too. Didn't know then that it was his brother. We watched it from C Flight. You know they've assigned us to S bay?"

The New Zealander nodded, and Douglas said: "It's influence doesn't seem to have lost any of its potency!"

"Don't think about it, Shern. Christ, what a bloody reception, we laid on for you boys!" His concern sounded sincere.

"Real friendly like! Too much has happened too quickly for my mind to grasp it all. What was behind that speech of Groupie's?" Douglas asked searchingly.

Kiwi swallowed, and took a sip from the cup beside him.

"What I more or less told you the first day. The squadron has been going downhill this last while. A new C.O. and a new Wingco move in. They've been told to get it back on its feet. Take it from me, things are going to be pepped up around here. We've drawn two tough babies!"

"Sometimes," Douglas said, "I wonder why I was sucker enough to get my feet off the ground!"

The New Zealander speared a chip, then looked up inquiringly. "Why did you?"

Douglas scraped back his chair. Slowly he lighted a cigarette and watched the smoke twirl and twist with the draught from the open window. A wrinkled smile played on his lips.

"Found myself in a T.A. outfit when war broke out. A.A. battery. Nothing more soul-destroying than an A.A. battery, especially one run by amateurs. Jumped at the chance to transfer after France fell. Always wanted to be a pilot. Used to imagine myself in a Hurricane or Spitfire!" Douglas smiled wanly. "Liked the appeal of being on my own. If I was going to be killed, it would be my own doing. The Yanks fixed that, or to be more accurate, that blasted Bund fellow I drew as my instructor. Trouble now is that I've had too many hours in as a pilot to feel at ease as a passenger. Not at all sure if I was wise to re-muster."

Douglas paused. "I look at it this way, Kiwi," he went on, "and it sorta makes it easier. I've had a pretty good time as a Sergeant Observer in Canada and the States. You walked into a bar and you knew folk looked at you. Not you really, but the wing. It was an open sesame to most things. I live well and the pay is higher than any other service job. We have a lot more cash in our pockets than Army Lieutenants. Now the bill has to be paid, and the price is thirty operations."

For a moment he was quiet and toyed with his fork. Then with a strange finality in his voice said: "They reckon one crew in three comes through a tour, with the odds getting smaller as you go on. I don't very much care if I come through or not. Naturally, I'd be immensely pleased if I did, but I just don't count on it! Instead, I've resigned myself to the fact that I won't come through. So I'm going to live every minute of my leaves. Easy-living Shern from now on!" He sat back in his chair and flicked his cigarette ash impatiently.

Kiwi beckoned the waitress, called for the bill and looking intently at Douglas said gently: "I knew when they washed me out, that I'd never make the grade as a pilot. Lacked the necessary co-ordination. I like flying, but I don't like being shot at. Now some fellows never turn a hair about going through a barrage. That's contrary to what a lot of people generally believe. Some just don't scare! It's darned ridiculous to say that all men are scared. Somehow it's become fashionable to say it. If one says, truthfully, he did three dummy-runs over the Ruhr and frankly enjoyed it, the majority of people would term him a line shooter. Yet I've known blokes like that, Shern," the New Zealander said earnestly.

The waitress came over and laid down their bill. Kiwi waited until she had gone, and went on sombrely: "It must be something in their mental make-up. Probably some stimulant to their nervous system. Perhaps by trying to prove something they're not quite clear about, they unknowingly unleash powers of self-hypnosis which quells their fears."

Pulling out his wallet, he extracted a note. "Shern, some would throw it in, only they're more frightened of what their mates would say. So they keep going out. If they get through their last trips, they're almost mental wrecks. Take this 'twitch' business. Great joke at the moment! People bandy it about as they do 'I couldn't-care-less' stuff. Look around the mess and you'll see that the 'twitch' is very real."

He shrugged his shoulder. "Hell, we're talking like a couple of quack psychiatrists! Let's get a drink," he said hastily.

"Where do we start?" Douglas asked.

Kiwi chuckled. "We'll leave the Phoenix for the moment and go over to the Atlantic. Most of the boys go to the Phoenix. Incidentally, Shern, you get a week's leave every six weeks here. Sometimes it comes round sooner if the crews before you go down. We've just come back from ours, so we should go about the same time."

Douglas said drily. "Fine, I'll save for it!"

8

THE hotel Atlantic had the faded, resigned look of an actress who had undergone her last face-lifting operation. An H.E. bomb dropped by a Heinkel on a night raid had levelled the hotel's wing. The once plush cocktail bar had been hurriedly repaired, with the result that it was now a cross between a gin palace and the neon-lighted foyer of a better-class cinema.

Kiwi draped a leg over one of the red leathered stools, and ordered two rums and ginger. Glancing at the long mirror behind the bar, he saw that the oblong room was half empty.

"Come on," said Douglas, "let's have a look at the lounge."

"You mean," Kiwi said lightly, "have a look to see what women are about?"

Douglas winked slyly, and they finished their drinks and moved down the bar.

They had downed their third rum and ginger when two girls seated at a table near the window smiled.

The New Zealander smiled back. "They don't look bad, Sherm. Shall I get them over?"

Douglas looked in the direction of the window. "Take it slowly. We can do better."

A little later Douglas rose suddenly, stubbed out the cigarette he had been smoking and, skirting round the crowded tables, made for the lounge entrance.

Kiwi following him with his eyes, saw two girls framed in the doorway. Even through the haze of tobacco smoke he could see they were unusually attractive.

As Douglas reached them, a young Army Lieutenant, who had moved from the bar, faltered and rather reluctantly, he thought, drew back. Kiwi took a long drink from his glass. Douglas, long practised in the casual 'pick-up', could charm a bird out of a bush. Kiwi had watched that same, seemingly innocent approach before, and seldom seen it fail.

He chuckled softly. There was a top drawer snub for him if they happened to be waiting for someone. He had known that happen before, but he didn't think it would turn out that way tonight. The girls were laughing, and Douglas was talking to them as if he had known them for months. Yes, he had to hand it to him. An accomplished operator who had long ago learned to play his own weakness for women against a woman's weakness for a smooth-looking fellow in a smooth-fitting uniform.

They were edging their way round the tables, with Douglas escorting them with the air of a wine waiter anticipating a big tip. He wondered which one Douglas had selected for himself. The blonde girl looked lovely but so did her friend. He thought he preferred the blonde girl.

"Suzan," Douglas said, his hand on the arm of the blonde girl, "this is Kiwi, one of the better types of New Zealander, though they're all grand fellows."

He rose and smiled at a pert face with two bright, sparkling blue eyes. Douglas, he mused, must be slipping, handing him a girl like this. She was slight and slender, with an almost beautiful face. She smiled back at him and the smile was radiant. No bar-room fly, this. Her voice was soft, musical, with no trace of accent. "You don't look as lonely as your friend has made out," she said.

Before he could think of a reply, Douglas interjected, "And this is Terry!"

A tall, slim girl with long black hair, which rested in shallow waves on her shoulders, nodded to him. God, she was lovely. Douglas had hit the jack-pot tonight. She sat down and her coat slipped open. He decided tight white sweaters suited her admirably.

"Kiwi, this is Terry's birthday," Douglas said warmly. "Twenty-one today. And I've pledged myself that she's going to have some fun." Smiling across at Suzan, Douglas went on, "As it happens, Kiwi is twenty-five today, and such a coincidence requires a slap-up celebration."

Suzan asked gaily, "Seriously, are you really?"

Somehow he hated to lie to this girl. Her eyes, a trifle grave, looked directly into his.

"It so happens," he said, and silently cursed Douglas. He would explain later if they ever got to know each other, for already he knew that he wanted to meet this girl again. Douglas waved airily to the waiter, and gave him their order.

Odd how he had never seen this girl in town or at any of the local dances. She said, in a honey cucumber voice. "Do you come here often?"

"As often as we can." His words tailed off, then he added. "We move between here and the Phoenix. But tell me, where have you been all this time? Are you strangers?"

She shook her head. "Not exactly strangers, but we don't go out a great deal," she said.

"What brought you here tonight?" he asked pointedly.

"My, what questions!" she said teasingly. "But I'll tell you. It was Terry's birthday and I thought she needed a change. You see, her husband was killed not so long ago—eight months, to be exact—and she has been rather in the dumps."

He glanced across at Douglas. He was deep in conversation with Terry, oblivious to anyone else in the room. But the words he had spoken so often came back to him. He couldn't recall the actual phrasing Douglas had used but it was something about peeling off when you saw a marriage ring in wartime. "Safer that way. You don't have to marry them," he'd said. Invariably Douglas had kept his affairs strictly to married women.

A strange feeling of foreboding came over him and as quickly went. Leaning over, he said: "I'm sorry about that. Tell me, are you married?"

She shook her head and he imagined he caught a glimpse of sorrow in the sudden curve of her lips. "No, but it was very close. I was engaged to an R.A.F. navigator. He went missing over Essen the week before we were to be married."

He fell silent and she said: "Now my turn for questions. What part of New Zealand are you from?"

He told her, and in telling her, amazed himself that he could talk so freely about things he had thought he had long ago forgotten. His life in Wellington, his family and his operations in a bomber. And in turn he learned her story and, with it, the story of Terry.

They lived together in the flat Terry's late husband had taken over when his mother died. Both had been shorthand typists, but were now working as time-sheet clerks in the local shadow factory. Terry's home was in Nottingham, while she herself was from Leeds, and it was there they had met when both were receptionists in the same hotel.

The waiter came over, and Douglas signed to him to bring the same again.

Terry said wistfully, "We always look upon your squadron as our own special one. We hear you go out and sometimes, if we're awake, we hear you come back. We always wonder where you've been!"

She opened her handbag. Her long slender fingers flicked through it, and extracted a packet of cigarettes, "But we have to wait until the news comes on before we know where you've been ... and our guesses are always wrong."

Douglas took a cigarette from her pack and tapped it deftly on his thumb. "I'm glad to know that. Hate to think our nightly visits were known beforehand," he said.

They talked on, and as their words flowed they drank a little more. And their glasses were always full. If they noticed it, they didn't care. Only Douglas remained ever watchful, speculating on the hours ahead and never completely relaxed.

Attentive, and equally alert, was the tall, hawk-nosed waiter with the stooping shoulders. Attentive he could afford to be, for each journey to their table brought him a tip from Douglas.

Carefully choosing his moment, Douglas said, "It's a great pity, but we have to break it up."

His words rang coldly across their laughter. "But why?" Suzan's voice was plaintive, her eyes puzzled. Terry looked quickly at Douglas, searching his face.

Kiwi jerked back in his chair. "Did I hear you aright, Shern?"

"Unfortunately," Douglas said, "it's eight minutes to closing time." Smoothly he went on: "I'd give anything for this evening to last a bit longer, but the town goes to sleep now. Birthday parties should end with music. Pity we couldn't take you back to the mess. We have a piano there. Maybe you'll come when we have a guest night ...?"

He trailed off his words and drowned them in his glass. Suzan, he saw, was talking in low tones to Kiwi.

The New Zealander looked up anxiously. "Sue's got a portable gramophone," he announced.

So far, Douglas reflected, it had been easy. But then they had no reason to suspect his motive.

"Bless you, Sue," he said; "you supply the music and we'll lay on the celebration bottles."

"It's Terry's flat, I don't know if . . .?"

Douglas caught Terry's hand under the table, and squeezed it gently. "It's up to you, honey, and I'm keeping my fingers crossed."

"Oh, I feel like dancing! I suppose it's all right, but we better not make much noise . . . the folk upstairs are an elderly couple."

Douglas called over the waiter, whispered to him and handed him some notes. Shortly, he came back to their table with a bulky brown paper parcel.

Douglas slipped him a ten-shilling note and he beamed widely.

As they rose, Douglas said to Kiwi: "Two quid, Cobber! That's your donation to your birthday celebration?"

Walking from the hotel, Terry said, "I don't want you to think we usually take men to our flat. It's just occurred to me that you might think . . .?"

"I know!" Douglas said gently. "I knew you were different as soon as you came into the room. That's why I came straight over. I've never done anything like that before and I was afraid of being snubbed and missing the chance of ever meeting you again."

She smiled softly, and he felt her sway slightly against him.

"Another thing, Terry. I don't have to look round any more. From now on I want to spend every moment I can with you, if you'll allow me to."

Her eyes searched his face. "Do you mean that, or is it just one of your lines?"

"I mean it very much, and I'll remind you of it a year from now, if I'm lucky enough to come through this tour."

She stopped and looked up at him. "Have you many to do?" The voice was strangely anxious, perturbed.

"Quite a few."

They walked on, and lightly and delicately he drew the story of her marriage from her. She had been married nine weeks when her husband had been drafted to North Africa.

"We'd gone to school together, but only started going out with one another seriously when he came home on leave. That was when he was stationed in Scotland. Both our families were then in Nottingham and we saw a lot of each other."

"Love at first sight?" he prompted.

"No!" the answer was slow and thoughtful. "I wasn't at all sure if I loved him enough to marry him. But he was so certain, so insistent. At the beginning of his embarkation leave he bought a ring and well . . ." A little sadness came into her voice. . . . "He was a sweet boy, not what you would call strikingly handsome but he was quiet, gentle and very much in love with me. We were married by special licence. I think if we'd had a little more time together I'd have grown to love him. It all seems so unreal now, yet his death upset me terribly."

Quietly he said, "Don't get depressed. Remember this is a double birthday celebration!"

Her eyes sparkled and she laughed softly. Douglas thought her laughter was a trifle forced.

Her flat was on the ground floor of a drab, grey bricked, two-storied house at the end of a cul-de-sac. A small hall separated the two bedrooms from the living-room. At the end of the hall was the bathroom.

"Here it is." Terry said. "Not much to look at but the rent is low and we have our own door. The one at the side is for the top flat."

The dying embers of a fire flickered in the low, tiled fireplace in the living-room.

"I'll get some sticks and coal," Sue said.

The room had the atmosphere of a place which had been well lived in. The frayed carpet and the heavy curtains, Douglas thought, were out of place among the solid, well-used furniture. Terry switched on two table lamps and the glow from their deep yellow shades sent a pleasant warmth through the room.

As the fire was being kindled, Douglas unwrapped his parcel and brought out the bottles. The drinks he poured were stiff, their potency veiled with liberal splashes of lime from the bottle he had asked the waiter to include.

"Swell to relax before a fire again," Kiwi said.

Sue shot a side-long glance at the New Zealander. "If you like, you could have a meal with us tomorrow night," she suggested.

"Like nothing better, Sue. Snag is, we could be operating. Saturday nights make no difference to Butch Harris. If we're not, count on us being here."

Sue rose, slipped on a record and hummed the opening bars. She stopped and asked, "Are these raids as big as they make out? I mean, if they are, why haven't the Germans cracked up? Surely no one can stand up to thousand-bomber attacks?"

Kiwi settled himself more comfortably in his chair: "When the news bulletins announce that a thousand bombers were out, a thousand bombers were out. Jerry is tough, though! They come out of their deep shelters and start putting up what's been knocked down. Like blinking ants, they are!"

Terry perched on the arm of Douglas's chair, spilling some of the contents of her over-full glass on his sleeve.

Brushing it off with a handkerchief, she said: "It must be terrible for them and awful for you. War is so senseless. There must be people in Germany who hate it as much as we do. I think of the children being maimed and killed in these mass raids. It's so ghastly!"

"It's pretty grim, Terry," Kiwi said solemnly. "I often think of the kids myself. But Jerry asked for it, remember!"

The warm tingling of the drink he had, merging with the heat from the fire, brought a drowsiness to Douglas. Then Terry's words and Kiwi's reply stung him, sending an icy blast of fury through the warmth of the alcohol.

"This war is not senseless! I want to see every town and city in Germany in flames and their inhabitants blasted into dust!" The voice was savage and steeped in anger.

Kiwi noticed how Terry paled. "God!" she said, "how you hate! You frighten me almost! I didn't think you were at all like that!"

Kiwi said sharply: "Don't mind him. He's rehearsing what he thinks he'll tell his pupils if he ever gets posted as an instructor. This has been a swell evening, so don't spoil it, Shern. Besides, I thought you were looking after the drinks! Mine's empty!" He snapped out the last two words.

Douglas winced. Easy, he thought; he had almost spoilt things.

Rising, he said: "I can do with another myself. Sorry if I flew off the handle."

They danced and, unheeded, he mixed them fresh drinks. Shortly afterwards Sue switched off the gramophone, swayed against the table, and caught it.

"Lor', is my head spinning? And look at Kiwi: he's practically out!" she said.

"Must be the heat from the fire. It's pretty hot!" Douglas said casually.

He bent over the New Zealander and gently tapped his face. That last drink had knocked him cold.

"Kiwi; we have to go." Glancing at the clock above the fireplace, he added, "We've about ten minutes if we're to get the last coach. Come on now, Kiwi—we'll never get a taxi if we miss that coach."

Kiwi's head lolled drunkenly against the back of the armchair. Terry, slurring her words said, "He'll never make it. Better put him in my room and I'll share with Sue. You can sleep with him."

Douglas straightened. "That's very decent of you, Terry. Fact is, my head is whirling. Guess if the air hit me, I'd go out, too."

They carried Kiwi into Terry's room and Douglas put him to bed. Suzan said she felt sick and left the lounge.

Douglas leaned against the mantelpiece, gazing into the fire.

Looking up, he said: "Shame to waste this fire, Terry. One more drink and I'll join Kiwi. How about you, darling?"

"No!—— Gee! I feel dizzy—drank more tonight than I've ever done! Certainly some party . . .!"

Her words rambled, and she sank lazily on to the settee. Slowly she rose and walked unsteadily to the fire, tossing in her cigarette.

"These lights are too harsh . . . firelight's soothing," Douglas murmured, and knocked up the switch.

He strolled leisurely back to the fireplace and lightly pulled her towards him. She reeled backwards, but his pull was firm. Her arms went round his neck and their lips met in a long searing kiss. After a while their lips parted.

"Darling! I've been looking for you all my life!"

"Have you?" she whispered.

"I'm crazy for you, Terry," he said softly. Slowly he caressed the warm flesh under her sweater, gently found and loosened her brassiere, his hand cupping a firm, up-tilted breast.

He stifled her protest with a smouldering kiss. She felt her head spin as she tried to fight against emotions weakened and sapped by the potency of the drinks he had plied her with.

The tight waist-band of her skirt was no longer biting into her, nipping her skin. Somehow it had slipped in a crumpled heap to the carpet. Easily she felt herself being lifted and carried to the settee. His lips locked on hers. Passionately her arms swept round him, pulling his head hard down.

"Be careful, darling, be careful!" she murmured.

9

THE khaki mud-caked coach pulled up at R bay. Corporal Watson saw it as he stepped back to scrutinise the broad yellow S stencilled on the dull black fuselage of the Halifax.

Beside him, critically appraising the newly painted letter, was Curly, his armourer. The rest of the ground crew stood by. They had not been idle. Since the aircraft had been handed to them the previous day they had checked the engines thoroughly, watching the oil gauges with alert eyes.

"Run her up again, Johnny!" Watson shouted to the L.A.C. in the pilot's seat. "Easy, though!"

When the four engines were throttled back, he turned to Curly and said: "Ticking like a well-oiled sewing-machine. Still, I'll be better pleased when we get the Mark III."

The armourer ignored the remark. "Wonder what sort of crew we'll get?" he asked.

Watson jerked a thumb towards the wagon lumbering from the R bay. "We'll soon know. Keep your fingers crossed."

He watched, apprehensively, as the coach turned in a wide circle, before backing on to the Halifax. The rear door burst open and he took a deep breath, feeling as a child does when it thrusts a hand into a lucky dip barrel.

He could not make out who the first three were. Their wings were dirty and could have stood for anything. Probably the gunners and the wireless operator. The others came out and they looked equally untidy. Only the last man seemed to have any pride in his appearance. His battle-dress was comparatively new and it had been recently pressed.

"Hiya, Tosh!" bawled the chubby-faced youth, who had jumped from the coach first. "We've come to take over our bus!"

Watson winced at the 'our'. Lord, what cheek! We maintain it, clean it, nurse it. We do a hundred and more things to it, and he calls it 'ours'!

He would have enjoyed putting this impudent dwarf in his place. Controlling his anger, he searched the tunics of the others for the pilot's brevet. How unlucky could he be? This scruffy bunch beat any he had ever had to keep flying. Must have been the new Wingco who had allocated him this crew. Things must be bad when the selection boards passed such material!

An hour ago he had been happy. Now he was depressed and miserable. It was bloody unfair to give him riff-raff like this.

His eyes settled on Carson and he reluctantly introduced himself, saying: "You've got a good aircraft there and she's in top condition."

Carson smiled wryly. He sensed something was wrong, but he wasn't sure what it was. "I'm sure she is and I hope to keep her that way. We are doing some circuits and bumps this morning. Shouldn't be up too long," he said pleasantly.

Carson introduced his crew and watched them mingle with the ground staff, trying hard to make themselves liked.

Two hours later he banked the bomber in a wide turn over the sea. On their starboard, eight hundred feet below, Flamborough Head, washed by the white tops, floated by, bleak and rugged.

He switched on his intercom. "Last landing! Wonder what they're churning up for lunch?"

But his thoughts were with Callaghan back in the rear-turret, Callaghan who had watched his brother die in the funeral pyre of the crashed Halifax, who had said nothing, but whose smouldering eyes told it all.

The Group Captain had been right, of course; yet no one knew, or would ever know, why Callaghan had not opened up and gone round again. On the face of it, his airmanship had been shockingly bad. Yet the thought niggled at him—Callaghan had brought a crew through thirty operations! Landing Halifaxes was easy to him. Maybe that held the clue . . . too easy, perhaps.

The gunner was leaving on the night express from York, and in the guard's van, lying in a sealed and carefully weighted coffin, was to be his brother. Maybe it would be better when he came back in three days time. Why send the body North? Better to have buried it in the village churchyard. No, they would have wanted it brought home. That way they could weep over something tangible . . . a long box . . . fortunately sealed.

He wheeled the Halifax into the funnel, straightened out and began the approach. As the bomber flashed low over the start of the main runway, he said "Cut!"

Douglas, his left hand on the four red-topped throttle levers, his right flat against them, pulled them smoothly back, ready to open them the instant his skipper gave the command.

Douglas knew the order would never come. Carson was coming in for a near perfect landing.

Each day of that week the new crews were airborne. They flew long, boring flights to Cape Wrath, on the jagged gale-swept tip of Scotland, turning and cutting down country to Carlisle, before slicing in a zig-zag leg to Barrow and across the Pennines to Flamborough.

Group Captain Dorton marvelled at his good luck. The bad weather, with thick impenetrable fog, which clamped over the Yorkshire and Lincolnshire airfields in the late afternoon and kept Air Chief Marshal Sir Arthur Harris's heavies grounded, lifted with the dawn.

Dorton sent off his new crews and prayed for another twenty-four hours of adverse weather. He knew that when the weather cleared, the teleprinter in the signals office would stutter at noon and the flash would be 'Maximum Effort—Tonight'.

Some nights the main force could have taken off. But they could never have landed. The fog belt forecast by Met rolled in and was heavily settled by 2030 hours. It seldom cleared before 0800.

Even so the sirens shrilled over Berlin. Fast Mosquito bombers carrying 4,000-pounders relentlessly carried on the Battle of Berlin from the fog-free bases of Southern England.

At Nissindon, as the fog swirled in, spirits rose with the nightly jaunts into town. In the out of the way hotel to which Carter had first brought him, Dorton toyed with his brandy glass.

"Surprisingly good meal, Bill. Not that it wasn't the other night."

Carter straightened in his chair. "I used to eat here before the war. It was always good. Fortunately few, if any, on the station know about this place."

Dorton mellowed by the brandy, leaned forward and his hand tapped restlessly on the tablecloth. "I was inclined to ask for another Wing Commander when Cartingham broke it to me that you had been posted to Nissindon. Why I didn't has been worrying me ever since." His voice sounded tired and curiously flat.

Carter put down his glass and his lips tightened. "That would have put you in a very awkward position. What grounds had you, in mind?"

"You damned well know, Bill . . ."

"That was a personal matter," Carter interrupted, "and there is nothing you could have done about it. I'm sorry I ever took you into my confidence. If you wish . . ."

This time it was Dorton who interjected. "We're old friends and I'll say what I think. I've repeatedly respected your confidence but for how long I can continue to is another matter. Frankly, you shouldn't be operating. After all's said and done, it's only a matter of time before they give you a command of your own. New squadrons are being formed and competent C.O.s are urgently needed. And they're not so plentiful. That's the price we have to pay for maintaining a small airforce in peacetime. That's why the ban has been put on G.C.s and above flying on operations."

"You intend to keep to that?" Carter asked sharply.

Dorton pursed his lips and said heavily: "The point I'm trying to make, Bill, is this. You are of far more value to me on the ground. When I said the squadron were lucky to get you, I meant it. Therefore, I shall see that you adhere strictly to the quota of trips needed for the completion of your third tour. Further, I will veto, if necessary, any trip you may select, if I think the circumstances warrant it."

The Wing Commander drained his glass. Shaking his head slowly he said: "Feather-bedding won't help. One can get it as easily over a so-called soft target as over the Ruhr. I appreciate your motive, Harry, but don't press it."

Dorton shrugged. "We'll cross that bridge when we come to it!" Quietly he added: "I suppose nothing has happened since I saw you last which might lead to a—ah—conciliation?"

Carter shook his head gravely. "Too far gone for that. I don't even know where she is. The children are still with my aunt. I've, of course, drawn a new will and adjusted my allowances accordingly. On the whole I'm not so worried about it as I was."

Dorton sipped his brandy. Carter's face showed that he was more disturbed about his children's future than he tried to make out. He decided to change the subject, for the Wing Commander was plainly uncomfortable.

"I think it's my call. Care to have it in the bar?"

They pushed back their chairs, rose and walked across the tiny dining-room to the cocktail lounge.

The cigarette-scarred piano in the lounge of the Phoenix tinkled out a rollicking tune as the thin bony fingers of a Pilot Officer rippled along the yellow-stained keys.

Every bar in the Phoenix was crowded. Men with full-wings, half-wings, sergeant's chevrons and officers rings, slouched from one room to another. Most had their tunics unbuttoned and were hatless. At the far end of the lounge, clustered round a rickety cane table littered with glasses, were the crew of F—Freddie. With them were the mid-upper gunner, wireless operator and engineer of S—Sugar.

The air reeked of tobacco smoke and stale, flat beer. Bursts of laughter rose above the steady babel of voices. Pilot Officer Martin, his tunic undone, his hat perched on the back of his head, sprawled in a wicker chair, one leg carelessly draped over the arm.

Surveying the trickle of coins in the centre of the table, he grunted: "The kitty looks as low as my pint . . . better chip in, boys . . . How much is left?"

Sergeant Donald Pastone, Sugar's six-foot engineer, poked amongst the loose coins. "Four-and-eight," he said.

"O.K., lads," drawled Martin's navigator. "Five bob apiece? That will bring it up to nearly three quid!"

Martin fingered the big red brush tickling his nose and watched the kitty swell. Looking at Pastone, he said: "Rather hard your rear-gunner had to see his brother splatter himself over the tarmac like that. How's he taking it?"

Pastone, his head cocked to one side, his face twitching a little said: "Think he's got over the initial shock, but he's naturally badly shaken. He wanted to go round to the morgue but the S.M.O.

wouldn't have it. He's gone home to Glasgow with the . . ." his voice trailed away.

Martin swung his leg off the chair arm, and caught his hat from slipping off his head. . . . "Poor bastard. We all get it sooner or later. Live for the day, me boy . . . don't let anyone tell you different. . . . We all get it . . . question of time."

Davis cut in. "Cheerful fellow, our Marty. Missed his vocation, though . . . Should have been an embalmer."

Martin laughed hollowly. "Davis never comes out of his office to know what goes on over a target. He might as well be a conductor on a blacked-out London—Leeds express. Seriously, I'm sorry for you guys. That S bay was always unlucky! Powerful hoodoo over it! You barely are allocated to it when it starts working on the Callaghan family. Thought they were going to scrap the lousy letter?"

"Ignore Marty," Davis said heatedly, "that's his way of taking the Mickey out of new crews. Pure coincidence, so let's drop the shop talk. Anyway, it was bad flying. Should have gone round."

"Don't worry about it! We got a good skipper!" Titch chirped.

"Sure, sure, the best there is; only he should be playing in a swing band!" Martin said icily.

"Oh, he's curing himself of that swing," Titch said with some intensity.

"I certainly hope so for your sakes!" Martin grunted.

They drank steadily and as they drank, their bantering became more boisterous. Pastone eyed the pint before him. It appeared to swell into a quart, to reappear suddenly as a half-pint. Hot needles of pain pricked the base of his skull. When they stopped, tiny hammers took over and beat incessantly somewhere under the bone.

He got to his feet and glanced at the laughing masks seated round him. They couldn't know how he felt. Even if they did, they would never understand.

"Excuse me. Think I'll get some fresh air."

Morphy, his wireless operator, looked up. "You feeling O.K., Don?"

"I'm all right . . . all right," he said, and pushed his way through the mass of blue uniforms.

For a few minutes he stood motionless on the wet pavement. The cold air hit him and the blackness made him blink. The sound of the piano and the snatches of an Air Force song drifted through the half open window of the bar, to hang limply on the still damp air.

"Four Group sent some Halifaxes to the Valley of the Ruhr. ....
 Oh, Four Group sent some Halifaxes to the . . ."

Pastone tossed away his cigarette and shuffled up the deserted street. His headache was gradually easing. Things were becoming clearer. As clear as they had ever been since he joined Carson's crew. His log book, he remembered, with today's flying, now totalled twenty-nine hours.

"Merely to get you acclimatised," the Flight Sergeant instructor at the Engineers training school had said.

Acclimatised—that was odd. He knew at the end of the Conversion course that he would never feel at ease in an aircraft. It might have been wiser if he had thrown it in then. Better than being classified L.M.F. and sent back from a squadron.

The letters scorched his brain. Lack of Moral Fibre, they called it. No doubt some psychiatrist had coined that one! Probably he had meant to be kind. Coward was an ugly word. Yet it had lost much of its harshness as it echoed down the dim, distant labyrinths of time. L.M.F. was a freshly-minted phrase. New and shiny like Spitfire or Hurricane. Say it in a cold, deliberate, contemptuous tone and the barbs bit deeper and hurt more than the old, outmoded word of coward.

His thoughts drifted back to the men he had left in the pub. They had accepted him unconditionally because he wore their brand on his tunic. But he was not of them, never would be.

Sometimes he believed he could be if his mother were not so wholly dependent on him. Her words came back to him. "When the war is over, Don, no one can tell the flyer, the submarine man or the commando, from the clerk or the conscientious objector. You're doing your bit. Be patient! It can't last long! The papers say it will be over very soon!"

She had pleaded hard against his re-mustering for aircrew duties. Pastone bit firmly on his lip as he recalled the day she first saw him with his wing up. Gently he had led her to her chair, sat awkwardly on the arm and waited until her quiet sobbing had subsided.

There were just the two of them. It had always been like that as long as he could remember. Since the day his father died, when he was three, she had fought with the ferocity of a tigress in sheltering him from the outside world.

It had drawn them closer, this knowledge that they were alone, making them more and more dependent on each other as time went by. He tried to tell her he had to fly. She had looked at him sorrowfully and her eyes had been unusually bright.

"You hadn't at all, Don," she had said softly. "It's some streak of vanity in you that never showed before."

She had been wrong there. The endless drill, guard duties, the petty chores and the bullying N.C.O.s. The short cut away from it all was a wing. So the idea was nourished and, for him, it eventually swamped her reasoning.

It was not that he had no intention of going on operations when he had first put in for aircrew training.

He wanted to fly; at least then. It was those letters from home, always written in the same strain, asking and pleading for his return. Thank God, they had eased a bit since he wrote saying he was now instructing. Pastone halted in the empty square and looked up at the grey hulk that was the town hall. The tower clock began to strike ten. In half an hour the first coach for the aerodrome would arrive. He curled up the collar of his greatcoat and leaned against the wall, idly speculating on when the next Maximum Effort signal would come through.

The few aircrew who had not gone into town lounged in the deep leather armchairs in front of the blazing log fire in the Sergeants' Mess. Across the road, the Officers' Mess seemed equally silent and empty.

Carson thumbed the pages of the current issue of *The Aeroplane*, his eyes scanning the official Air Ministry casualty lists. Meticulously he went through the alphabetical columns of type. Already he had found the names of three pilots who had been on the American B.F.T.S. with him. He wondered how they had got to squadrons so quickly. None of them, he reflected, could have done many operations.

His watch showed it was nearly ten-fifteen. He tossed aside the magazine and rose to his feet. He wanted to get clear of the mess before the coaches pulled in with their boisterous liquor-flushed cargoes.

A full night's rest held more appeal to him than a drinking session round the mess piano. As he reached the hallway, the main door swung open and Masters, his navigator, came in.

He swayed a little on his feet. "Hello, Lew, thought you were turning in early?"

Masters' grey eyes looked at him with surprise. His light brown hair was wind-blown and ruffled. It made him seem younger than his twenty-four years.

"On my way now. Been in town?".

"No," said Masters, "met a fellow I knew at I.T.W. and we went into the village. Stick around and he'll be here in a moment. Then we'll have a drink?"

"Thanks, Larry. Some other time. I'm pretty tired tonight." Masters said lightly. "See you tomorrow, then."

Pedalling along the perimeter track, Carson whistled softly. On the whole he felt good. Mentally, he checked over his crew. Not particularly bright, with the exception of Masters and Douglas. But then his own rating was not so high. That could be turned into an asset. For, knowing his limitations, he would leave nothing to chance.

Easy for them to think he was unsociable. Six lives, apart from his own, were in his hands. There was nothing wrong in being over-conscientious about that. He had never mixed drink and flying and he was not going to start now. If they couldn't realise that, they were dimmer than he thought.

The gunners were a long way from being sharp-shooters, but they had guts. Callaghan was safe in the rear turret. Morphy was an efficient wireless operator. Reliable, too. Masters was a first-class navigator, with an ice-cool calculating mind. Never a trace of excitement in that precise, sardonic voice. If he was any judge, he was cooler than Douglas. Or colder, a more apt description. Douglas, for all his detached aloofness and fatalistic outlook, could be downright rash.

Maybe Douglas would settle down now and keep clear of the entanglements he always landed in, like that time he was playing around with the Flight Commander's wife at O.T.U. It had made their trip through O.T.U. harder than it need have been. He got tired of Douglas and the perpetual chip he had sewn on to his shoulder-strap. Better men than his bomb-aimer had been scrubbed as pilots, under the U.S.A.A.F. scheme.

The low roofs of the sleeping quarters loomed in black irregular oblongs in front of him. He swung off the perimeter track and rumbled over an uneven path. The iron stove in the room, he shared with masters, glowed red in the darkness.

Douglas had a single room a couple of doors from them. It was in darkness. He recalled how Douglas had taken over the room on the same morning that its late occupant's personal effects were being moved out, urging the orderly room Sergeant to hurry up.

"Callous bastard!" the Sergeant had remarked later to him. "Maybe we'll sort out his one day!"

"You'll be doing mine too then," he had said. "I'm his skipper."

The Sergeant had reddened and mumbled an apology. But he was right enough, he mused, Douglas seldom thought of anyone but himself. He himself had gone out of his way to make things easy for him. It came from the sympathy he had for one who had come so near to getting his wings. The memory of the relief which came over him when he heard he was going to a British Flying Training School was sharp in his mind. The only time he ever remembered Douglas looking happy was when he asked him to take over the controls of the Halifax.

It was all part of the bomb-aimer's duties in Halifaxes. They were expected to be able to fly the aircraft, excluding of course take-offs and landings, and he had never any qualms about handing over to his bomb-aimer. Some skippers, he reflected, were not so eager in having their bomb-aimers at the controls. Others, he chuckled softly, bragged that they had taught their bomb-aimers to fly almost as well as themselves.

With him, he had shown his confidence by leaving Douglas for long periods in the pilot's seat while he squatted with the navigator . . . and he always allowed him to follow through on the controls when they took off and landed in the dual machine at O.T.U.

He had done everything possible to make his bomb-aimer feel happy.

Then there was the new man—the Flight Engineer. Quiet and likeable, but somewhat bewildered. The bewilderment would go, he told himself, after the Engineer did a few more flights. Yes, Pastone would be all right. As he undressed, he thought again of his first operational trip as a second pilot, when he had gone with a screened crew from Conversion Unit. The next time he would be on his own.

10

AT 1130 hours the following day the first alert signal stuttered from the master teleprinter at Group . . . and on the squadrons the bomb trolleys and the petrol bowsers crawled towards the flights. It was going to be a "Maximum Effort".

"It's the Big City again! Can tell it from the bomb load and the juice they're to carry. Lay you two to one," Curly said to Corporal Watson.

"A mere thousand-pounder, the rest incendiaries and oil bombs. Could be, Curly," Watson said quietly.

Half an hour after the mess orderlies had cleared the luncheon tables, the loudspeaker system blared. Douglas heard it with Kiwi as they were leaving the mess.

"Attention! Attention! All pilots, navigators and bomb-aimers report to main briefing room at 1500 hours . . . Attention . . . All pilots. . . ."

Douglas shot a side-long glance at the New Zealander. "Wonder where Butch is sending us tonight?" He still felt rough from the drunken orgy of the night before and the early rush to get back to camp.

Kiwi said tersely: "I'll check your tracks, courses and pre-settings once we know the target. After a couple of trips you'll soon get the hang."

Peering over the heads of the jostling aircrews surging round the Ops board, Douglas ran his eyes down the letters. Chalked against F was Martin's name. His eyes focused on S and the name Carson written alongside. So tonight was to be the culmination of two years—two years of bitter disappointment and frustration.

He found himself trembling slightly. He put it down to excitement, but he knew in his heart it was nerves.

Carter stood before the huge mercator map of Western Europe.

The clamour of conversation had died down and the aircrews were seated quietly on the wooden forms in front of the plain tables.

The Wing Commander toyed with a bright red pin. Attached to the pin was a long narrow red cord. He surveyed the room for a few moments . . . "Tonight—it's Berlin again!"

He waited until the low murmur of whispered comments died. "For the benefit of the new crews, I must remind you that you do not divulge the target or anything which may identify it—not even to the rest of your crew. They will know soon enough at the main briefing at 1700 hours."

Carter handed the red cord to the Squadron navigation officer and watched him plunge the pin into the black square that was Nissindon. Deftly the navigation officer placed another pin in a minute triangle over a D.R. position in the North Sea. Swiftly, from there, he laid off the legs to the enemy coast, then across Germany to Berlin.

When Carter completed his briefing of the pilots, the navigation officer took over. Then came the bombing officer. Slowly and clearly they gave their instructions, repeating some points, stressing others.

Kiwi finished work on his chart and began to help Douglas. He pointed out where the flak belts were, where the concentrated batteries of searchlights could be expected.

After checking Douglas's computations, he said softly: "That's all you can do for now. They'll run through the general points at the full crew briefing. This is only to allow us to work out the tracks and courses. Saves a lot of time once we're airborne."

Two hours later, the main briefing hall was packed. This time the gunners, wireless operators and flight engineers were in the big room. There was one additional name to the crew list chalked earlier on the Ops board. Beside B—Baker was the name of Wing Commander Carter. And Carter, standing beside the Group Captain, was now in battle-dress.

Dorton ran through the preliminaries, pausing now and then to let his words sink in. "Lancasters will make up most of the main force. You know why, and I want to impress upon you all that, should any of you be unlucky enough to be shot down, you must forget everything you have heard about the Group converting to Halifax IIIs. . . . Remember that the vital thing in a mass raid is to get the maximum concentration of aircraft over the target in the minimum amount of time.

"The Target Indicators will go down at 0001. You will be in the first wave and your bombing time is 0002. The whole show has been timed to be over by 0024. Keep to your flight plan. It has been carefully worked out to achieve this concentration. . . . And fly the heights you have been given. They have been scaled to avoid collisions over the target. You must keep to them."

Dorton slapped his thigh with his gloves. "Wing Commander Carter is flying with you tonight, so I will hand the rest of the briefing to him. If there is anything you are not sure about, please ask."

Carter, a billiard cue in his right hand, traced on the map the course and heights they were to fly at, the estimated time of arrival at their turning points. He told them—and there was a sigh of relief at his words—that twenty minutes before they crossed the enemy coast sixty aircraft from the O.T.U.s would make a dummy feint a hundred miles from their landfall. Half an hour later marauding Mosquito bombers would attack targets from the Ruhr to Bremen as an extra diversion to fox the night fighters.

The Bombing Leader said his piece, thankful he himself was not going out; he had an unpleasant memory of the last time he had gone to Berlin. He revealed that the Pathfinders would take as their aiming point the Unter den Linden. They would mark it with red indicators. The backers-up would aim at the reds with green markers in as tight a circle as the Mark 14 bombsight would allow.

"So your primary aiming points are the reds. If they are bombed out or otherwise obscured, bomb the greens." He moved over to allow the Met Officer to be seen. Suddenly he hesitated . . . "Remember," he added sternly, "check your bombing stations for hang-ups."

The Met Officer, a mild soft-spoken man with large horn-rimmed glasses, nervously unrolled his chart. He might as well keep it rolled, he thought. It was always the sign for a ripple of laughter to go round the room.

He resented deeply this enforced role of briefing jester, for there were only two questions they ever wanted to know. The rest were phrased either to raise a laugh or make him look foolish.

Glancing apprehensively at his weather chart, he was about to amplify a point he was making, when a long-haired bomb-aimer with a Cockney accent rose to his feet. "Say, what's it like over the target? Is it likely to be clear?"

He waited for a moment. Group Captain Pittle would never have stood for an interruption like that. He half turned to Dorton. The Group Captain and the Wing Commander were smiling faintly, but still, they were smiling.

He spun round quickly, flushed, and icily retorted: "I was coming to that. Obviously, since you are to bomb visually, we expect fairly clear conditions."

A loud cheer burst from the centre of the hall as they applauded his retort.

Reddening, he switched the chart to his left hand and traced with a finger the portion west of Berlin. "This front should pass to the south of the target and should be clear of the area before you arrive. On the other hand, there is the chance, which we do not rate highly, of the wind changing. If this happens, the top edge of this front here . . ." he tapped it with his finger . . . "should bring about five-tenths cloud over the city."

Martin snorted and said to his navigator, "Ifs and buts and shoulds, that's all we ever get from those wallahs! They don't bloody well know themselves!"

A Warrant Officer Pilot lumbered to his feet. "What's it likely to be when we get back?"

The Met Officer eyed him bleakly. "Visibility should be fairly good, with cloud base at 3000. A slight drizzle below, with gradual deterioration in visibility, is expected about 0500; but you should be in your beds before then."

He smiled in a sickly way. They could have their little joke. He didn't really mind. He would be in bed in another hour, while they . . . he shrugged, and asked, "Any more questions?"

Dorton stepped briskly forward. "That's all then, except— Good Luck, Gentlemen, and Good Bombing." He was irritated with Carter. It was not until the afternoon briefing that he had casually announced he was going with them. His first reaction was to remind the Wing Commander that he did not have to pick the toughest targets for his third tour.

Flight Lieutenant McGrath, with twenty-five operations behind him, nudged Martin. "Hell, if I was the Wingco, with the record he has, Berlin would be about the last place I'd include in my quota."

Martin fingered his moustache. "Christ, maybe he's after another bar; but he can have it. Imagine the last one picking on the Big City?"

"I can't, not even in my wildest dreams," drawled McGrath.

As the crews filed out of the big briefing room, a slim fair-haired gunner with a flying officer's cord on his shoulder straps and a D.F.M. on his tunic, tapped Martin on the shoulder. "I happened to be behind you when you made that remark about the Wingco. Don't ever say it again, or I'll personally tear that ugly brush from your top lip!"

A squat, broad-shouldered W.O., with the wing of an engineer, at his side said tersely: "He ain't kiddin' none! You get some ops in, son, before you make cracks about our skipper. We don't like it, especially when it comes from bums on a squadron he's trying to make operational!"

Martin coloured, and was about to reply, when Davis said: "You got it all wrong, fellows. It was meant as a compliment."

The Warrant Officer said menacingly. "It better be," and pushed past them towards the door.

Group Captain Dorton, his ears tingling with the concentrated roar from twenty-two Halifaxes warming up, climbed into his car after chatting with Carter and his crew. When he came to S bay, he pulled in, braked and got out.

Carson, watching his port-inner engine spring to life leaned out from the open cockpit window and glanced down at the Group Captain. Gently he throttled back and moved to get out.

Dorton waved him back and shouted, "It's all right! Just came along to wish you a good trip!"

Carson smiled broadly. Dorton entered his car and drove in the direction of the secondary runway.

He parked well off the concrete and waited, as the first of his Halifaxes taxied slowly down the perimeter track and on to the start of the runway.

Behind the first bomber came the rest of the squadron in a long snaky chain. Flashes of yellow flame pierced the darkness as engines were run-up and eased back. The end of his cigarette glowed from the darkened interior of the car. The flashing exhausts of A—Able led the spaced out line of black Halifaxes. Her pilot taxied on to the runway, cleared his engines and the noise from its four airscrews, running at full throttle, shattered the stillness of the night.

A green Aldis lamp flickered to the port of the runway from the control wagon parked on the grass triangle.

The roar from the bomber's engines increased to a thunderous snarl. Slowly, picking up speed with each second, the Halifax, heavy in the belly with a full load, rolled smoothly down the runway. Reluctantly she lifted and climbed steadily into the night, her navigation lights twinkling.

Other evil-looking black shapes lumbered past him. They reminded Dorton of racehorses but, he thought, rather old, tired racehorses, being led past the stands to the starting post.

Once again the Aldis lamp flashed green and B—Baker with Wing Commander Carter at the controls roared down the runway to take off into the blackness.

Douglas, sitting in the co-pilot's collapsible seat, tightened his safety belt and slammed shut the side window. It was quieter in the cockpit now.

Carson evenly pushed the four throttle handles open and curtly called "Lock!"

Douglas's left hand closed over the hand of his skipper's, his right pulled back on the locking lever. Silently he prayed that Carson would keep the bomber straight.

There was no margin for any of his skipper's wild swings. A bad swing, coupled with the weight they were carrying . . . the thought chilled him, for this was the first time Carson had taken off with a full load.

The Halifax was half-way down the runway when the blood drained from his face. His body tightened. The bomber was swinging, gently at first, then wilder.

"For God's sake!" he felt like screaming, "you'll kill us all!" His first instinct was to brace his feet against the panel in front of him, but the safety belt tight round his waist, made the movement impossible, for his feet were clear of the floor, swinging over the entrance to the navigation hatch.

He fought back the panic which swept over him, his mind gradually clearing. No hope of coming out of a crash at this speed, he thought. It was then that he remembered the bombs. The utter hopelessness of it qualmed him. His eyes fixed on the engine gauges in front of him. That would be about the spot his head would smash against when the Halifax's undercarriage folded under the unequal strain of trying to go forward and sideways at the same time.

He thought of the bomb-aimer who had flown on that fatal trip with his rear-gunner's brother. He must have experienced all this.

Tearing his eyes from the instrument panel, he glanced at Carson. Thin riverlets of sweat trickled down his skipper's forehead as he exerted all the strength in his right leg on the starboard rudder, in a last effort to counteract the pull to port.

The blue lights marking the edge of the runway whipped towards them at a fantastic speed, but their angle was all wrong. The tip of their port wing should have formed a clean 90 degrees angle with the lights. Instead, they were yawing towards the boundary markers at an acute angle.

Any second now the wheels would flash over the lights, bounce on the grass verge, and then ... The hoodoo couldn't be blamed this time, surely, Douglas reflected. But those who hadn't flown with Carson would not know, and so the myth would grow and gain in power.

His face ashen and haggard, Carson hauled back on the control column. The Halifax shuddered and sluggishly dragged itself from the runway. Carson eased the control column forward to scrape above stalling speed. Douglas saw his teeth bite sharply into his lower lip.

It was then he saw the vague outline of the white-washed building hurtling towards them. Frantically, Carson pulled back the stick.

In the rear turret, Callaghan knew the bomber had developed a swing. He sensed it get worse and tried to gauge the extent of it from the angle of the flare path lights. He saw the lights pass under him and he knew they had left the runway. They were airborne—but only just. His stomach muscles twisted violently and his eyes glazed as the chimney of the farmhouse flashed beneath his feet. He fought back the giddiness that had come over him and pounded his right boot against his left toe-cap. He felt no pain. He slumped back in his seat, his heart pumping madly as his breath came in sharp, short gasps.

Seconds later he looked down at the tiny blue lights. His fear left him with the knowledge that somehow they had got off. The giddiness vanished and a tiredness came in its place. But then, he had not slept since he had returned from burying his brother.

He switched on his intercom. "Jesus, skipper! You missed that farmhouse by inches!"

Down below, Group Captain Dorton found his hands tremble as he lit a cigarette.

Had the swing developed earlier, parts of the Halifax would have been scattered over the airfield, for they would never have gained the speed necessary to lift her.

Dorton shuddered. His mind flashed to a fleeting slide of the buxom, rosy-cheeked woman and the three children he had seen that morning feeding some cockerels from the kitchen door of the farmhouse. They would have been blasted into nothing. His hand brushed across his brow, wiping away tiny beads of ice cold sweat.

The rest of S—Sugar's crew never fully realised how death had pardoned them on the take-off. They were in the fuselage, braced against the main wing spar in accordance with take-off and landing procedure. They saw nothing and knew nothing until the rear gunner's voice came over the intercom system.

At 2030 hours the squadron kept its rendezvous with the main force, 8000 feet above the North Sea. And, like them, they kept climbing to operating height.

Ten minutes before they were due to turn on to the last leg leading to Berlin, Morphy leaned round from the transmitter and handed Masters the broadcast wind.* The navigator discarded his own and worked out the course to the target from the new wind. He smiled faintly seeing that it was practically the same wind as he had been using.

---

* Result of Wind Speeds and Wind Directions worked out by selected aircraft in main force and transmitted to England. It was analysed and the mean average broadcast to all aircraft in the bomber stream. It thus ensured that all would navigate on same wind and keep concentration intact.

Switching on his intercom, he said: "Course for target 063 magnetic! Speed 185! Turn on NOW!"

Carson repeated the order and altered course. Masters laid down his dividers. Way down there—any moment now, he reflected, someone would lift a telephone over a broadcast line and bark an order. Down through the closely co-ordinated commands it would flash until it reached the tense waiting gun crews and searchlight batteries of Berlin's massive ground defences. Then, and the thought chilled him, all hell would be let loose.

He swallowed his two Pep tablets and debated with himself whether he should slip into the nose when they sighted the target. He decided he would look at Berlin's defences on the next trip. There would be more time then. At the moment he had enough to do and had still the course out to watch.

The fighter flares floated down ahead of them when they were eight minutes from the city. They burst in brilliant pools of light on each side of the bomber stream. And they burned lazily as they lit up the broad avenue to Berlin.

At first they drifted in strings of twos and threes. Then rapidly they fell, wiping away the cover of darkness shielding the bombers. Out in the nose, Douglas saw them as he completed his pre-bombing check and knew that the elaborate diversion had not come off. The FW 190s and the JU 88s were waiting for them. Already he could see the tracer criss-crossing ahead.

The first combats were on. An orange glow splashed the darkness below and he caught the fiery outline of a Lancaster plunging earthwards, tracer streaming from her rear-turret.

Douglas pulled off his leather gauntlets. Dragging a pair of newly washed white silk gloves from his pocket, he thrust his hands into them. He screwed and twisted the silk until his fingers fitted smoothly into the sockets. The heavy flying gloves were too bulky for him to feel sensitively in the blacked-out nose for the delicate switches on the bomb panel.

White gloves. It brought to his mind the executioners of old, masked men in hooded headgear, bending slightly as they leaned on their axes. He smiled into his oxygen mask and looked out of the transparent nose. The smile died on his lips.

A searchlight flashed on, dead, straight and blinding. As rapidly as it appeared it went out. Suddenly it was there again, slowly toppling backwards as if pointing their course to the fighters hurtling through the night to the defence of Berlin.

Within seconds the darkness was pierced by hundreds of other groping beams. Must have been one of the master searchlights, he decided. A voice crackled over the intercom.

"There's dozens of combats going on. Shouldn't you weave, skipper?" The tone was eager, anxious and very near to panic. He cursed the Engineer. Did he think they were bloody blind?

Carson's voice was harsh in its reply. "Be quiet! They're not dozens! Don't talk again unless you see a fighter coming in!"

Again the intercom buzzed. This time it was Masters, cool and unperturbed. But then, Douglas told himself, he could not see what was happening, lulled in the flimsy security of his hatch.

"Shern, you should see the T.I.s in another two minutes."

He swore into his oxygen mask. Did the navigator think he was asleep? God, he was praying for them to burst, so he could let the bombs go and get the hell out of it.

"Thanks," he replied, "but I don't think I'll miss them. It's rather bright out here!"

The words had hardly flowed from his lips before he was wishing he had never spoken. His nerves must be worse than he thought, getting irritable like that. Another batch of flares burst above and ahead. Specially converted JU 88s were, beyond any doubt, flying along the bombers track, releasing them at timed intervals, making it easier for the fighters to select their 'kills'.

The flares threw the black floating puffs left by the spent A.A. shells into sharp terrifying relief. He was grateful he could not hear the mass thunder of the barrage below, above the roar of the bomber's four engines. The spine-tingling crump of the shells as they burst uncomfortably close spewing out their shrapnel jarred his tensed nerves.

The petrified sky was getting brighter. He looked up sharply and saw the dim silhouette of a Halifax, below his port quarter, suck in long lines of tracer and burst into a rich deep glow. The exploding bomber cart-wheeled slowly and illuminated a Lancaster on its starboard bow. The Lancaster pilot corkscrewed violently away from the stricken bomber, to be caught relentlessly by a searchlight.

Christ, Pastone was right. There were combats all over the sky.

Bombers were exploding ahead, below and on each side of him, sky-writing their death trails in spirals of black smoke.

"Master Switch On! Bomb switches selected and fuzed!" he shouted.

Then he saw the red target-indicators sail down, plump in the centre of the forest of searchlights, trailing through the flak in a leisurely fall of fiery bells of colour.

They splashed lazily over the ground, beckoning impatiently to the armada above, gurgling voraciously as they waited to receive the bombs. After them came the secondary markers, equally vivid clusters of bewitching greens. Douglas thumbed forward the drift handle.

"Left-Left-Steady!" The reds were coming nicely into sight.

"Bomb Doors Open!"

Carson repeated the order and watched the light appear on his panel as the belly of the Halifax yawned. In the rear turret, Callaghan swung his Brownings in a half arc, his eyes looking, above and then below. Two searchlights had fastened on to a Halifax. A third, like a vulture disputing its right to kill, weaved across the sky, transfixing the bomber, blinding its occupants.

Callaghan tore his eyes from the corkscrewing Halifax and continued his watch. Dexterously he swung the electrically operated turret in a full sweep from port to starboard, straining his eyes as he searched the sky, The cold seeped through his electrically-heated flying suit in short, sharp needle thrusts of excruciating pain. Always it was cold in the tail turret. He shut his eyes tightly and quickly opened them again. Stare too long he had found and he began to imagine things.

Gently he felt for the knob controlling the brilliance of his graticle sight and dimmed it slightly. Better that way if he had to focus on a fighter. No glare. Unless the fighter saw him first. The thought disturbed him. When was the bomb-aimer going to press the 'tit'? Bomb-aimers, he considered, were as bad as navigators. Worse, when the target was sighted. Concentrating so much on their blasted bombsight, they momentarily forgot about the angry, shattered night sky around them.

Douglas pressed the bomb-release button as the red T.I.s crawled over the cross hilt in the graticle sight. Carson felt the Halifax rear.

"Bombs Gone!" Douglas called. At the same time his right hand flicked down the four switches controlling the bomb stations he had purposely left unselected. Then he shot across the jettison bars. That lot should fall clear of the markers to burst, he hoped, in the suburbs.

Carson pulled on his jettison toggle and then closed the bomb-doors, unaware of his bomb-aimer's personal vendetta with the citizens of Berlin. His intercom was still on, for he heard Douglas snarl to himself: "Burn, you bastards! Bloody well burn!"

He wondered for a moment at the cold fury and venom in the voice. To him, piloting a bomber and its load of destruction was a detached, impersonal job, a necessary surgical operation conducted with the minimum of feeling.

The blast from a bursting A.A. shell well to their port tossed the bomber's port wing up. Carson pushed forward on the stick and shoved on right rudder. So far, it had been fairly easy. They had slipped through the night fighters going in, and with a bit of luck, they might miss them going out.

Banking the Halifax on to the course for the coast he saw a bomber burst into a dark red ball to port of them. Titch sighted it at almost the same instance and saw two parachutes swing open, almost immediately, below the flaming aircraft.

Seconds later a long finger of burning debris fell on the white canopy of one of the 'chutes. The flimsy nylon burst into flames and trailed with sickening speed down into the blackness, dragged by the black blob dangling in the harness.

The blazing shape, that was once a four-engined bomber, was spinning faster in wide twisting circles. Fascinated Titch watched it disintegrate, scattering hundreds of flaming matches into the dark sky.

The gunner ripped his eyes from the scene knowing it would always be in his mind, traced and etched by the indelible fire which had consumed the aircraft and the hapless wriggling puppet swaying to and fro beneath the flaming nylon shroud.

"Weave, Skipper, weave! Two combats dead astern, and I think a F.W. has flashed beneath us!" Callaghan's voice from the rear-turret was urgent, yet cool.

Carson threw the Halifax into a steep diving turn to port and watched the height slice from his altimeter. They crossed the coast dead on E.T.A. But it was not until they were half-way over the North Sea that Carson reached for his coffee flask.

Six Halifaxes had landed when they circled Nissindon. Eight more were in the circuit, stepped up above one another to avoid collisions. He heard others calling as he made his approach. Ten minutes later he waited as Curly made a snap check of S—Sugar, flashing a heavy torch along the fuselage.

"Lor'!" said the armourer. "It looks like you've come through without a scratch on the paintwork!"

Watson grunted. "We better check that undercarriage thoroughly in the morning."

The words wiped away the elation Carson had felt. He climbed into the crew wagon, wondering what Dorton would say about the take-off. Until now he had completely forgotten about it.

The briefing room was crowded. He saw from the Ops board that fifteen were down. There were three in the circuit. That left four to come in. They finished their de-briefing and were about to get up from the Intelligence Officer's table, when Carson saw the Group Captain coming towards them.

"Don't get up," Dorton said. "What kind of trip did you have? Your first, wasn't it?"

Carson swallowed. "Yes, sir. On the whole, it was pretty good."

Turning to Douglas, Dorton asked: "See the T.I.s all right?"

"Couldn't miss them sir! But I'll wear anti-dazzle goggles next time!"

Dorton laughed for a moment. Then the smile vanished. His eyes looked hard at Carson.

"What happened to you on the take-off? Couldn't you hold her? You may not know it, but you missed our farmhouse by inches!"

Carson flushed. "The bomb-load gave it a different feel."

Dorton said, his eyes still on Carson: "Naturally, the feel would be different. You should have allowed for that. You'd better watch it next time," he rasped.

Kiwi sauntered over. The tenseness slipped from the Group Captain's face.

"Well, MacArthur, back first, I see. Your skipper tells me they dented Freddie's fuselage a bit."

89

"Spent shrapnel, sir; nothing serious."

Dorton moved on, and Kiwi took a sip from the pint pot of steaming tea in his hand and said: "Well, Cobber, you know all about it now?"

Douglas smiled wanly and lit a cigarette. The New Zealander nodded to Carson:

"Think the chop rate will be fairly high? I saw three going down myself!"

Carson looked past him at the Ops board, his eyes resting on the four blank spaces in the column headed 'Time Down'.

Kiwi, who had followed his gaze, said: "Looks as if they've had it. Course, they may have lobbed down on one of the emergency 'dromes farther down the coast." He looked thoughtful for a moment and added: "You wouldn't have known Rossie, A Flight Commander? He was flying C—Charlie—looks as if he's bought it. Tough. He had only four to do!"

Pastone said quietly: "Wasn't one of his gunners called Bluey?"

Kiwi nodded "Bluey is as hard as they come but he's one of the best. Hope you're wrong with your use of the past tense, but I've a feeling they're not coming back."

Pastone coloured. "Sorry; it was a slip."

Martin came over, chuckling into his red moustache. "Quilbey's off again! He's like a hound in heat!"

The New Zealander grinned. "Marty's got a real nasty mind. He's always baiting poor old Quilbey. He's the driver of, Y—Yorker. Nice guy; only married four weeks ago. He's got a wife fixed up in a furnished cottage in the village and cycles the three miles there after every trip." He paused, then picked up his mug of tea from the edge of the table. "I've met her once or twice. She's a good type but gets worried when the squadron goes out. Never can sleep until he comes back."

"Like hell," said Martin, "they don't sleep. Quilbey never takes his Pep pills until he hits the coast on the way back."

"Baloney!" laughed Kiwi.

"They make me sick," Martin retorted firmly; "they're like a couple of love-sick kids. Anyway, he's no damned right having his wife on the squadron's doorstep."

When the films taken from the cameras were developed and pinned to the intelligence board, much later that morning, they

90

showed that twelve out of the eighteen aircraft which had come back to Nissindon had clear aiming points. They would never know what was on the plates of the four missing aircraft. Their cameras, like those of the forty-four bombers the Command had lost that night, lay among the twisted wreckage along the route to Berlin and back.

Braced against the side of Dorton's desk, Wing Commander Carter sent a neat smoke ring curling upwards and flicked the ash from his cigarette on to the well-worn carpet. "Yes," he said thoughtfully, "four is too high! Keep that up, and after five more raids we'll need a new squadron!"

Dorton's eyes were grave. "The devil of it, Bill, is that they were all experienced crews. Might be a pointer that, huh? Carelessness—we've-done-it-all-before attitude, eh?"

Carter frowned. "Trouble is, neither of us has been long enough here to know what kind of crews they were."

11

TWO nights later, the main force crossed the enemy coast between Ameland and Borkum in the West Frisians, flying on a course which took them south of Hanover. Wheeling sharply east, on a broadcast wind, they slipped between Magdeburg and Leipzig, to turn again and attack Berlin on a northerly heading.

The heavily concentrated raid took exactly twenty-eight minutes. From 186 Squadron twenty Halifaxes went out. Seventeen came back, one so badly damaged that it was 'written off' the next day as totally unserviceable.

The German ground controller sent the bulk of his night fighter force circling the Hanover-Brunswick orbit, later changing his mind and making Magdeburg the target. By the time he had decided the true objective of Bomber Harris's striking force and switched his frustrated 88s and 190s to Berlin, the Target Indicators of the Pathfinders were almost out.

Even so, it was the night fighters, kept in reserve and operating from the airfields round the capital, that took the greatest toll of the bombers.

The weeks passed and the Halifax IIIs promised by Air Commodore Cartingham swept low over the aerodrome, their great radial engines deafening the watchers on the ground.

These watchers were many, for the entire squadron personnel from the Waaf cooks to Dorton himself, were out on the windswept perimeter track, necks craned upwards.

Conversion from the inline engines which powered the Halifax II to the Hercules engines of the Mark III was rapid and smooth. It had to be. There was little time to waste. The saturation raids were to be intensified and more and more cities deep in the heart of Hitler's Reich were to reel under Harris's sledge-hammer punches.

With a maximum speed of 280 miles per hour, a service ceiling of which was modestly put at 20,000 feet and capable of carrying 7,000 pounds of high explosives on a round trip of 1,985 miles, nearly twice that load on trips under a thousand miles, the Halifax III was to lighten the burden so long carried by the Lancaster.

Dorton, like a mother hen keeping watch over her brood, observed with critical eyes his squadron convert to the new aircraft. They took to them easily and confidently.

All but Carson. On his first take-off he nearly took Hangar B with him. On his second, the torque from his powerful radial engines beat him again and sent the Halifax swinging madly. Douglas, mistaking his cuss word for 'Cut it', promptly cut the throttles and the bomber lurched to a stop on the grass between the two runways.

Carter suggested flying with him to find out what his trouble was. Dorton viewed him as a man contemplates a potential suicide, shook his head and firmly stamped on the idea.

Yet Carson held the Halifax straight on the next three take-offs. So 186 converted, but to the crew of S—Sugar the experience was worse than any raid they had yet gone out on. The neat six-inch bombs painted in deep yellow on the gleaming black fuselage of S, below the cockpit, crept to four. Corporal Watson felt better than he had for months. Only one of his late Ss had completed seven trips. With one more trip, taking into account the three they had done on the old Halifaxes, there would be eight raids to the credit of Flight Sergeant Carson and his crew. Just one more trip, and they were going out again tonight, and there would be five symbols on the fuselage. He decided he would personally stencil on the bomb tomorrow.

Group Captain Dorton, surveying the past month, was not quite so elated as his Corporal. Nevertheless, he was quietly confident that, considering the major targets attacked by his squadron in that period, his losses were not unduly high.

With the new aircraft had come a new spirit. He sensed it among the ground crews and the men who flew the bombers they nursed so carefully. On his part, he nourished this spirit gently, acutely uneasy that two bad nights could cancel out the slow but steady progress he had so far achieved.

Yesterday he had sent to Group H.Q. four Flight Sergeant Pilots and two navigators he had recommended for commissioning to

Pilot Officers. Their appearance before Cartingham, he knew, would be a mere formality. The Air Commodore would ask a few questions about the raids they had been on and how they found life on the squadron. Then he would scribble his signature on the forms. Six new officers would be transferred from the sergeants' mess to the officers' ration strength.

Carson was among them. Why, he didn't quite know. Peculiar, the interest he had in Carson's aircraft. Last night he had tried to analyse it, refusing to accept his earlier theory that he had unconsciously made the S aircraft the material vortex round which the squadron's bad luck could be broken.

The jinx, the squadron believed they were under was either transmuted directly from the losses of aircraft bearing the letter S or else came from the over-all losses which the bay magnified.

Damned silly reasoning, he told himself, but he could think of no other thesis which might explain the hoodoo outlook.

A knock sounded on his door and Carter walked in.

"Sit down, Bill," he said. "I feel things are coming our way. Cartingham was on the phone this morning. Fairly pleased with our results this last month. Aiming points up, meeting maximum efforts and all that. Losses still too high, though! Told him I owed the results mostly to the way you whipped them back into shape. Could hear him chuckling as he said, 'That's why I sent you Carter'."

The Wing Commander snorted, but he looked faintly surprised when Dorton added: "Keep it under your hat, but he told me I'd shortly be losing you. Your Group Captaincy has come up! He wouldn't say more."

Dorton rose, walked to the window and stood with his hands behind his back.

"I'm going out with them tonight, Bill!" Turning abruptly, he faced Carter. "Don't look so worried; I'm not taking your crew." He smiled and added: "I know they wouldn't like it."

Plainly puzzled, Carter asked: "Who then?"

An impish gleam came into Dorton's eyes. "Some people around here who could do with some refresher hours . . . the Navigation Leader, the Bombing Leader, the Wireless Leader . . . in fact, all the heads of departments!"

Carter whistled and raised his eyebrows. "Thought of what

Group's going to say if you're all dangling under 'brollies before the night's out?"

"I'm not planning to tell them. When I come back I'll put it down to observation flight, refresher or something like that. Might even fiddle the log like Davis of F—Freddie and cut courses."

The Wing Commander laughed outright. "So that's how Martin's always first back!"

Dorton winked broadly. "He won't be tonight, and I'll watch his navigator's face as I tell him how I did it. That alone should be worth the flight."

Carter frowned. "There'll be hell to pay if anything happens."

Dorton shrugged impatiently. "Well, I won't be here to face it! You can carry that one!"

Two hours later, exactly three hours before the main briefing, the station grape-vine picked up the news. . . . "The Groupie's flying tonight!"

Pilot Officer Martin laughed loudly, and with an exaggerated gesture twirled one end of his bushy moustache.

"Must be a real cushy job tonight!"

Davis smirked. "Coast job and straight back. You don't get Groupies sticking out their necks on major targets!"

Kiwi cycled breathlessly up to them. "Jeez, what's going on round here? The Bombing Leader's flying, the Navigating Leader's flying, the whole gol' damn bunch are getting airborne!"

"You come from the Flights?" queried Martin. Kiwi nodded, and Martin demanded, "What they loading us with?"

"Thousand pounders and incendiaries. Can't be a long trip. Bomb load up. Petrol down. Seems like the Ruhr."

Martin scratched his chin thoughtfully. "What's the old man going for then?"

"It can't be the Ruhr," Davis said finally; "not if he's going with all that highly precious cargo."

"Maybe," said Martin, "he wants to dump them somewhere and start from scratch!"

Leaning against one of the bay windows in the mess talking to Morphy and Masters, Pastone saw Douglas come in with a Canadian bomb-aimer. They went to the bar and he idly watched them stroll over.

Douglas put down his can of beer. "Think you've met Micky M'Call; flies with F/O Tomlinson all Canuck crew P—Peter."

"You came the same day as us, I think?" said Masters. "Know your navigator, Ham Roemer."

"Then you're Masters? Sure, he's told me about you." The Canadian smiled blandly. "And the drinking sessions you two have at the Ostler."

A crooked grin creased Masters' face but his eyes were cold. "Well, we do our drinking a little more discreetly than some."

M'Call's lip tightened. The hint was plain enough. Come to that, it was only a matter of time before the Wingco heard about it, and then Tomlinson would wonder what had hit him. He had nearly called a show-down with his skipper that morning. At the last moment he had called it off. Even with a drink, Tomlinson was a good pilot. Should be too, he mused, being a former bush pilot in Ontario. All right in those days to fly with a hip flask. Plain stupid in a Halifax. What infuriated him was that Tomlinson needed no alcohol to bolster his nerves. Never drunk, but then never exactly sober. He carried it well. Too well, for one had to know him intimately to be aware of how much he had.

Douglas fumbled for his cigarettes, brought out a packet, and broke M'Call's train of thought.

Easing himself from his prop against the window, Pastone took a letter from his pocket and glanced through it.

"She put a picture inside?" Morphy asked, winking at Douglas. Pastone's eyes flicked up sharply, "What?"

"Gee! You got it bad, huh?" The wireless operator grinned broadly.

The engineer's voice was wrapped in anger, "Got what bad?"

"Take it easy! I only asked if the girl-friend enclosed a picture?"

"Oh, the letter?" Pastone said absently. "It's from my mother."

The obvious relief in the voice made Douglas wonder what was behind the fleeting flash of temper.

"Not bad news?" he asked indifferently.

"No, except—nothing really," Pastone looked at his wrist watch. "Guess I'll go in and have an early lunch."

When the Engineer had left, Douglas said: "Queer guy, that.

He's as nervy as a kitten. Acts as if he had ants in his pants. Maybe he's got some wench into trouble."

Morphy caught the malice in his bomb-aimer's voice. "Don's O.K. Bit too sensitive, though."

Pastoné brooded over his lunch. After a while, he pushed back his chair and walked out of the mess.

Back in his hut, he flung himself on his bed and stared vacantly at the whitewashed roof, deliberately trying to clear the confused tangle of thoughts in his mind. Along the corridor a door slapped loosely as the wind caught it.

He sat up and re-read the letter. It would have been better had he told her the truth. But then, how was he to know that Ginger Bromley was on the station? When he had met Ginger coming from the orderly room where he was a clerk, he had thought nothing about the meeting. They had lived a few streets from one another but had never been close friends. He smiled cynically. God, it was ironic. Ginger writing home and describing him as a hero. That would have been the word all right. Ginger's mind had never got beyond the comic strips. It didn't take much imagination for him to picture Mrs. Bromley meeting his mother in the local grocery store.

"How could you have done it, Don?" The words really meant, "Why crucify me like this, son?"

The thought twisted in his mind that he was grasping, groping for some excuse to drug his conscience. That wasn't quite right. The tug was equally strong both ways. He must go one way, but which way? The issue was plain, only the answer was obscure.

That was contradictory. That was how he had thought yesterday. It would be easier if he could confide in someone. Put the burden of supplying the solution on his confessor and abide by his advice. The elusive equation came out effortlessly enough in the air. Once on the ground it receded again, became hazy, to rub itself out in watery outlines of indecision.

At such times he believed he could go through with it. That too was a lie. Not with Carson's take-offs and Douglas's dummy-runs. Lord, why had he to get a skipper like Carson and a crazy bomb-aimer who counted dummy-runs as points towards a D.F.M.?

He had given it a fair trial. Whatever they said, they couldn't deny that. Many, a great many, who had never seen the hell over a target, never heard a shot fired in anger, would brand him 'Coward.'

Let them! He'd at least made an effort. God, he had tried to be true to himself. With every take-off the odds were getting smaller. He had had enough, he suddenly decided. He would request a personal interview with the C.O. Too late today to see him but he would write the letter and hand it in tomorrow.

Dorton, they said, was human. Perhaps he would understand. Of course he would have to take down his wings. His stripes would go to and the letters L.M.F. would follow him throughout his service. The war couldn't last long now. His mother was right.

Yet . . . he had a fleeting glimpse of the squadron. They probably wouldn't call him yellow to his face but their eyes would scream it. He rose from his bed and walked to his locker. He took out his writing pad and began to write. Sealing the letter, he placed it in his drawer. Then he remembered that they were going out tonight. He reached for the knob of his drawer, hesitated and looked at the unlit stove. No, backing out at such short notice would clearly condemn him.

What was it they had said about tonight? Easy target! Coast and back! Groupie and his leaders flying. Well, they were due for an easy one after the trips they'd had.

12

CARTER took the briefing. He told them the target was Dusseldorf. He was certain he detected a slight jarring note in the buzz of conversation which usually followed the announcement of where they were going. When the muttering faded, he went on to tell them that seven-tenths cloud was expected over the Ruhr and the technique of sky marking would be used. If the cloud cleared sufficiently, bombing would be on visual markers.

Twenty-three aircraft were going out. Take-off would be at 2030 hours. "Runway 090 will be used, so it will take you directly out to sea," he said.

B—Baker, with Group Captain Dorton at the controls, took off first.

Carter, watching from control, saw the black Halifax roll down the runway in an arrow straight take-off. Smoothly it flashed out to sea, its navigation lights fading into needle points as it climbed for height.

A—Able, C—Charlie, G—George, F—Freddie and D—Dog flashed past at minute intervals. They were not keeping strictly to the take-off order. P—Peter was now at the head of the runway, her skipper clearing his engines before pushing the throttle handles through the gate.

Flying Officer Tomlinson and his all-Canadian crew roared down the concrete. Carter followed the Halifax as it picked up flying speed, saw it lift from the runway and skim over the cliff edge.

What happened in the next few seconds came so fast that only blurred images were photographed by his eyes. The bomber sank as if a gigantic magnet had sucked it down. For a moment, its powerful radial engines pulled against the down-drag, then it hit the sea and bounced with the flexibility of a table tennis ball.

The square tipped port wing sliced through the wave tops, sending up a sheet of spray. The Halifax reared, plunged and sank from his sight. The roar of an aircraft racing down the runway drowned the death dive of the bomber. A red Very light burst, across the runway.

Carter waited for the deep muffled growl of bombs exploding under water. It never came. Unfused, they somehow resisted from detonating on impact.

The clanging of the fire-bell on the crash-tender drifted above the impatient snarl of the bombers whose take-offs had been halted by the red Very signal.

Carter turned to the Corporal Waaf at the table beside the controller. "Get on to A.S.R. Tell them to get a launch out right away," he snapped. To the controller he said: "Not that I think anyone will get out of that crash."

He strode back to the window, then swung round. "Better have a green fired. We can't hold up the squadron. The runway's clear."

The muted sound of the crash-tender's bell filtered into the astro-dome of S—Sugar, where Pastone was standing. Puzzled that he had heard no explosion, he stepped down and went back to the take-off position in the fuselage. He was positive the bomber had plunged into the sea. One moment he had seen the rear light, the next it had vanished.

Carson released the brakes. Douglas's stomach coiled into a tight spring. Slowly his muscles relaxed, as he realised that this time the take-off was straight. He sensed the great wheels trying to leave the concrete as the bomber's momentum crept over the flying speed necessary to lift her.

He glanced at Carson. They were far along the runway and Carson was still holding the Halifax down.

Twenty yards from the end of the concrete, Carson eased back the control column. The Halifax soared over the cliff edge and Douglas felt the aircraft slip down as if they were flying across a vacuum. His skipper, he saw, was keeping the nose down slightly. Suddenly, as quickly as the down-draught came, it vanished. Carson pulled sharply back on the stick and the Halifax climbed steadily and surely.

Switching on his intercom, Douglas said: "Lew, that was real sweet! I felt we were slipping into the drink. What a hell of a pull!"

For the first time, Carson, relaxed in his seat. His shoulders sagged. His voice was cool and matter-of-fact, "Either that or an air current. Might, of course, have been someone's slip-stream. But I've never experienced a drag like that!"

A little later Carson said, "Care to take over, Shern?"

Douglas clambered into the seat and Carson said, "Keep her on that course and climb to twenty-thou'."

After sitting for a while with the navigator, Carson rose and squatted on the step leading into the glass-house. From where he was, he could see the Flight Engineer. He switched on his intercom button and called up the gunners to check if they were all right. Pastone, he noticed, jumped as his voice broke the silence. For some time now he had had a feeling that something was bothering his Engineer.

Carson took a deep swallow at the oxygen. Squadron life, he reflected, suited him. He would have his P/O. up soon. A D.F.C. on it would look well. If they were holed, but not too badly, and he managed to bring the Halifax back, it was fairly certain he would get it. Better getting an immediate award like that than having to take pot-luck in the draw for one at the end of a tour. Even then he was almost sure to get a ribbon. Now it was awarded to almost every bomber pilot who finished a tour. It would help him too in his ambition to get a permanent commission. That was looking well ahead.

Pastone's voice broke into his thoughts. "Skipper, pressure on starboard inner falling!"

Pulling himself into the cockpit, he stood behind the engineer. Like most of the squadron pilots, he knew nothing of the finer-points of engine mechanics. His job was to fly the aircraft; others were there to maintain the radials.

Sure enough the pressure needle was dropping. He moved over to the pilot's seat and tapped Douglas on the shoulder. Back at the controls, he glanced sideways at Pastone, and said into his mask: "How's the pressure now?"

"Still falling . . . wait a minute . . . port inner also fluctuating a bit. Yes, it's beginning to drop, too."

A little later, Masters said, "Gee,* Box has packed up. Looks like something's wrong for it gets its power from that engine."

* GEE—Radar navigation worked from ground transmitters in England and picked up by receiving set in aircraft. Effectiveness limited as enemy jammed it.

Carson looked at his watch. "Where are we now?"

"Coast should be coming up in ten minutes," Masters said shortly.

"Sure you switched on to the correct tanks, Engineer?"

"Positive, Skipper. Dammit, pressure on starboard inner now on the red line!"

A few seconds later the starboard inner coughed and stuttered. Carson feathered the engine and watched the three-bladed airscrew gradually spin to a stop.

"What do you think, Engineer? Is the pressure on the port inner holding?"

"Don't like it at all, Skipper. Think we should turn back?" Pastone's voice was urgent, pleading.

Carson thought rapidly. The idea of turning back held no appeal to him. Yet no one would expect him to go on with one engine feathered and another about to go. With the full load he had, he could not maintain height. Six lives were in his hands. They trusted him, and he must not violate that trust with any foolhardy decision to carry on. There were other nights . . . He had made up his mind to turn for base when he called Masters.

"What do you think, Larry?" he asked.

Masters said slowly. "If you decide to go on, I can navigate on dead reckoning and the astro fixes I get from Shern. My last wind was a good one, and I've an accurate fix to work on. Anyway, Gee would be jammed shortly."

Carson frowned. He might have banked on Masters to throw it right back in his lap. He called Douglas.

"What do you think, Shern?"

His bomb-aimer, a trifle too casual, he thought, said, "You're the skipper, Lew!"

As if he didn't know it! He regretted ever asking them. He had sounded them only to stress that they were an integral part of each other, a close working team.

How bloody silly they were. Masters and Douglas, vying with one another, like two schoolboys, vainly trying to see who could be the coolest. Carson half thought of going on. See how they'd be then, he urged himself. He remembered the gunners and wireless operator. He admired them again for refraining from making any unsolicited comments. Over the intercom he said: "Okay, we're going back!"

He banked the Halifax in a steep diving turn. "Give me a course for home, navigator."

With deliberate preciseness, Masters said testily: "I will, when I pick my bloody instruments off the floor. Wish you'd let me know before you bank like that!"

Carson felt himself grinning in spite of his mood.

"Shern, you'd better get ready to jettison the bombs. Let me know when."

"I suppose so, but I hate doing it," Douglas retorted, and the regret in his voice seemed genuine.

"I don't like it either, but we can't land with the bloody things," he snapped.

Ten minutes later he called the bomb-aimer again. "You ready to unload yet?" God, what was the matter with Douglas? He was getting damned tired of his messing about.

Watching the gauges, Pastone bitterly cursed the bomb-aimer. A cold rage surged through him. He could kill Douglas. Once Douglas jettisoned the load they could never turn back for the target. Then he began to shake. The pressure gauge on the port inner had picked up for some unfathomable reason. It was steadily climbing back. His hands suddenly shook uncontrollably.

Carson would notice it, and when he did, would decide to bomb on three engines. The orders made it clear that when only one engine was unserviceable they were expected to bomb on three.

He fought back the hysterical urge he had, to scream at Douglas to jettison the bombs. God! Why was he taking so long? It was just a big act, this show of reluctance to let them go. Who did he think he was fooling?"

Carson's voice seared through his earphones. "Engineer! Port inner seems to be picking up. What's the pressure say?"

Pastone inhaled deeply from his mask. He felt sick and weak. "Just a moment! I'll look. . . . Good Lor', it's gone back, practically at normal now. Think that dive and the loss of height must have had something to do with it?"

"I'm going to unfeather the starboard inner and see if it picks up," Carson said firmly.

The engine spluttered, the airscrew spun slowly. The next

instant the engine growled deeply and the three-bladed propeller merged into a continuous circle of motion as Carson pushed the throttle lever into line with the other three.

Satisfied, he thrust forward the four levers and swung the Halifax into a tight turn to starboard.

"Give me a course for the target, navigator." His voice was crisp, curt. In the navigation hatch, Masters did some rapid calculations. After a while he said plaintively: "No use keeping to the flight plan. We're too far behind the stragglers—if there're any stragglers!"

He paused. "Of course, it will mean flying at the height we are at now, 11,000 feet. We would lose too much time getting back to twenty-thou'. Let me know what speed you can manage."

They flew on in a weird silence, all seven acutely aware of the risk they were taking. Now they were alone, isolated completely from the protective numbers of the main stream, a solitary and distinctive blob on the screens of any German radar sets which might, and probably would, scan their section of the sky. An easy sitting target for the night fighter vectored on to them. Out in the nose, Douglas was the first to notice that the thick cloud layers they had been flying above were breaking, leaving clear patches through which he could see the black surface of the earth below.

Gradually the clouds dissolved to mere wisps of vapour. Their last flimsy cover against the night fighters had gone. Ahead, he could see the searchlights, slim lines of light groping for the stragglers in the last wave.

The next time he looked, the lines of light were distinctly broader and they were going out, switching off in uneven groups. The flak, too, was thinning, tapering away to a half-hearted barrage, as the last of the bombers headed into the night on a course for the coast, a course which would pass them.

He thought of the sweating gunners below and how they would curse at having to 'stand to' again for a mere nuisance raider. Some of the contempt he had for the battery he once served with came back to him and for a brief moment comforted him. Their ambition, he recalled, was to become part of the London A.A. Defence, but their 'shoots' delegated them to an obscure area on the West coast. Eventually it led to them being disbanded and dispersed to more efficient regiments.

Two chances he had tonight to jettison the bombs. They would have been on the way home if he had. He wondered what had held him back. There was something, an uncanny feeling, in the dark halls of the mind that they would go back. He shrugged, dragged his head from the bombing panel and searched the darkness ahead.

The industrial haze which nearly always screened the Ruhr cities swirled below. Nothing that could be called a fire glimmered through that haze. A few cans of incendiaries, burning themselves rapidly out, flickered faintly from below. The raid showed every sign of being an abortive one. What fires there had been, if any, had gone out.

A dying red target indicator twinkled through the mist. "Target ahead!" he called urgently.

"Can't see a thing!" Carson said, as he opened the bomb-doors.

"Hard left," he snapped; "there's a red glowing dimly on the port quarter."

By the time Carson had banked the Halifax and levelled out, a patch of broken cloud blanketed out the red.

Douglas called: "Dummy-run—sorry, but cloud blotted that marker!"

Carson's first impulse was to jerk the jettison toggle on the panel above his throttle-handles and to hell with explaining—if they ever got back.

Cloud or no cloud, the bomb-aimer could have let them go. Either way there was going to be no trace on their camera plate. Reason tugged at the urge. No, Douglas had done the only thing possible. They had not gone through the torture the night had brought, only to slap their bombs anywhere.

The intercom clicked. The voice was Pastone's. "Searchlights are springing up all over the place. Hell, Douglas! Jettison them, and let's get away from here!"

The words stung Douglas, but before he could reply, Callaghan from the rear-turret spoke, and his tone was coldly, objective: "Flak port quarter, and are they pumping it up!"

The guns were on to them. Short brilliant flashes of yellow

were bursting, ripping through the black velvet in erratic lines on his starboard. No use. Only one heading could take them on to the spluttering T.I.s. He steeled himself and said: "Lew, it will have to be a heading of 135 degrees. It will have to be quick, too! It's the only red I can see!"

The Halifax turned in a tight, blood-draining bank. Douglas was thankful no one spoke. The heading would mean a longer run into the heart of the Ruhr. There was no other way.

Spent shrapnel clattered sickeningly against the fuselage. God, how he wished he had jettisoned the load. "Hard right!" Thrusting forward the drift handle, he glanced into the bomb-sight.

"Left—steady! Steady...!" A muffled growl as a A.A. shell burst dangerously near them. The starboard wing kicked, fell, and the pale pink smudge swung a little from the sword sight. Slowly it swung back as Carson levelled the bomber. As it crossed the hilt of the sight, he pressed the bomb-tit.

"Bombs gone—jettison bars across! Close bomb doors!" He waited for a voice smeared with relief to say something. No one spoke.

Two broad beams of light staggered in front of him, toppled into the nose, blinding him. The bomber twisted, lurched, reeled and side-slipped as Carson vented his wrath on the controls.

Masters grasped the tubular alloy spar running from the gee-box. And doing so, his eyes skidded across the panel in front of his table. The altimeter needle wavered at the 9000 mark, swaying crazily as it waited for the time-lag.

Over the intercom, a voice said: "Good work! You've lost them!"

It was then that Douglas, sprawled in the nose, realised that the darkness had again clothed him. When he opened his eyes, swirling eddies of grey vapour sheathed the perspex of the nose.

The tension of those last two hours brought a tiredness to Masters. He stood up, lifted his parachute from his seat and placed it in the rack. He had taken it out and laid it within easy reach when Douglas called for a dummy-run. Some madness had come over them tonight. From the beginning they had tempted the fates. Once they decided to turn back they should have kept going. There was no future in such indecisiveness. He would have this out with Carson when they landed, and that shouldn't be long.

Their luck had been amazing. It had even held on the second run up. The bomb-aimer was really to blame. If he had jettisoned the load when he was told, everything would have been fine. He reached under the table for his coffee flask, and for the first time became aware of the draught. He looked at the panel below him. Three inches of the metal casing of the fuselage had been ripped back. He lifted up the thermos. A trickle of ice-cold liquid ran up the sleeve of his battle-dress. A two-inch jagged hole ran diagonally above the base of the flask. That near burst on the bombing run had hit them, after all!

They landed at Nissindon twenty-five minutes after the last air-craft had touched down. Most of the crews had left the briefing room when they climbed down from the crew wagon. Dorton saw them come in.

A smile replaced the anxious look that had been on his face as he had waited for their call sign. Tonight he had lost two Halifaxes from the squadron—three, including the aircraft which crashed on take-off. But that would not be included among the missing listed in the B.B.C. news bulletin later that day. They knew where Tomlinson and his crew were. And a crash squad would bring them up, or what was left of them, when the tide ebbed.

Dorton listened to Carson's account of the delay, rubbing his chin thoughtfully.

"Looks like we'll have to go back there. We saw some fires, but they couldn't be very large if they were out by the time you arrived. Think they were strong enough to show a trace on your film?"

Carson shook his head. "Doubt it, sir; but we're hoping!"

"Has your fitter any idea of what might have led to your engines seizing up?"

Again Carson shook his head. "Whole thing mystifies him as much as it does me."

Dorton smiled but there was no humour in his eyes. "Looks then, like a Gremlin job. Maybe they'll find a reason when they do a full check in the morning."

It was over the flying supper that Douglas first heard of the fate of P—Peter and its crew.

"You knew the bomb-aimer?" Carson asked.

"We first met at a bombing school in Manitoba. M'Call was a grand guy. Pity he got it like that," Douglas said.

Callaghan stabbed a chip, looked up and said: "Buzz is Tomlinson was well shot. The Wingco's finding difficulty in proving it, though. No one wants to come forward and say it outright!"

"By the way, Lew," Douglas said, "there's something I think we should get cleared up for everyone's satisfaction!"

Carson's eyes fixed steadily on Douglas. "Think I know what you mean. Larry has already mentioned it, but for the benefit of you and the rest there won't be any more mess-ups like tonight..."

Pastone interrupted angrily: "If you'd dropped the blasted load when you were ordered to, there never would have been any mess-up...."

Douglas flushed, leapt to his feet, his right arm jabbed back. Carson caught his arm, swung him round and rasped: "None of that! It's over now!"

He waited until his bomb-aimer sat down, and said quietly: "It's shot all our nerves to bits; but from now on, if we ever decide to go back, we'll go back! As it happened, it wouldn't have looked so good if we had turned back with four engines running smoothly—as ours did afterwards."

13

PASTONE waited for the dawn to seep through the uncurtained, windows of his room. Many times before he had waited for it in the cold, bleak hours that heralded the morning, with only the steady snores of P—Peter's engineer breaking the silence. But now the bed alongside the window was empty.

For Reynolds, and the rest of P—Peter's crew, dawns didn't matter any more. They wouldn't even feel the firm tug of the ebb tide which, in another hour, would partially reveal the wreckage of their metal coffin.

To him, the lengthening shadows meant a new lease on life. By nightfall he would be free from this limbo of half-life, half-death, which had engulfed him since his posting to Nissindon.

Pastone's eyes smarted and his head ached. All night he had lain awake, trying to stop the endless cavalcade of past events flashing through his mind, tumbling one upon the other with the speed of a motion picture projector.

Sometimes the images were blurred. More often they were sharp, frightening in their vividness. Tonight there would be another fully developed spool in the mind's camera. A picture he would forget in time. It would fade like an old photograph, making identification of the outlines it once held difficult. One day, it could not be so far off, the war would end, and the picture would fade too.

He noticed it was getting lighter. He rose, dressed and cycled leisurely to the mess. In the dining-room he sat down at a table near the window. There were only two other men in the mess. He lingered a long time over his breakfast. Lighting a cigarette, he looked intently over the big room. Every week it held new faces. Any gaps in the old familiar faces were never allowed to become conspicuous. Quietly but quickly they were filled. They had to, he reasoned, if the squadron was to meet a Maximum Effort.

Well, it would not bother him much longer. He looked at his watch, pushed back his chair and rose.

For half an hour he walked aimlessly through the station. Then he turned towards the administration block. The Waaf Corporal in the Adjutant's office smiled at him thinly as he handed her the letter addressed to Dorton.

Dorton, although he had not been in bed until 0003 hours, was at his desk by 1030 hours. Lounging in his chair he looked through half-closed eyelids at the cigarette stub smouldering in his ash-tray. There was nothing he could do but wait.

A crash crew had left at dawn to bring in the bodies from the wreck. With them had gone a bomb disposal squad to render the bombs safe. With a pencil, he poked out the burning butt and began to clear the wire basket marked 'IN'. He read the letter written on the cheap N.A.A.F.I. paper and scowled.

Usually they threw it in at O.T.U. or at the Conversion Unit. The majority of them had no intention of ever flying on operations. They banked on some undefinable miracle coming along to keep them from being posted to a squadron.

They had not the guts, he decided, or the moral courage to honour the contract they had made. He didn't like L.M.F. cases. The Air Force liked them even less and hustled them with incredible speed to a special holding station, where they were reclassified.

Now he had one on his squadron. On S—Sugar, of all aircraft. Just when things were coming along nicely with the S—bay.

Yet the man had done eight trips. He was puzzled. God, he would have him posted to an L.M.F. holding and off the station by that afternoon. He read the letter again. Possibly written on the spur of the moment and sent to him in a fit of depression.

That was probably it. After all, he had done eight trips. Maybe he already bitterly regretted his impulsiveness. He would see him and find out what was wrong.

Pastone heard the Tannoy system blaring for him to report to the Adjutant's office as he walked towards the Flights. He turned and made his way back to the central buildings.

As the Adjutant rapped on Dorton's door, he felt the same tension come over him as he had experienced when climbing into the

Halifax. Farley closed the door behind him, and Pastone watched Dorton's eyes coldly flick over him.

In turn he searched the Group Captain's face for the look of contempt he expected to find. Whatever the Group Captain was thinking, his face showed no sign of emotion.

His voice was toneless. "Why have you asked to come off flying?"

The clock on the wall behind him ticked louder. A voice, strangely unlike his own, shattered the silence. "I haven't the guts to go on! I never had, sir!"

Dorton noticed that his right hand had abruptly stopped tapping the blotter beside the 'IN' tray. The frankness of the engineer astounded him. Usually they had elaborate excuses worked out, mysterious ailments, and heart-tugging tales of home troubles.

"You had the guts to do eight operations against some of the heaviest defended targets in Germany?" he said, stiffly.

Pastone's eyes, wide and childlike, held Dorton's then wavered. "I tried to give it a fair trial, sir. Instead of getting used to it, each trip made me feel worse!"

"Would you care to reconsider your decision?"

"No, sir!"

"When did you write this letter?"

"Yesterday afternoon."

Dorton's lips tightened. "Why didn't you give it to me then? You might not have come back, you know, or didn't you think of that?"

"I thought of it, sir, but I just can't go on. . . ."

The words tailed off, flat and dejected.

At least, Dorton mused, he's honest. Half turning in his seat, he looked at the engineer sharply. "No other worries?"

Pastone hesitated, fumbled in his breast pocket, brought out a well-thumbed letter.

"I'm not making any excuses, sir, but if you care to read this. . . ."

Dorton leaned across his desk and took the letter. Reading it quickly, he handed it back. He remembered the case of Carter and a similar letter.

Icily he said: "Most of the aircrews have mothers, some have wives and a few have children." The voice was harsh and grating now. "No, that's no damned excuse at all. Get out of here, and get packed. You will be posted at once to a place where they handle cases like yours."

Pastone winced, saluted limply and stumbled from the room.

As the door closed behind the Engineer, Dorton picked up the telephone and asked for the Adjutant. He had hardly replaced it, after arranging for Pastone's departure, when there was a soft tap on the door.

Wing Commander Carter poked his head round.

"Come in!" Dorton said.

Carter thought he detected a trace of annoyance in the tone.

"I think," he said, "we can conclude the inquiry into P—Peter. There's no doubt Tomlinson had been drinking during the afternoon. I wouldn't say he was drunk but at least half-cut. Difficulty is, proving it. Everyone who knows anything shut up like clams. The padre has, off the record, confessed that Tomlinson had a flask on him that day. Steel one which he accidentally dropped and quickly picked up. He's adamant, though, that he will do nothing to add to the grief of the next-of-kin or smear the memory of a gallant pilot. . . . They're his words, not mine!"

Dorton's lips twisted. "Looking back on it, Bill, I can't see much point in holding a full-scale inquiry now. But I think we must tighten up the lunchtime rule on drinks."

Carter shook his head. "Tomlinson was an exception. Fortunately, they don't come often. It wasn't from the mess he got it. Seems he kept a quart bottle in his billet. Incidentally, they've got the bodies up. Expect to get the bombs off shortly."

"I don't think," Dorton said, "we'll find anything wrong with the aircraft. There was a down-drag over that edge. Might possibly have been the slip-streams of other aircraft. I didn't experience it myself, but then, I was first off. Carson of S—Sugar mentioned it to me. Said it was fairly strong. Tomlinson may have felt it, too, and not having all his senses about him, failed to correct for it."

"That could well be it," Carter agreed.

Picking up his gloves from the edge of the Group Captain's desk, he added: "I'm going down to the flights. By the way, Met reports forecast fog tonight for nearly all our area. Anything you want done?"

"No; nothing for the moment. I expect the stand-down will come through soon if the weather is likely to be that bad."

Dorton rose from his seat, walked round the desk and sat lightly on the edge.

"S—Sugar will need a new engineer. The one they had has gone L.M.F. He was quite open about it . . . but then dragged in his old mother. I had him in here."

"They usually drag in their mothers!" The Wing Commander's tone was detached, disinterested, as if he disdained to discuss the matter. "I'm sorry he had to land with us."

"He'll be out of here by tonight!" Dorton said sharply.

"Glad to hear it." Carter walked to the door, opened it, and over his shoulder said, "See you later, then."

Dorton strolled to the window and idly looked out. Pastone had unknowingly made up his mind for him. He would drive to Group next week and get Cartingham to take the Wing Commander off operations. Cartingham would do it damn quick when he heard the story.

And he would do it discreetly, so that Carter would never know about his breach of confidence. It would be easier now that the Wing Commander had been ear-marked for promotion to Group Captain.

No, he swore to himself, Carter wasn't going to carry his problem any longer while a man like Pastone could get away with it so easily.

Pastone packed faster than he had ever done since joining the Air Force. He wanted to be clear of the hut before the crew of S—Sugar were awake. Then the personnel people would be arriving shortly, to sort through the kit of P—Peter's engineer. He didn't think he could stand that, and the look in their eyes when he told them why he was leaving.

His watch showed it was nearly noon. He'd never get away from the station in time! Carson and his crew were bound to meet him before he received his clearance papers and travelling warrant. He decided to go and see Carson and forestall him. His skipper had always been decent to him. Seemed the only reasonable person in that crazy crew.

Pastone went into the corridor and walked to Carson's room. Half-way down, a door opened and Douglas came out, half-dressed.

"Christ, you all dolled up? Stand down through already?"

Pastone stopped. "I wouldn't know! But I have something to say to the skipper. You'd better hear it too," he said heavily.

Carson and Masters were dressing when they walked in. Masters made a mock bow. "To what do we owe this honour?" he asked.

Pastone said flatly, "I'm leaving this afternoon!"

He saw the quizzical, perplexed look come into their eyes and went on, in the same dull tone. "I felt I should see you before I left. I had a talk with the Group Captain." He paused, faltered for a moment and his eyes clouded. "I'm LMF. Can't take any more . . ." He looked at Carson. "Your bomb-aimer shattered any doubts I may have had last night. God! I admire you, but . . ." His voice broke and, before they had recovered from the initial shock of his announcement, he had strode to the door.

Half-way through, he turned. "I wish you all the best of luck," his voice broke again; "I hope you get a good engineer. You deserve one." He turned on his heel and they heard his footsteps ringing against the bare boards of the corridor.

Douglas was the first to speak. "Hell! What do you know? Just like that!"

Masters snapped, "He was a jittery bastard, but I didn't think he was that bad. Seems you've ruffled him; how, I can't guess." The sarcasm in the voice was thinly veiled.

Carson rose and hurried along the corridor. He caught up with his engineer as he was going through the rear door.

Pastone turned. "Sorry to be letting you down like this."

"I'm sorry, too. Is there anything I can do or should have done?"

"No, nothing you could have done."

The utter deadness in the voice sent a spasm of sympathy through Carson. "Don't take it too hard. Everyone isn't built the same way. Last night must have been hell for you."

The sincerity in Carson's voice triggered off the tight, taut, hairspring which had previously kept Pastone's emotions in check. His throat muscles contracted.

"I'd like you to read this before I go. It's no excuse, but . . ." His voice trailed off as Dorton's comment on the letter came back to him.

Carson scanned the letter and handed it back. Pastone had taken enough without any comment from him.

When Carson got back to his room, the rest of the crew were there.

"He's bloody yellow, and if I see the bastard I'll tell him so!" Titch, the mid-upper, was saying.

Douglas looked up, puzzled at Carson's expression. "He been weeping on your shoulder?" he asked.

Carson sat rigidly on the edge of his bed. His voice sounded flat.

"You could call it that. Personally, I agree with your sentiments, but yet I can't help feeling a trifle sorry for him. His mother has found out, from an erk here, that he was flying. He's not made that the excuse for his action. He brought it out as we were saying good-bye. I read the letter. Rather pitiable."

"Are you a sucker for a sob story?" Masters said drily.

As if talking to himself, Carson said, "Still, he did do eight 'ops'."

Douglas made an abortive effort to blow a smoke ring and frowned. "That doesn't mean a thing, except that he now knows what it's all about. He's looked at it quite clinically and decided he didn't like the odds. Cold, calculated cowardice. They shoot men for that in infantry regiments."

Morphy said emphatically: "You're so right. Bet his pants were dirty, when you called those dummy-runs?"

Titch laughed coarsely. "Next time you do that, Shern, I'll give you a burst through the nose. There's one thing, though: the next engineer we get is a lucky fellow. He'll get a free gift of eight trips. His tour will finish with ours."

"If we finish!" Douglas said caustically.

Carson looked at him, and glanced at Callaghan. He wondered what the rear-gunner's thoughts were. Probably he was thinking of the brother he had seen killed and of how his own mother felt.

"What do you think, Jock?"

Callaghan eyed his skipper. "We're better rid of him!"

The words were frosty and as hard as the glint which had come into the gunner's eyes. They were the eyes, Carson thought, of an old man, and yet in the face of a boy.

"Hey!" shouted Titch, rising suddenly from the bed. "This is Friday, pay-day. What are we waiting for?"

14

FOR seven days the crew of S—Sugar could plan ahead comforted in the firm knowledge that they would see each dawn without remembering the odds against such a likelihood. And with this confidence came a boisterous and carefree attitude.

Their leave passes were waiting them in the orderly room but before they collected them they caught the wagon to the Flights. There was another reason too for their high spirits. On orders that day, Corporal Tubby Watson, had been up-graded to Sergeant. The news had been broken to them when they were drawing their pay, travel vouchers and the Nuffield bounty for senior N.C.O.s and Pilot Officers on operational leave.

Squadron Leader Farley had readily agreed that Watson should get the news of his promotion from them. The cowlings were off two of the Halifax's engines when they alighted from the flight wagon at the S bay.

"Special overhaul," Watson winked broadly. "It'll take us a few days. We don't want her being taken over as a spare kite when you're on leave. Reckon she needs a break too!"

Curly jerked a greasy thumb at the row of bombs painted on the fuselage and said, "Sure growing!"

Masters screwed up his lips and an expression of dismay contorted his face. He had been thinking the same, only he wondered how many more symbols would go up.

"One of these days," said the mid-upper, "you're going to break that line with a neat little Swastika."

Callaghan laughed, the first time, Carson realised, since his brother's death.

"Well, it won't be credited to you, Titch, for you're as blind as a bat," he said.

Titch turned on the rear-gunner furiously. "What do you think I fired at last night?"

"Bats," chipped in Morphy; "or more probably some poor suffering Lanc! Lor', not so long ago they wouldn't have given you a licence for an air-gun!"

Carson said lightly: "Joking over, Tubby. We came here to congratulate you on your third hook."

Watson cocked his moon-face sharply sideways. A look of incredulity came into his eyes.

"No kidding," Carson said. "It's just come through. Come on; we're pushing the boat out."

Group Captain Dorton, his hands clasped behind his back, watched them from his office as they went into the mess. Above Watson's Corporal's chevrons, he saw a third stripe had been chalked in.

There was genuine pleasure in his smile as he picked up the leave list the Adjutant had earlier placed on his desk. Skimming through it, he noted that all S—Sugar's crew were going to addresses listed as their homes.

All, he corrected himself, but their bomb-aimer, who had made out his application for a rail warrant to London. That was not the address listed on his personal papers. Come to think of it, he could not recall any home address or next-of-kin on Douglas's documents.

He fidgeted uneasily with his tie. London was all very well if he had a home there. Otherwise it was not the place for his aircrew to rest. He had too often seen the effects of leaves in London. Washed-out crews, tired and red-eyed from too many all night parties. Not that he could blame them. But still, the fact remained that some of them were lucky. They managed to get a full night's rest before they were operating again. Others found they were operating on their first night back.

He turned from the window, walked to his desk and picked up the telephone.

"Group," he said to the Waaf switchboard operator.

When the operator put him through, he asked for Air Commodore Cartingham. A few seconds later his receiver crackled. "I'm sorry, sir, but the Air Commodore is away this week-end."

Dorton replaced the receiver. He wanted to speak to Cartingham about Carter. Well, he would keep him on the ground until he had a chance to have a talk with Cartingham, and get him grounded for good.

One other crew was going on leave with S—Sugar, the crew of F—Freddie. They were standing at the bar when Carson and his crew came in. Kiwi drew Douglas aside.

"So you're going to London?" he said bitterly.

"You know damned well I am, Kiwi, and you promised a long time ago to come with me."

"That," the New Zealander said, "was weeks ago when we hadn't any other place to go to."

"And what other places were you thinking of?" Douglas smiled mockingly.

"Come off it, Shern. We've a standing date, remember, with Sue and Terry."

Douglas drank some of his beer. "What of it? We can't bed them and de-bed the denizens of the Ruhr all at the same time...."

"That was bloody well uncalled for! They're fine kids!" Kiwi retorted heatedly.

"So we buy them a diamond ring apiece, I suppose?"

Kiwi blinked. The flicking of his eyelids was getting a bit worse lately. He would have to do something about it. Rubbing his right eye gently, he looked at Douglas. "Let's be sensible about this, Shern. I like Sue a lot and I thought you liked Terry. They've a nice place, and we could have it to ourselves when they're at work. Frankly, I'm all for the quiet life. I've had enough of London," he said wearily.

Douglas sneered. "What a helluva exciting picture you've drawn!"

"Christ! Let me finish!" The New Zealander's voice was sheathed in anger. "We save money for one thing. Look at it rationally. We have a couple of real smart lookers. Even if we meet any girls near their standard in London, which I doubt, our leave'll be over before we get on nodding terms." Kiwi picked up his glass and drained it. "No, Shern, we've been lucky meeting them. That kind of break doesn't come often. If you can't recognise it, that's your tough luck; but we'd be crazy to throw them up. Anyway, I feel that way about Sue."

"Are you quite finished?" Douglas's voice was disinterested, sarcastic.

"For the moment," Kiwi said bluntly.

"All right then! You're the crazy one if you think I'm going to stay put in this dump of a town and listen to those blasted 'Halibags' going out every other night. What kind of a rest is that? Might as well stay on the bloody station, like that half-mad wireless operator of yours."

Douglas paused. "Trouble with you, cobber, is that you fall for every girl you meet," he added scornfully.

Kiwi shook his head. "You know damned-well, Shern, who's the skirt-mad genius around here. Time and again I've got you out of trouble. Most of the time it left a nasty taste in my mouth but they were your women, not mine. This time it's different. I'm not in love with Sue—I hardly know her—but she could be a very easy person to love. There's another thing. She telephoned this morning. I told her we would be going on leave today and had nowhere special in mind, so she . . ."

Douglas interrupted angrily. "You bloody well should have kept your mouth shut! Now you've probably messed things up for me with Terry when I come back!" His voice dropped and he said: "Okay. You made the date; you keep it!"

"Shern!" Kiwi said sternly. "We've known each other for a long time, but each week since you've come to this squadron you've grown a bigger bastard. You don't care one damn about messing up my leave. You haven't even given it a thought. I'm just the boy who tails along with the great Shern Douglas! But let me tell you this: your own crew aren't so hot on you. I've heard a few things that you wouldn't be flattered to know! Oh, hell! . . ."

The New Zealander glared, as he fought against his rising temper. "Shern! Be reasonable! You can't walk out on the girls just like that! You could spend one night in town and travel to London if you must, on Sunday. I'm asking you as the best friend you've got on this squadron! Don't mess things up for me. . . . You see, I like Sue a lot." There was an earnest plea in his voice.

"Sorry, Kiwi. I'd like to; but I hate travelling on Sundays. Don't let's quarrel over two pieces we picked up in . . ."

The New Zealander stared contemptuously at Douglas for a moment.

"To hell with you, Shern!" he snarled and walked out of the mess.

15

FOR two days Douglas mooned round London, cursing that he had ever decided to come. Everything was going wrong, not at all the way he had planned.

American servicemen had taken over in most of the clubs he had once known so well. What rankled him was the fact that the majority of them were U.S.A.A.F. flyers, men who would spend in a day more than his whole week's pay, and never miss the money. Two of his girl friends, who had usually welcomed him warmly when he was in London, were polite and cool when he telephoned.

"Sorry, Shern," one had said that morning; "you should have written. I thought you had left the country? No! I can't possibly make it tonight—Phil is coming on leave."

When he had asked who Phil was, the voice laughed teasingly, "Oh, he's cute, Shern! An American Air Force Captain. Met him last month, and he already wants to take me back to America with him. Tell me: you were there—what's Michigan like?"

He'd banged down the receiver and spent the next two hours in a drinking club. Bringing out a well-thumbed address book, he went into the telephone box in the basement and spent forty minutes dialling fruitlessly.

There was a fair chance, he considered, of Julie being in now. When he had telephoned earlier there had been no reply. It had been so long since he'd rang her number, she might well have moved from the flat.

As he checked with the directory, he regretted never having kept in touch with the women he had known before he had gone to the States. Ten minutes later he put down the receiver and went upstairs to the bar. He ordered a small Scotch and sipped it pensively.

Harry, fat, jovial and in his sixties, slid on to the stool beside him, and beckoned to the barman. "Large Scotch for my old friend here! He don't look so good!"

The barman smiled slyly. Harry could afford to give a large Scotch away, now and then, at the prices he was charging.

"Well, now, Shern, what's the trouble? Young lady stood you up?"

Douglas grunted, swung round lazily on his stool and eyed the proprietor. "Remember Julie?"

The fat man nodded.

"Well, she's asked me along to her engagement party tonight. A Lieutenant Commander, U.S.A. Tell me, Harry, have they any privates in the American Forces?"

"You're angry, my friend. He's not a bad fellow. Julie has taken him in here sometimes and he spends freely."

They talked for a while and Douglas made two more telephone calls before he left. Each brought a blank. In the end he reluctantly decided to attend the party.

He hailed a taxi in Lower Regent Street. Might as well admit it, he was damned lonely. Anyway, he wouldn't be buying his own drink. And he could always leave if he didn't like it. Her engagement meant nothing to him. It was just, he reflected, that his ego had been badly deflated since his arrival in London.

He was wondering what a psychiatrist might have thought of him. He certainly hadn't acted rationally since he was a kid. He thought of his brother and wondered, not for the first time, where he'd ever got to. Strange how he'd gone out of his life. He seldom remembered he even had one. Only on occasions like this—when he felt lonely and his thoughts wandered back into the past.

For a fleeting moment he thought he saw a glimpse of disappointment in Julie's eyes when she opened the door of her top floor flat.

"I hope a mere Flight Sergeant doesn't lower the tone of your party?" he said mockingly, as his eyes ran over the officers' greatcoats hanging on the wall rack.

"You're being silly, Shern. It's just that—well, I thought you were going through as a pilot. When did you change your mind?"

"I didn't; they washed me out," he said icily.

She led him into a softly lighted lounge. Once there had been two rooms. He remembered them well. Must have cost her quite a bit to have them knocked into one long studio type lounge.

About twenty people were talking and laughing in little groups throughout the room. And still it looked half empty. There were two British R.A.S.C. captains and three lieutenants from an R.A. battery. Apart from three U.S. Navy officers, the rest were women. That was probably why he had been asked along. Julie, he mused bitterly, should have rung up the Y.M.C.A. and balanced the numbers.

Julie's Lieutenant Commander was a big, broad-shouldered all-American footballer type. Somehow, he decided, he looked a bit out of place in dark navy serge and gold rings.

The whisky he took from him appeared tiny in that large, beefy hand.

As he raised the half tumbler he said, "Cheers!"

The American grinned, waved towards a table at the far end of the room, stacked with bottles of American liquor, and said, "Drink up; we've a lot to get through."

He was not sure whether it was the raw whisky or the warmth in the Commander's voice but some of the tension slipped from him.

"Do you like it over here?" he asked.

The Commander swallowed his drink before replying, "Sure, great to get into the war zone! Guess I'd rather have the deck of a destroyer under me and a Pacific gale chafing my face; but then, you can't kick against where the top-brass send you. But you know that."

He nodded and his eyes scanned the room. Some of the girls were better looking than he had at first thought. Difficult, though, to know who was paired with whom.

Julie and the Commander started to dance to the strains of a slow tempo record. He strolled towards the tables where the bottles were, splashed some water into his whisky.

A girl was leaning gracefully against the radio-gram, studiously flicking through an album of records. A plain black jersey wool dress clung to her petite, beautifully moulded form. Her honey blond hair was curled Grecian fashion, accentuating the delicate loveliness of her face.

Leisurely, he moved down the side of the room, deftly skirting couples who were dancing to the radio-gram.

Quietly he asked for a certain record. She looked up, and he detected a little sadness at the corners of her mouth.

"'Fraid that's not here: at least, I haven't noticed it. I've been trying to find 'That Old Black Magic'. It should be here! I was with Julie when she bought it."

"Let me try," he said. As she stepped back from the record-holder, to tilt a disc she was holding, he saw the plain gold ring on her left hand. Leaning over he lifted it gently. His lips curled in a rueful smile as he dropped her hand. "Whenever I meet a beautiful woman, she's already married!"

She laughed, a low, warm laugh. "That's very gallant, Flight, but rather stereotyped for the R.A.F."

"What do you know about the R.A.F.?"

Their eyes met, and he was conscious she was searching for something in his face. "My husband was a fighter pilot," she said quietly.

"Was?"

Wistfully she replied: "He baled out of a Hurricane over France in 1940 and is now a P.O.W."

"I'm so sorry," he said.

She sipped her drink and said evenly: "The great thing is that he's alive and out of the war."

Douglas raised his glass. "Let's drink to him!"

"I think I'll have a long drink this time," she said.

"In that case, have a Cuban Libre."

"I like the sound of that. What is it?"

Douglas took a tall glass from the table, slipped into the kitchen, and stuck two ice cubes in it. Julie was laying out plates of sandwiches. He waited until the two girls with her moved out with heavily laden plates.

"Julie," he said, "I congratulate! He's a swell guy, that Commander, and I'm sure you're both going to be very happy."

Looking up sharply, her eyes, wide, she said: "I'm so glad you like him, Shern. You haven't told him that we were once . . .?"

"No," he said; "anyway, we were just friends. Right?"

She nodded happily, and, glancing at the glasses in his hands, said:

"That's the boy. Circulate and keep the party going. Who are they for?"

"The blonde girl in the black dress," he said; "so far I haven't got her name."

"Oh, you must mean Loraine Davis? She's a friend of Nancy's. Works in the Admiralty with her. But you're going to be disappointed. She's married, with a kiddie of three. Her husband's a P.O.W.—Battle of Britain boy, I think. . . ."

A quizzical expression came into her eyes. "If you're thinking what I think you're thinking, forget it! Lori's one of the faithful types."

"God, what a mind you have, Julie! I was only getting her a drink. How about you?"

"No, thanks! Later, maybe, and remember what I've said!"

Loraine raised an eyebrow when he came back with the glasses.

"This is the foundation," he told her, as he poured in a little rum; "but to make it correctly one should use one part Cuban rum to one part Jamaican rum."

"I don't think I like rum." Her voice was slightly hostile.

"People," he said, "are usually misled by the preconceptions they have about their likes and dislikes. Watch what I do with the rum."

Splashing in some lime juice, he added a half bottle of coke, then stirred the glasses.

She sipped it gingerly and smiled in surprise. Then she took a longer swallow.

"Why, it's lovely! Where did you learn of a drink like this?"

"In Florida," he said airily.

"By the way, I can't keep calling you Flight. I think I heard Julie introduce you, but I missed the name."

"Shern Douglas; and I missed yours."

"That's the worst of those general introductions. I'm Loraine Davis."

She told him of her three-year-old son Johnny, who lived with her parents in Reading, and whom she visited every weekend.

"I'd like nothing better than to be with him all the time, but I have to eke out my allowance as a Pilot Officer's wife, and it doesn't go that far."

"No," he said thoughtfully; "the R.A.F.'s not the world's best payers."

He took her back to her flat when the party ended at midnight, and he noted the look of concern in her eyes when he paid off the taxi.

"You shouldn't have done that! You won't find it easy at this hour to get another."

"It doesn't matter," he said. "I want to walk a bit, anyway. Have a cigarette with me before you go in?"

She took the cigarette he had lighted for her, and again he was aware of her eyes watching him carefully as he lighted his own.

When she spoke, her voice was warm, yet firm, as if she had studiously weighed what she was about to say. "Shern, if you promise to be good you can have a coffee with me; but then you must go, understand?"

"I promise, but you really don't have to."

Her flat was small and compact. A lounge led to a bedroom and off that was a tiny hall, which in turn led to a bathroom. Adjoining the bathroom was a six-by-four kitchen.

"One thing about these bombing raids is that you can get a flat cheaply and easily," she said.

He drank the coffee slowly, then looked at his watch. "Lord, it's nearly one o'clock! I'll go and let you get to bed!"

At the door he turned and slipped on his forage cap.

"Won't you change your mind and see me tomorrow night?"

"No," she said, and the voice was toneless; "there's no point. I'm married and still in love with my husband."

He shrugged his shoulders. "Then there can be no harm in it." His voice dropped, and he added: "I'd appreciate your company. Fact is, I'm plain lonely, and this might well be my last leave."

She looked up at him and her eyes softened. "It's a date, then, but if you'd tried to be fresh, I wouldn't have made it."

"Will you keep it, or is it just a nice way of getting rid of me?"

"You'll see! 'Bye now!" As she closed the door, he saw again that faint sadness in her smile.

From the window of her darkened room she watched him walk down the empty street. And she marvelled once more at his likeness to the man whose ring she wore, whose little mannerisms she had once again witnessed that night when a stranger walked into a crowded room. Not as she had been picturing him lately, through high broad fences of barbed wire, but young, laughing and carefree, the Johnny she had always known.

Each memory brought a fresh ache to her heart. If the Flight Sergeant had worn a moustache, she wondered if she would have been able to tell them apart. Even so, he had sent her heart racing when she had first seen him. Only his voice had shattered that first wild delirious thought which had sent her body tingling with the hope that somehow he had managed to escape from his prison. The next time she went home she would bring back the enlarged picture of Johnny and show it to the Flight Sergeant. . . . But no, there could be no next time. It was madness even agreeing to meet him tomorrow. Yet his attraction was magnetic, at times disturbingly hypnotic, in the fantastic likeness of his to Johnny.

Every evening of that week he was waiting for her in the little coffee bar off Trafalgar Square, where she had her mid-day meal. With each meeting the still small voice, warning her of the danger of her pent-up emotions everflowing, grew fainter, less insistent.

But it was the steady off-beat rhythm from the four piece band, in the smoky basement club he had taken her to one night, which swept away the last of her wavering qualms.

That, and the heady, fiery drinks he had plied her with, unleashed the desire surging within her. Her head whirled giddily and an exhilarating sense of levitation swept over her as he helped her from the taxi and guided her into the darkened flat, later that night.

Her leg stumbled against the soft quilted edge of the bed. She felt herself falling. Her arms tightened round his neck. She clung to him tightly as his lips crushed on hers with a hunger equal to her own.

Gently her coat slipped from her shoulders. As it fell, she pressed away, only to be drawn back into another long smouldering, pulse-throbbing embrace.

The mists cleared on a flimsy waft of reason. She tore her mouth from his. This was not Johnny, she thought wildly. This was . . . The gyro spun faster and the whirling breathlessness of the moment ripped the mind free from the pull of the past.

Her arms locked round his shoulders. Her lips sought, held his, as her finger nails bit deep into his firm flesh.

"Darling Johnny! Darling! . . . Darling! . . . Put me to bed. . . . It's been so long! . . . So very long . . . !"

Through the mists, the whispering sound of his own loved voice came to her.

"Darling Lori! How I've missed you! Wanted you so much through all those years. . . ."

Slowly she felt him undress her, lifting her in all her nakedness, and carrying her to the big, wide bed. His lips, hot and eager, seared on her parched trembling mouth. Then his hands were caressing, confidently and expertly, her firm taut breasts, exploring firmly and daringly the loveliness of her body.

Her arms tightened round his bare shoulders and the smoothness of his flesh sent an electrifying tremor jerking through her body. Passionately she pulled him towards her, surrendering in eager, utter abandonment to his fiery kisses.

Many hours later, after the floodtide of passion had ebbed, she lay awake, quietly sobbing into the pillow. God, she had had too much to drink and allowed her emotions to take her off in a dream-world of her own making.

The sleeping figure at her side stirred and awoke. She felt his arm tighten against her and pull her towards him.

She tried to push him away, then his lips were on hers. Violently, she clung to him as his kisses blotted up her tears.

"Shern darling, darling! . . . Love me again!" This time it was no make-belief dream in which Johnny figured. She wanted this man as much as his body ached for her. There was no excuse now, the dream was shattered, the idol in her mind toppling over into nothingness.

A steady drizzle of rain was falling, when they arrived at the station. He found her a corner seat and placed her suitcase on the luggage rack. They stood on the platform, smoking idly, anxiously glancing at the splotched face of the railway clock.

"This isn't the end, Lori?" he asked eagerly.

She drew heavily on her cigarette, and looked at it thoughtfully before flicking it away with her thumb. For a moment he watched the sparks cascade from it as it slid off the edge of the platform, to disappear on to the line. Strangely it was symbolic of something, something he couldn't quite place.

When she spoke her voice was limp, almost inaudible. "I don't really know, Shern. For years I've held out against what we did, and now I'm terribly ashamed."

The voice was dead and toneless, and he winced at her words.

His answer sounded unconvincing as his ears translated its words: "Lori, with us it was bound to happen. Nothing we could do about it . . . stronger than ourselves. . . . I'm crazy about you, darling! . . . Must see you again!"

She smiled wanly. "I don't know, Shern, and what is worse, I can't think straight. Once it was all clear. I was in love with Johnny. Now, everything is confused. I can't be in love with two men, and the terrible thing is I think I'm in love with you. I should never have met you that first time!"

"Do you love Johnny?" he demanded.

"I did. I still do. Oh, I'm not at all sure! It's been so long. Both of us must have changed so much! I'm a stranger even to myself." She paused, and her eyes again switched to his face. "No, darling, it won't be easy! Harder than ever now!"

"It's you and me that matters, Lori," he said softly.

"There is his son—my son and . . ." Her words trailed off, as a whistle sounded along the platform.

The train jerked and the coupling hooks clanged. The carriage in which he had placed her case moved and abruptly came to a stop. He pulled her quickly to him and kissed her long and hard. For a moment she went limp in his arms. Then she broke away and said softly: "Darling, I'll miss this train."

He pulled the carriage door open and watched her get in and lower the half-open window. A whistle again shrilled along the platform and her carriage moved slowly past.

"Write, darling! Write me!" she shouted through the open window.

Vigorously he nodded and, turning on his heel, walked to the station buffet. He drank the rum slowly, but his thoughts were on the night before. On the dinner he had in her flat; the dinner that he had called on Harry to supply from the club. Then there was no doubt as to how she had felt.

But then, the bottle of Canadian Club and the soft firelight had helped.

Strange, the pull she had on him. It seemed he had always known her, met her a long time ago, and that their meeting at Julie's was merely a reunion after a long parting.

The announcer's voice came over the radio at the end of the buffet bar. "... Forty-two of our aircraft are missing from this and other air operations. ..."

16

A LOW thick fog crawled from the sea, rolled up the cliff face and sprawled over the aerodrome. Dorton watched it drape the black shapes of the Halifaxes in a mantle of murky yellow, and remembered it was Sunday.

The padre, he mused, would not have to deliver his evensong service against the background roar of warming-up Hercules engines. Both of them, in their different ways, had their problems and neither, he reflected, could help the other much. Looking back over the past month, he felt he had been more successful in his own field than had the chaplain. Getting the aircrews into the air was easy enough. Talking them into a church parade needed a Billy Sunday. Since he had cancelled the compulsory church parades, the Chaplain had been cool, almost hostile, to him.

Still, it had been by attending to the little, seemingly insignificant, pin-pricks of service life that he and Carter had remoulded the squadron. Compulsion of the wrong kind might well upset the delicate balance of their framework.

Now Cartingham was sending him H2S—the new blind bombing and navigation device—hitherto only used by the Pathfinders and a few select squadrons.

Crews had to be of top quality, yet not too near the end of their tour, otherwise it would be a waste of time training them in the new technique. But again, they must not be too green. On the whole, he did not think he had made a bad selection in allocating the sets to B—Baker, F—Freddie, S—Sugar and Y—Yorker. All four had been withdrawn from operations until their crews had mastered the intricacies of the sets.

The bomb-aimers of B—Baker and Y—Yorker had already been given ground tuition in operating the device. Tomorrow they would begin the first stage of air instruction. The crews of

F—Freddie and S—Sugar would start, he had decided, immediately they returned from leave.

With Carter handling the training, it would be smooth, efficient and intense.

Kiwi MacArthur lolling in an armchair in front of the fire, happily watched the room darken as the fog shrouded the town. Suzan rose from the settee, switched on a reading lamp and smiled.

He rubbed his hands. "Sue, old girl! I hope this weather clamps in for a few more days. This marvellous week's leave's spoilt me for service life"

They had heard the squadron go out twice that week to rendezvous with the main force which attacked industrial targets in the Ruhr. Once he had stirred in the small hours of the morning when they had straggled overhead in twos and threes, loping off height as they circled the town and waited to land.

He was in love with Suzan. And it was not all physical love. He had learned a great deal about her during his leave and found that underneath her facade of gayness lay an extraordinarily sensible and practical character. His commission would be through shortly; and he had asked her to marry him when he finished his tour.

Kiwi stretched luxuriously. It had been the best leave he had ever had. Only one thing had marred their happiness—Terry's disappointment at Douglas's absence. It took them a long time to dissuade her from leaving the flat, for she had felt she was in their way.

He reached for the cup of tea, Suzan had placed at his elbow, and hoped Douglas had had a lousy time in London.

He must brief Douglas on the excuse he had made for him. Douglas would be furious. But why should he mess up his own leave because of S—Sugar's bomb-aimer.

On second thoughts it might be better if he explained the whole farce to Suzan. He did not think she believed the story that Douglas was spending his leave with his parents.

S—Sugar's bomb-aimer had never talked much about his life before the war. Once he had told him that his parents were dead; had died when he and his brother were quite young. Until they were eleven they had lived with a grandmother. On her death, they had been separated, Douglas going to an orphan home while his brother was boarded out with foster parents He didn't know whether they had ever met since.

Perhaps that accounted for the unstability of Douglas. Often he had spoken of how fortunate his brother had been in entering the Merchant Navy as a cadet officer, his foster parents having paid for his apprenticeship. That had been the last he had heard of him.

For the third time that day, he wondered how Douglas had got on in London. If he was any judge, Douglas would have found a woman, and the odds were she would be a married woman.

Douglas had looked at him once with mock pity when he had asked what was wrong with single girls.

"Single women want an engagement ring after they know you a few weeks, Kiwi. Better keep to married women; they're a lot safer."

He chuckled as Douglas's words came back to him.

Suzan, watching his face, asked what was amusing him.

"Nothing, darling; only something Douglas once said. It wasn't repeatable."

"I can imagine that, if it came from him. I can't think what attraction his friendship has for you?"

"He's not bad, really, Sue. He's his own worst enemy."

Funny, he mused, but Suzan had never taken to Douglas.

She came over and sat on the edge of his chair. "Are you going back then tonight?"

"Yes, I'm afraid I'll have to. If this fog clears, we may be on tomorrow night, and I've a few things to sort out."

She kissed his brow. "I wish to God you were finished with it all."

He stroked her hair and thought again how lovely she was.

"I wish that, too, Sue. It won't be so long now," he said.

Wing Commander Carter waited until the crews of B—Baker, F—Freddie, S—Sugar and Y—Yorker had taken their seats in the navigation briefing rooms before he uncovered the rough diagram on the blackboard.

Tapping it with his hand, he looked round the room. "The H2S set looks something like this. You'll get a better idea when you go down to the Flights, as your aircraft have now been fitted with the device.

"Basically, the H2S set is a jam-proof navigation aid. It will be operated by the bomb-aimer. I don't know very much about the technicalities of the set. However, that is not our problem. Our job is to operate it and operate it efficiently!

"Briefly, the set gives a picture similar to that on a television screen. As the receiver and transmitter are both in the aircraft, it can't be jammed or its picture deflected."

Carter adjusted the light above the blackboard and brushed some chalk from his hands. "For example, if you are flying in from the sea towards Flamborough Head, the set will send out radar pulses at fantastic speeds. These will hit the coast line within a certain radius and return to the receiver, giving a clear outline on your screen, of towns, cities, lakes and sometimes the estuaries of rivers, if they are large enough."

With a piece of chalk he illustrated how, by operating different knobs on the set, distances and bearings could be taken every other second.

"These bearings and distances you will plot on a Mercator chart, specially designed for use with the H2S radar aid."

Carter talked for the best part of an hour, explaining how they could bomb a target 'blind' and still put their load down with accuracy, how they could use the device for timed runs and for picking out definite coastal characteristics invaluable for split-second alterations in course.

"In fact," he said, "the set makes navigation simpler than it has ever been."

Indicating a young Flying Officer who had been sitting behind him but who had now moved to his side, Carter said:

"This is Flying Officer Sanderson. He will take the bomb-aimers and navigators of Freddie and Sugar down to the Flights and give them their first practical course. The rest of you will get your chance when he's through with them."

He stepped forward, his hands thrust deep into the pockets of his battle-dress. "One thing more! We haven't much time. You will be expected to operate the sets efficiently by the end of the week."

Carter paused, and smiled thinly. "But you will still be called on to meet any maximum effort, so you'd better learn quick. After all, it's to your own advantage."

For the rest of that day they checked and rechecked their operating drill. Watching them, correcting them and guiding them, was Sanderson.

As dusk fell, he called an end to the instruction and walked back with them from the Flights.

"I reckon," he told them. "you have the hang of the 'magic-box'. If the weather is anything decent, we'll try and get a cross-country flight in tomorrow to give you practical experience."

They were at breakfast when the Tannoy system called them to the Flights. Carter was waiting as they filed into A Flight office.

"Met," he said tersely, "expects it to be clear until late afternoon, when fog is likely. Flying rations for a five-hour cross-country are on the way down for you."

A light drizzle was falling as Carson taxied S—Sugar on to runway 090, cleared his engines and waited for the green flare.

Above, the cloud was grey and sombre, with base at 2,000 feet. As the green cartridge burst a hundred yards from the Halifax's nose, Carson pushed the throttles forward, before taking his feet from the brakes.

"Lock!" he called, and Douglas locked the throttle levers.

The bomber began to swing, slowly at first, then gradually building up to a vicious swaying movement. And Carson, momentarily forgetting the feel of an unloaded Halifax, over-corrected on the rudder.

Faster the Halifax slewed round, as Carson slapped on right rudder. His hand tightened on the control column as the bomber whipped slowly to heel. The left rudder bar kicked against his taut leg and he saw the white concrete of the control tower swing towards his centre vision panel.

They either sliced off the top or cleared it by inches, but first he had to lift her from the runway, otherwise they would hurtle straight into the tower.

It was as simple and as terrifying as that, for he could never bring her to a stop now, he thought. He prayed he had the flying speed to play with and eased back on the control.

Douglas saw a black form rush along the roof. Arms out-stretched and legs splayed, it disappeared frog-like over the parapet.

Petrified, his brain registered that it was a human form. Some-one who knew they were going to crash, burying him in a crumbling tomb of petrol-seared concrete.

His hand clawed at the release clip on his safety belt. A split second contradiction from the mind-box and his hand fell limply. No time even to get out of the seat. The glass-fronted control tower, with the white terror-stricken faces against the big, wide panels, was dead in line with him.

God, it must be even more terrifying for them! They were static, paralysed by the black wings hurtling towards them.

Men were electrocuted strapped to a seat, and this must be how they felt. Easier that way, for they never saw the hand that flung the switch.

"Oh, Jesus! we've missed it!" The voice came on and as suddenly faded.

Strange, ghostly and unreal. He'd never heard that voice over the intercom before. As the mists of fear cleared from his mind, he identified it as that of Sanderson's. The H2S instructor must have stayed in the nose.

"Jeez!" The accent was Glasgow, wild and loud. He'd never heard the rear-gunner shout like that. "Christ, you've hit the aerial . . . !"

"Sorry, chaps." God, how cool he could be! "I'd forgotten she was so light . . . over-corrected that swing, but we're all right now!"

Releasing his safety belt, Douglas looked contemptuously at Carson and slipped, half tumbled, into the nose.

Sanderson was leaning limply against the Gee set. He shook his head dazedly and Douglas noted how deathly white his face was.

"My Gawd! I'll never fly again with your mucking skipper. Tell me, has he ever flown a Halifax before?"

Douglas sank on to the navigator's bench, his brow, sticky and wet, resting on his hand. He shouted back. "You ain't seen nothing yet! Once we nearly took a farmhouse with us!"

Sanderson looked down at him with glazed eyes.

"Ops," croaked Douglas, "don't mean anything. It's the take-offs that scare us!"

His body was trembling and he marvelled at the mind's power of recovery. Then he heard Sanderson say: "I believe that."

The Flying Officer plugged in his intercom, and called up Carson:

"When I get over the shock of that take-off, I'll try and show your bomb-aimer how this set behaves in the air. But fly around for a while until my arms stop shaking," he said vehemently.

Carson's voice was quiet and subdued. "Sorry I upset you."

"Upset me? Christ, man, you nearly killed me!" snarled Sanderson.

"By the way," he snapped, "you don't land like that?"

Carson flinched. His finger was on the intercom button, but he decided to let the remark go. There'd be enough to explain when he got down.

A little later, when the temper left him, he called the rear-gunner.

"Callaghan here."

"You really got wire round that turret?"

"Gun barrels look like Christmas trees, dripping with tinsel!"

"Do you think we took anything else with us?"

"Fellow took a nose dive, but Jock wouldn't have seen that," Douglas interrupted.

"What fellow?" Carson asked.

This time the voice was Sanderson's. "Some fellow with a lot of sense took a header from the tower. . . ."

"God," Carson said, "how high's that tower?"

The instructor's voice was steeped in sarcasm. "'Bout thirty feet, but you were going a little too fast for me to measure it. Now, if you'll stop marvelling about your flying, we'll get on with some instruction."

At 1539 hours Carson brought S—Sugar down through the cloud base, breaking clear at nine hundred feet over the sea. Twenty-five minutes later, a sickly grin on his face, he came out of the Administration Building and rejoined his waiting crew.

"That fellow broke an ankle and sprained a wrist," he said. Ruefully he added, "Don't ask me what Groupie said. Easier to tell you what he didn't."

Then turning to Douglas, he said: "I think I know what you must feel like, sitting with me on take-off, just watching! But there'll be no more like that! I've got the hang of the ship now, know how that swing starts and how to stop it."

Douglas was having a beer with Masters when Kiwi came into the mess. He strolled up to them and, grinning broadly, said: "Hear you beggars nearly took the control tower with you this morning!"

They nodded, and the New Zealander said: "They don't come much closer than that. Reckon you must be the luckiest guys around here! Incidentally, what sort of leave had you, Shern?"

"Swell, Kiwi," Douglas replied, winking broadly at Masters. "So good, that I'm going back to London next time. What sort of leave had you?"

"One of the best I've ever had, Shern."

Cocking his head at S—Sugar's bomb-aimer, he said anxiously: "Don't mind me mentioning it, but you don't look so good. Maybe it's the delayed action from that take-off?"

Douglas glared, and Masters emptied his glass. "Guess," he said, "I'll push along. Have a couple of letters to write."

After he had gone, Kiwi said: "I hope you appreciate, Shern, that I'd to give some explanation for you not showing up?"

"There was no need to," Douglas replied haughtily.

"Oh yes, there was, and you know it damned fine!"

"Okay, what did you make up?"

Kiwi held Douglas's eyes for a moment. "Said you were spending it with your parents. I think Terry believed me, but she was still very upset. Nice kid, that!"

"She's got her points," Douglas said dourly.

"Well, you won't have to worry unduly about her, Shern. I introduced her to Jack Hogarth, Y—Yorker's bomb-aimer. He came into the Atlantic when Sue, Terry and I were having a drink one night."

As Douglas's eyebrows rose, he added: "He's taken quite a fancy to her. She sorta likes him, too."

"Christ, that's big of you, Kiwi! I originally fix up these dates, and as soon as my back's turned, you start farming out my girl-friend to all and sundry...."

The New Zealander cut in sharply and heatedly. "You're bloody well impossible! But you don't fool me none. You'll toss Terry over as soon as you're tired of her. But this time it happens that she's Sue's best friend and I'm not going to stand for it. You see, Sue and I are getting engaged."

"So it's like that then?" Douglas's tone was low and surprised.

"Better lay off entirely, Shern. It would be better that way." The New Zealander turned on his heel and strode towards the bar.

Douglas watched him for a moment, shrugged his shoulders and walked out.

The fog which lay over the Yorkshire bases of Bomber Command, late every afternoon that week, obligingly lifted with the first rays of the pale February sunlight. And regularly with each dawn, aircraft B, F, S and Y rolled down the main runway on long cross-country flights. Everyone on the squadron knew they were special radar flights. The big black bulges of the H2S scanners under their fuselages gave the Halifaxes the appearance of pregnant whales.

One evening, long after the four crews had left the Flights, Douglas worked on a spare H2S chart, carefully plotting in the latest intelligence reports on the movements of German flak and searchlight concentrations.

The door creaked softly and Masters came in.

"Hello, Larry! What's brought you down?"

Masters walked to a table near the window, picked up a white silk flying glove and dusted it against his leg. "Left this, and didn't want to find that it had been 'knocked'."

He came round to glance over Douglas's shoulder.

"What do you think of the new box of tricks?"

Douglas scratched his left ear thoughtfully. "Should make navigating easy. As for bombing there's not a city safe in Germany from a precision attack above ten-tenths cloud."

"Yes," Masters said, "it's going to make our work a lot easier, but it means we have to work closer together than before. I've been thinking. If it's okay with you, I believe the best technique is for you to plot the H2S fixes on your own chart after giving them to me. I'll mark them alongside the Gee fixes. That way, we have a double check."

Douglas nodded. "Sounds foolproof. Incidentally, have you said anything to the rest of the crew about how the set works?"

"Well, yes, I have. They'll know sooner or later, so they might as well know it now," Masters said. Flicking some dust from his glove, he added quietly: "You know Titch has some notion that Jerry can vector on to the set?"

Douglas frowned. "He's bloody daft. How can they, when we carry the receiver and the transmitter in the aircraft? No beams to intercept!"

"True," Masters replied, "but nevertheless Titch has an unshakeable hunch the set will end our spell of good luck . . . and you know how very lucky we've been this past while."

"Titch," Douglas said with emphasis, "has a bee in his bonnet. Thinks he knows better than the boffins who put this thing together."

Masters smiled thinly as they walked from the room. "Out of the mouths of babes and sucklings, they say . . ."

"Forget it," Douglas said; "pure cock!"

But Titch was to be proved right. Bomber Command's statisticians, working detachedly over the figures of the Command's losses, were one day, very soon, to know that the Germans had in fact found a way of vectoring their night fighters on to the H2S aircraft.

But in the lapse between the present and the time when the JU 88's were fitted with the homing device to guide them with uncanny accuracy beneath the bellies of the radar aircraft, there, unseen, to pour long lethal bursts from their fuselage turret into the scanners, Douglas and Masters fattened on the new-found confidence the device gave them.

17

FEBRUARY slipped into March, and the long row of bombs on the fuselage of the Halifax crept to fifteen. Carson was now wearing the broad ring of Flying Officer. Masters, with the thinner braid of a Pilot Officer, moved into the Officers' Mess a week after Flight Sergeant Kiwi MacArthur.

Slowly new names were being chalked on the Ops board, new faces appearing at the bars of both messes. Dorton, leaning back in his chair, his eyes resting on the dullness of Flight Sergeant Douglas's buttons, realised with some reluctance that S—Sugar and her crew were one of the few old ones left. Not quite the oldest, but nevertheless the thought was disquieting. Still, he reasoned, Cartingham seemed pleased that he had somehow managed to bring down the squadron's losses.

Not by a lot, but they were lower than they had been. His smile was warm, his voice confidential and friendly when he spoke.

"One thing more, Flight. Clean these buttons when you go to Group tomorrow. The Air Commodore's deputy is a stickler for clean brass and doesn't appreciate how such things are overlooked on operating squadrons. It would be a pity if it held up your commission."

He leaned over the desk. "That's all, Douglas, except, Good Luck!"

When the door closed behind the Flight Sergeant, he pulled out the top left-hand drawer of his desk. Taking out the letter he had written to Cartingham about Carter, he slowly ripped it to pieces. It would be better, he considered, to explain the matter of the Wing Commander to Cartingham personally. He would miss Carter, but lately he was finding himself getting tense and taut when the Wing Commander was flying. He sighed, some squadron was going to get a first-class Commanding Officer. Dorton rose from his desk and paced the floor restlessly. The squadron were ticking over as an operational squadron should, and much of the success they had achieved lately was entirely due to Carter's handling of the aircrew.

What was more, he ruminated, they were bringing back clear-cut proof that their bombs were finding the targets—flak-streaked night photographs with the target indicators boldly portrayed on the plates.

F—Freddie and S—Sugar were particularly consistent. Their bomb-aimers came to his mind and abstractedly he compared the two men, so different in character, yet with an all-powerful common denominator linking them relentlessly together. Mac-Arthur, level-eyed, boyish, with his unruly mop of sun-bleached blond hair and the firm determined outline of his finely chiselled chin; Douglas, dark, lean, a trifle too handsome and suave, with his swashbuckling clean-cut features.

Strange, he contemplated, but MacArthur had the look of the men usually associated with Spitfires and Hurricanes, while Douglas had the air of the buccaneer, whose courage and loyalty were gauged by gold.

MacArthur's eyes had sparkled that day he had told him he was commissioning him; Douglas had eyed him speculatively, a trace of a sardonic smirk plying his lips, and politely but pointedly reminded him that his Warrant Officer was through.

"Financially, sir, I'll be better off as a W.O. and it would mean more to me."

God, the conceit of the man infuriated him for a moment. Not the Air Force he was thinking of, but himself and the warrant on his sleeve, which would show to everybody the service he had: the man who had turned down a commission. Oh, he saw through that part easily enough. But, Lord, the man had guts, the dummy-runs he had done this last few months.

Dorton thought of Carson, and decided that S—Sugar's skipper had earned any award coming to him. Come to that, Martin of F—Freddie was long overdue for a ribbon.

He made a mental note to put both aircraft captains in for the D.F.C. when the squadron's next allocation came up.

Douglas was reading a letter that had come that afternoon from Loraine, when Kiwi telephoned him from the Officers' Mess. The ever-changing names on the Ops board had drawn them closer than they had been for weeks.

"Damned glad you're taking your commission. How'd it go?"

"It's gone through, but it leaves me cold. The old man cut up a bit rough when I told him I'd prefer my Warrant."

"So what? You'll have your F/O through in no time. They back-date it quite a bit on a squadron and you won't look so much of the sprog you obviously think you will."

"What makes you think Groupie will back-date it?" Douglas asked.

"Baloney, Shern! Look, this is more important, we've a date tonight, remember? So for Christ's sake, play it easy! You've no idea of the oil I've poured on!"

"I played it sweet the other night, but it didn't get me far. . . ."

Kiwi interrupted sharply. "Hell, you can't blame the girl! How were we to know that she'd found out you'd no parents to spend a leave with?"

Douglas said metallically: "I like your use of the 'we'. Sure it wasn't that bastard bomb-aimer in Y—Yorker you introduced her to?"

"No, Shern; it wasn't Hogarth. Jack doesn't play low."

"I'm in two minds whether I should keep this date tonight!"

"Forget it, Shern. You're just annoyed. By the way, I hear you had a big win in the crap school the other night? Hear you raked in about seventy-five pounds playing some new system you've worked out."

"Nuts, every damned win or loss in that school is exaggerated. I was lucky, that's all."

"How much you take?"

"'Bout fifty-six pounds, but I'm not advertising it. Wild horses won't drag me back into that school. That little roll is for my next leave in London."

The New Zealander lowered his voice. "Say, Shern, you know where I can pick up a motor-cycle cheap?"

Douglas stuck a cigarette in his mouth, pulled a match from his pocket and scored it down the cream-painted wall of the kiosk. "Fellow in the village has one. Tried to sell it to me in the Ostler the other night. I'll tap him next time I see him and find out what he wants for it!"

"Okay, Shern, I'll be grateful. See you outside the mess in thirty minutes."

Douglas heard the receiver click down, returned his own and slipped out of the telephone box.

On his way to his room, he wondered how much the villager would take for the motor-cycle. If he could make a little on the deal it would help towards his next leave in London. He'd need every penny then. He cursed the time-lag behind his pay being transferred to a bank on his commissioning and reflected his leave would fall around that time . . .

No, perhaps he'd let Kiwi have the bike without any strings. The idea of making anything on the deal brought a twitch to his lips. The New Zealander was the only friend he had ever had and he had always been square with him.

They were sitting over their second pint in the low-beamed room of the saloon bar when Suzan came in. Kiwi rose, his blue eyes soft and tender, and pulled in a chair.

"Hello, darling!" Douglas noted that his clipped New Zealand accent was this time slow and deliberate.

She kissed him lightly and when she had sat down, he asked: "Where's Terry?"

Coldly, Suzan glanced at Douglas before her eyes swept back to Kiwi.

"It's his date, darling. He should ask that!"

"What have I done now?" Douglas asked.

She eyed him with the same hostile look she had flashed him when she first came into the bar. "Terry's hurt, Shern! She feels she has been cheap with you. I didn't know what she meant at first. Then she told me, and I'm still furious."

Kiwi toyed sheepishly with his glass and shot a quick look at Suzan. Her hand squeezed his arm gently. "It's better to say it, Len. I've been thinking it for a long time. You are quite a heel, Douglas, and it was her birthday. Her first night out for a long time!"

"You have it all wrong, Sue. I'll go round and see her. But, God, how temperamental some women can be!"

Douglas rose, and saw her eyes flash angrily, as she muttered to the New Zealander something he could not quite catch.

As he walked out of the bar, he pondered again as to why Kiwi's girl had taken such an instant dislike to him. He had sensed it almost from their first meeting.

Terry opened the door and her long dark eye-lashes fluttered in surprise.

"Can I come in?"

She hesitated and stood aside. The hall light was soft and it flattered her delicately shaped face. She had changed her hair style slightly from the last time he had seen her. It hung in full bold waves which caressed her shoulder.

She was lovelier than he had imagined.

She closed the door behind him and made to move past him. He caught her lightly by the shoulder and gently turned her round.

"Don't move, Terry! Just let me look at you. Now I know. It's the hair. You should always wear it that way. My, but you're adorable. Slip on a coat, darling. I've so much to tell you, so much to put right. Please, Terry, just this once!"

She laughed nervously. It was musical but a little forced, he thought. Her eyes glanced inquiringly over his face. "It had better be good, for I've . . ." she broke off, tossing her head airily. "Go into the living-room while I change."

Surprisingly soon, he thought, she came back into the room. He let his eyes roam over the tight white silk blouse, the black pencil-slim skirt, the sheer gun-metal nylon-sheathed legs, in the black patent leather shoes, with the three-inch high heels, and wondered again why he had ever spent his leave in London.

It was over a meal in the Atlantic that he told her tenderly: "There's not a great deal I can say, Terry. So I'll just tell the truth. I couldn't stand another week near the squadron. I had to get away. I wanted to ask you to come with me, but I knew you wouldn't have been able to get away from work."

Pausing, he added softly: "It was Kiwi who made that excuse about my spending my leave with my parents. They died a long time back. For the record, I had a lousy leave. Spent it in a service club."

She laid her hand on his arm. "It's all right, Shern. I think I understand what you and Kiwi must be going through."

He noticed that she shivered slightly. "It's rather cold here. Let's have the coffee at home," she said shortly.

As they strolled down the street, he told her casually about his coming commission.

"I'm glad for you," she whispered, "but I'd rather if the news had been . . . you were finished with operations."

He squeezed her hand. "We could emulate Kiwi and Sue, then . . . couldn't we?"

He felt her finger nails bite into his palm. "You really mean that?"

He kissed her gently. "Every word, Terry."

18

THREE days elapsed before Dorton telephoned Cartingham and discussed Carter's case. Before he rang off the Air Commodore told him:

"Very well. As you are aware, new squadrons are being formed and Carter has already been selected to command one. However, in view of what you have just said I shall have him posted from Nissindon this week-end. He'll go on leave first—a long one—and by the time he comes back I'll have a command for him."

Cartingham paused. "Either Conning or Strange will replace him. I think Strange is the man. He has already selected his crew and is impatient to get back on operations. Better come over and see me tomorrow. There are some things I want to discuss with you. . . . Fine, then . . . we'll have lunch together."

Dorton heard the receiver being replaced. For a few seconds he relaxed in his chair. Carter was off his hands and his mind was at rest. He had never any qualms, he assured himself, of Carter coming through. But the matter had troubled him and it was comforting to know that no longer would the Wing Commander's name appear opposite B—Baker on the Ops board.

Dorton was parking his car outside the A.O.C.'s office when the signal '—Maximum Effort—Tonight—' stuttered over 186's direct teleprinter link with Group.

An hour later the teleprinter rattled again, and Carter knew the target, route, bomb load and the Command's latest Met forecast.

So it was to be Frankfurt! He had a feeling it had been coming up on the list. It had been a long time since he had been there, back in early '42; as if he could ever forget that night.

Now it was March 1944. It was over Frankfurt he had won his D.S.O. when he had brought back the burning Wellington, with a dead wireless operator and a half-blinded navigator lying in the fuselage. The blast from the A.A. shell had torn a gaping hole in the nose. A little further back and he himself would have had more than just flesh wounds in his left thigh. He had been lucky that night; but then, he had been lucky all through his operations. Now his operating days were over—a Group Captaincy—a squadron of his own. And three weeks leave. He'd take the kids to Scarborough. Cold at this time of year, but the sea air would be bracing.

Just one more trip, one more raid. Looking down again for the last time over the Halifax's great radial engines at a target burning. The same old melancholic spasm he had experienced on ending his first tour, but even more pronounced on the last trip of his second, came over him. The anti-climax was always bitter.

Would have been easier to meet it had he known that the last take-off with a full load was the final trip. Coming like this, it had caught him unprepared. Had not Dorton gone to Group, he would have led them himself tonight.

Maximum Effort—eight hundred to nine hundred bombers were going out, and the diversions were elaborate.

'Gardening'* operations in the Baltic, feint attacks by fast Mosquito aircraft carrying 4,000-pound bombs were to be made on Berlin and Hanover. The Hun controller was going to be in a dilemma tonight, and the odds were he would decide it was another large scale attack on Berlin. But it was going to be Frankfurt instead. He smiled faintly. Someone had a sense of humour about the selection. It was the anniversary of Goethe's death and to mark it—taunting again at Goering's empty boast that no enemy aircraft would ever penetrate the skies of the Third Reich—they were to put on a firework display, a lethal one, in the German poet's birthplace.

There was a sharp rap on his door. Looking up, he saw it open and Flight Lieutenant Rodern, his navigator, poke his head round. "Can I have a word with you, Skipper?"

"Certainly."

Rodern closed the door behind him, and he saw he was far from easy.

"First of all, Skip, congratulations on you getting a Command. . . ."

* 'Gardening'—Mine-laying operations.

Carter frowned. "Is there nothing secret on this squadron? Look, Rod, who told you about this? It's not official yet, and I only knew it a little while ago!"

"Sorry, but . . ."

"Oh, that's all right! But these leakages can get damned annoying at times. May well be dangerous to our security. Far too much talk going on among the crews when they get jugged up a bit. One of these nights Jerry is going to learn of the target before we get airborne; then we'll know what losses really are!"

Rodern glanced sheepishly at the floor. "Nothing like that, Skip. I happened to be in the Adjutant's office when the signal came in about Wing Commander Strange coming here. Just put two and two together."

Carter grunted. "Well, they're taking a damned long time bringing that signal over. I haven't heard officially that it's Strange, but I fully expect it. What did you want to see me about?"

Rodern eyed him anxiously. "Frankly, we are wondering—that is, the crew and myself—what's going to happen to us? You won't be doing any more trips as a G.C., so you won't need us. . . ." Rodern accepted a cigarette from the packet Carter brought out. "We'd like to know if Strange will take us over. It might be, though, that he has his own crew and will bring them over, as you did with us. Bluntly, we don't want to be farmed out on any sprog!"

Carter thumbed his lighter, and applied it to the end of his navigator's cigarette. Their eyes met for a moment and held. He reprimanded himself mentally for forgetting about the crew. Naturally, they were apprehensive. They were four short of the quota required before they could be screened. Two, probably three, they would overlook, but four? The chance was, they would have to complete it as spares. And as spares, flying with whatever crew had a man on the sick-list, their hopes of finishing diminished. He couldn't have that.

"I more than appreciate your point and I'm glad you brought it up. I'll get on to the Group Captain right away. He's at Group, and should be able to get a ruling on this."

As the Flight Lieutenant went out, Carter stubbed out his cigarette and lit a fresh one. They deserved better treatment than being classed as a stand-in crew. They had stood by him, trusted him, and he in turn trusted them. The contract was clear enough. They had agreed to fly their second tour with him as skipper, and with no one else.

He lifted the telephone and asked for Group. Ten minutes later he replaced the receiver. Good thing he had telephoned straight away. Even Dorton was not at all sure of the position, since Strange was bringing his own crew. He would have the Group Captain's signal on the query after Dorton approached Cartingham.

He was with the Engineering Officer when the message was handed to him.

"Seems crew are one short of minimum required. Nothing to worry about. Will be personally responsible for them."

He read the message again before thrusting it into his pocket. Back in his office, he picked up the telephone and asked for A Flight. When the operator put him through, he told the Flight Commander: "Get B—Baker bombed up! I'm taking her myself tonight!"

He sat for a long time, thinking. In his mind he had already decided he was going. Knew he would, when the target was named. Ethically, with Dorton away, he was Commanding Officer of the squadron and as such should remain on the ground.

Dorton wouldn't like it, but he'd at least understand. Anyway, the Group Captain would be back by take-off time, certainly before they returned. Come to that, it would be squaring things with Dorton for the times he had slipped off on trips himself, leaving the station under his command.

Dorton drove through the main gate at Nissindon two hours after the squadron's twenty-three aircraft were airborne. Automatically he swung towards the briefing room, remembered they would be about approaching the enemy coast, and turned round the Administration Building to pull up outside the Officers' Mess.

The mess was almost empty. It was always the same, he reflected when the squadron were out. When they went they took its warmth and friendliness with them, leaving an uncomfortable tension behind.

He went into the bar. Farley and the Intelligence Officer were lounging against the oak counter, chatting with the S.M.O. The Adjutant smiled politely. "Good evening, sir. Had a nice trip?"

Dorton nodded to the white-coated aircraftsman behind the bar and motioned him to bring them another round.

Turning to Farley, he asked: "Have you seen the Wing Commander?"

Farley said lightly: "Why, he's operating tonight and extremely happy at getting twenty-three off. Said he'd have beaten your record had not T—Tommy's navigator been grounded."

The Senior Medical Officer interjected: "That leg of his has opened up again. Seems the wound hurts more than he has made out."

Dorton grunted and inwardly cursed Carter. He drank with them for half an hour before excusing himself. He pulled his car up outside his darkened office and slowly got out.

Big things were coming off. Cartingham had made that plain. He doubted if the Air Commodore knew exactly what his "big things" were precisely, but at Group they could pick up and assess fairly accurately what was in Command's mind.

Carter, he contemplated, would find it a lot more difficult going out on raids when he took over his own squadron. Cartingham had made the Air Force's new ruling clear when he made his caustic comment on his own flagrant breach of orders.

He had tried, and failed, to find even a glimmer of a smile on the Air Commodore's face when he summed up his displeasure at the times he had put himself on.

What was it he had said? "Not at all necessary. Administration requires more subtle methods."

That had hurt. He stretched his legs over the desk and eased himself into a more comfortable position. Then he reached for the telephone at his elbow and told control to ring him immediately the first returning aircraft called up.

Flying Officer Geoffrey Martin flicked out 'George'*, unfastened his oxygen mask and extracted a cigarette from the packet tucked into his Sutton harness. The altimeter needle wavered at the five thousand feet mark. He decided to slice it down to three thousand feet. He pushed the control column forward, his right hand slid towards the four red-tipped throttle handles, hesitated and, instead, reached for his lighter.

* GEORGE—Automatic pilot.

Switching on his R.T., he spun the flint and cursed. For the last ten minutes he had been steadily calling base. Kiwi twisted in the second pilot's seat. "Take it easy! We're still outside their range."

Martin stuck out his tongue and flicked up two fingers at his bomb-aimer.

Kiwi whistled jauntily. They could afford to be light-hearted. In a short, sharp two-second burst Sergeant Best, in the rear-turret, had sent an '88' down in flames. He had seen the JU silhouetted against a fighter flare on the way out from the target. For a fraction of a second it had hung naked two hundred yards above and astern of him. The German pilot, as Best related afterwards, could never have seen them. Had no inkling of the turret's four Brownings being elevated until the '88' was ringed boldly in the illuminated sight. Probably, Kiwi decided, he was scanning above for an easy kill when the stream of tracer from Best's turret smashed into his cockpit and sprayed into his fuel tanks.

It was over so fast that Hobson in the mid-upper turret barely managed to squeeze in a half second burst as the JU spiralled past his starboard quarter, deep red flames belching from its wings.

Yes, Martin was happy tonight, Kiwi mused. Then there was that bet he had with the Wingco, about getting home first, and everything pointed to F—Freddie winning the bet for Martin.

Martin called again. This time, base came through faintly and far away.

Dorton, a mug of steaming tea in his hand, heard F—Freddie's call-sign. Sometime later he heard the roar of her Hercules engines as Martin swept in a low banking turn into the circuit.

The first twinge of agonising worry niggled at his stomach after he heard Carson in S—Sugar call. She was late, the thirteenth air-craft to sweep into the funnel. He wondered idly if Carson would ever manage to get down first. Lord, he had tried often enough. Six Halifaxes were stepped up in the taxi-rank above, waiting to come in.

The clock in the big briefing room ticked on. All were down now, and on the Ops board, he saw, were four blank spaces. B—Baker, Q—Queenie, R—Robert and P—Peter. He flinched. Their losses were heavier tonight than for some time.

He glanced at his watch and checked it with the clock. Still time. It couldn't happen to Carter and his crack second tour crew. God, not tonight of all nights. Something must have gone wrong. Probably they had made an emergency landing on a 'drome along the South-East coast.

The telephone, at his elbow, would ring in a moment confirming it. He let his eyes roam the room. It was crowded and there was acute expectancy in the air. Crews who were down were hanging about, deliberately taking their time over mugs of tea, forgetting the hot flying suppers waiting for them in the messes.

The muted drone of a circling Halifax lit up the faces round him. The R.T. set crackled through the loudspeaker which was linked with the control tower.

A taut, nerve-twisting silence draped the room. His own voice, irritable and edgy, shattered it as he heard a strange voice and a stranger call-sign. "Some bloody clot can't identify his own beacon!"

The Halifax circled again over the red flashing squadron identification beacon. Gradually its engines faded, to be drowned in the low hum of conversation which rolled over the cream and green painted briefing room.

Slowly the crews filtered out to the crew wagons. He watched them go until only F—Freddie and S—Sugar remained. He saw Carson fidget as he leaned against one of the tea-stained tables. Beside him, Martin drew heavily on a cigarette, his head sideways to catch something his navigator was saying to S—Sugar's bomb-aimer.

The telephone shrilled and the group round him started. Their tired eyes, he noticed, suddenly became alert and anxious. He snatched the receiver from its cradle and his facial muscles relaxed slightly.

A half-minute later they saw them tighten and the lips merge into a thin white line.

Dorton's face aged. In a gravel voice they heard him say: "Q—Queenie . . . you are quite sure . . . ? I see. . . . Any one hurt . . . ?" the tone was detached, normal again. ". . . Good! Yes, ring me immediately."

Slowly his hand felt for the cradle. The receiver fumbled twice in his grip before he found the notch. Speaking in a far off voice, he said flatly: "Q—Queenie crash-landed! Navigator and mid-upper dead!"

He picked up his hat and walked slowly down the room. Their eyes followed him, until the door closed behind him. then Martin said: "Never seen the old man so upset."

Kiwi slid off the table on which he had been lounging. "They were pretty close old friends. I feel bloody grim myself . . . the Wingco was one of the best."

Callaghan dropped his cigarette and ground it out with his flying boot. "What's the chance of him lobbing down somewhere in the drink off the coast?"

Martin shook his head. "No Mayday signal has been picked up, so that's out." He pulled out his lighter, thumbing it idly. "No hope at all, and the old man knows it. Come on; we'd better not keep that wagon waiting much longer!" he said quietly.

The telegram arrived that afternoon as Dorton was sorting out the Wing Commander's personal effects. It was addressed, he saw, to Carter. On opening it, he found it was from the police station near where Carter's aunt lived. Something screwed inside him, bounced from his stomach and his breath came heavily. He rapidly scanned the words on the rough paper: "Regret to inform you Jayne Minster died St. Mary's Hospital here. Result of road accident last night. Children in care local authority. Please advise this station immediately."

For a long time Dorton stared at the telegram. Then he asked the switchboard for the exchange number in the flimsy. He afterwards called Group. This was out of his hands . . . out of Cartingham's. It was up to the Welfare People now.

Carter's aunt dead, her nephew missing and two confused, bewildered kids wondering why they couldn't have slept in their own beds last night. He looked again at the enlarged picture of a boy and girl. Gently he wrapped it in tissue paper and enclosed it in the brown paper parcel on his desk. Lifting the parcel, he placed it inside a large cardboard box. This he would send by registered post.

Some day they would want it. He leaned back in his chair and remembered there was now no address to send it to. He'd keep it in his safe until the Welfare People sorted it out. He speculated quietly on the chances of Carter having successfully baled out. Trouble was, he did not know what had happened to him. Might never know, for that matter. Baling out and spending the rest of the war as a P.O.W. was the best he could hope for.

He reached mechanically for his 'IN' tray and saw from the leave list that the crews of F—Freddie, S—Sugar and R—Robert were on six days' leave from noon.

He tore up the passes of R—Robert. Telegrams would be going out to their next-of-kin. Signing the leave vouchers of Martin's and Carson's crew, he recalled vaguely that it seemed only the other day since they had returned from leave.

19

DOUGLAS was sitting on his bed when the two gunners came in. They dumped their suitcases on the floor. Callaghan stuck a waver of gum in his mouth, chewing thoughtfully before he spoke.

"No chance, then, of you changing your mind and coming with us?" he asked.

Douglas shook his head. "I'd like to, but I've already fixed up to spend this leave in London."

Titch said: "Well, have a good leave. Reckon we won't see so much of you now? It'll be the Officers' Mess when you come back."

"Oh, we'll still have our jugs," Douglas said. "I'd have one with you, only I've to collect the grant for my uniform. Should have it within the hour. Care to hang on a bit?"

"Haven't the time," Callaghan replied; "we want to get the connection for Glasgow at York."

They had been gone fifteen minutes when Kiwi came in, immaculate in the uniform of a newly commissioned Pilot Officer. Douglas noted that, like every other operating officer on the squadron, he had removed the wire stiffener from his hat. The crown had been carefully pushed back and pressed. Now the hat was a cross between the cap of a bus conductor and that of a Luftwaffe officer's. On the station they always wore battle-dress and he had been unable to persuade the New Zealander to put on his new outfit and give him a private preview.

"You look a typical sprog!" he observed bluntly.

Kiwi grinned. "You'll be exactly the same in a couple of days."

On the way into town, the New Zealander said moodily: "I'm not at all sure that Terry's going to swallow this line about you having to go up to the Air Ministry. Bit ambitious, isn't it?"

"I don't like doing it, Kiwi, but I'll make it lie-proof. Have some important things to attend to in London."

"Yeah," Kiwi said drily; "I can imagine all one of them—that woman you met the last time!"

Terry took more convincing than he thought. Eventually she reluctantly resigned herself to his being away for the best part of the week. As the train neared King's Cross, the first doubts of his own emotional feelings towards her came to him, shattering his complacency. God, she would have ended it there and then, had she had the slightest suspicion his commission was already through.

He tried to analyse the reason for his emotions fluctuating between her and Loraine, but all attempts to tabulate them into a simple equation failed. Time was running out, too. Bigger raids were to come. He'd had a fair run, so there was no use in planning more than a few days ahead. Easy living had been his only formula, but a new and complicated factor had come up.

He shrugged suddenly and picked up the magazine he had bought before boarding the train at York.

He met Loraine as she finished work at the Admiralty and the solution was no nearer to the problem his feelings had aroused. He told her quietly that he had been commissioned.

"Tomorrow," he said, "I want you to come along with me and see how the new rags fit." He laughed unsteadily but stopped short when he caught the look of dismay which clouded her eyes.

"Oh, I'd love to, darling, but it's impossible! You must have forgotten! I go home Saturdays!"

Of course, there was her young son. For a moment he thought of going to Reading with her; but then realised that was out—her people were there.

"I'm sorry, Lori; I forgot."

The disappointment in his voice made it easier for her to agree to his suggestion that he should stay in her flat while she was away.

She glanced at him anxiously. "But be discreet," she added. "Don't answer the door or anything like that."

After she had changed, he took her up town, where they danced in a small, smoky club in Leicester Square until the early hours of the morning.

He was asleep when she brought him breakfast. Gently shaking him, she said: "I'll have to go, darling. But I'll be waiting for you at lunchtime."

He spent the morning getting fitted out. When she saw him on the pavement outside the Admiralty, her face paled.

"Lord, how that uniform suits you!" she said, but her mind was on the man behind the barbed wire and their remarkable resemblance. The smooth cut cloth, the gold and scarlet cap badge on the peaked hat, had accentuated, even magnified, his likeness to Johnny. She watched him wave carelessly as her train drew out and she was still bewildered and confused by her thoughts. By Monday, Douglas, after two days cooped up in the tiny flat, was fretful and irritable. Many times he had thought of leaving London and catching the first train to York, but each time he had rejected the impulse. Had she not been coming home tonight he doubted if his self-imposed discipline would have been strong enough to hold him alone in the flat another evening.

Loraine observed the rush-hour evening crowds streaming into the Trafalgar Square underground station, as her bus halted at the traffic lights. Solemnly, she speculated as to how many of the smartly dressed women scurrying down the stone steps to the tubes had problems similar to her own . . . wartime love affairs that in peacetime would merely have been taunting thoughts.

If only she could be sure of her feelings. There was no way of knowing for certain whether she was in fact in love with Douglas or only with the living image of her husband.

It had been three years ago. They could have grown apart. Barbed wire soured a man, twisted his soul, sometimes completely changing his outlook. Picking up the threads of their life, so short a life together, would be thwart with difficulties. She had no illusions about that. But then, there was young Johnny, their child. Surely that would help, and even be the deciding factor to their problems.

The bus lurched forward. How awful it would be to come face to face with Johnny and suddenly realise, beyond all reasonable doubt, that he was only a stranger to her. The prospect worried and alarmed her.

Douglas had a large Scotch in his hand when she came in.

Funny, but he always seemed to have a drink close to him. Her husband, she recalled, like beer. She trained her mind on the tall, lean figure coming towards her trying to forget Johnny.

"Lori . . ." the smile was slow and infectious, "I am glad to see you!"

He took her firmly in his arms and kissed her eagerly.

She broke away. "What a welcome to give a girl!" she said breathlessly. "Be a dear, Shern, and bring me a drink. Take it into the bedroom. If we're going out tonight, I'd better get changed."

He poured her out a liberal Scotch and brought it into the bedroom. She was sitting on a low stool brushing her hair with rapid straight movements. Again he marvelled at her loveliness.

He watched her take the drink and sip it slowly.

"Nice week-end?" he asked.

"Lovely, Shern; but I'm afraid it would have been too domesticated for you."

A flicker of a smile played at the corners of his mouth. "How do you know? You've never given me the chance to prove how domesticated I could be."

She laughed softly and said: "Take out my black cocktail dress and give it a brush."

She saw him in the mirror stride to the wardrobe, take out the dress and toss it on the soft rose-coloured bedspread. Then she remembered the picture.

"Oh! I've a surprise for you, darling!" she cried. "Open my case; it's not locked. On the top there's a picture of your double —my husband. At least, if you'd a moustache, you could be twins!"

Douglas swallowed the contents of his glass, frowning. Why had she to bring up this blasted husband and spoil everything?

He doubted, as he always had, whether there was really any strong resemblance between them. Merely balm to her conscience. He'd experienced it before with married women.

Viewing him in the big mirror, Loraine saw him open the case. The picture, she knew, was lying face downwards. He picked it up, twisted it round, and then she saw his face change to a ghastly greyish hue.

He moved directly under the ceiling light. She noticed his hands were trembling as they held the picture in his outstretched arms.

Half turning on the stool, she said: "Darling, you look as if you'd seen a ghost! Didn't I say you could be his double?"

His voice wavered, coming across to her gravel-toned. "Is there a long white scar along his upper lip?"

The warm glow of the Scotch switched to vapour ice in her stomach. How could he have known that? She did not know why, but sudden panic swept over her. The scar was why he had grown the moustache! God, they must know each other—have met on some R.A.F. station!

"You've met somewhere?" The words she phrased were barely audible to her ears.

Douglas's eyes were transfixed on the picture. "Had he a brown-shaped birth-mark on his right shoulder?" he demanded in a piercing voice.

She rose from the stool. A fleeting glance in the mirror showed her own face as pale and drawn.

"Yes," she said shakily; "but for heaven's sake, tell me what all this is about. . . . How could you know?"

His words came to her as an echo threading through a vast empty auditorium. Toneless, yet deafening, they flooded and pounded in her ears: "This is my brother . . . my twin brother!"

Her legs trembled violently and she sank heavily to the bed. He had moved over to the dressing table and laid the picture across the satin runner, face downwards.

Swinging round, he looked past her. "There was just the two of us. We were separated when we were kids. Last I heard he went into the Merchant Navy as a cadet. . . . Never heard from him since."

He strode out of the bedroom. Faintly she heard the clink of glasses and liquid. He came back with two large glasses half full of whisky.

Grasping her shoulders, he shook her roughly. His eyes stared at her, dull, lifeless and cold. Draining his own glass he thrust the second tumbler into her hand. The pressure of his fingers over hers made her wince.

"Lori, snap out of it!" The voice was forceful, calm again.

The raw whisky hit her stomach and a feeling of nausea welled in her throat. She stumbled past him and groped for the door handle.

He heard her retching in the bathroom. Then a tap splashed distinctly.

When she came out of the bathroom, a dressing-gown was wrapped tightly about her.

"Give me another drink, but put some water in it this time," she said in a miserably flat voice. She huddled before the fire, her mouth twitching in uncontrollable tremors.

He lit a cigarette and dragged deeply on it. Looking down at her, he said: "He had no gol' damned right to change his name like that! It's not us to blame, can't you see that? He's brought all this on himself!"

She looked up sharply and her voice was harsh. "How can you talk like that?—and you his brother!"

"Don't act like a child, Lori. I've told you we were separated when we were kids. He went to a foster-family and must have taken their name," he said passionately.

Despairingly he ran a hand through his hair. "Why? God knows! The last letter I had from him was in '38, care of a shipping company. So full of damned nonsense about the sea and the great life he was having. It made me sick, and I never replied," he said viciously.

He walked over to the fireplace and his voice was smeared with anger. "Come to think of it, he enclosed a photograph and signed it 'John Douglas' something or other, but he was such a rotten hand with a pen that I could never make out what the last word was. Thought it was a rank category or something like that!"

She sipped her drink mechanically and, without glancing at him, said: "Yes, that would be about right. He told me he left the Mercantile Marine at the end of 1938 and joined the R.A.F. I met him in January 1940 . . ." her voice trembled, broke . . . "We were married three months later."

Her eyes went back to the flickering flames in the grate. "He often told me he had a twin, but he never mentioned the name of Douglas, and I naturally thought the name would be the same as his. He always talked of Mrs. Davis being his mother. She had put up the debenture for his apprenticeship. He said she knew she was dying, and it was her way to make things easier for him.

Douglas heard her sob softly and saw her body shake, but he could feel no pity for her, only cold fury that this affair should have to end this way. Now, the initial shock over, he was cool and discerning.

It was twelve years since he had parted from his brother. Time had long since sapped away what love they had had for one another. But even so, he would not knowingly have seduced his brother's wife.

Still, there was nothing he could do about it now. This was just another fickle twist of fate, which had tricked him, frustrated him, all through his life. He watched the girl crying and the fury arose once more.

"Listen, Lori, don't take it like that! There was nothing we could do. This thing had to happen. Don't do anything silly, in a fit of remorse, and write to him. Only the two of us need ever know."

He walked over, sat on the arm of her chair and slipped his arm round her shoulders. "Get dressed, Lori. We'll go out and you'll feel better. . . ."

She flung her head up, her hand brushing his arm away. "I think you'd better go," she said coldly. "I've had a bitter lesson, but it won't ever happen again—never!"

With an effort she eased herself from the chair, her eyes flashing angrily. "No, he'll never know. But I know now what a wonderful person he is. . . ." She laughed hysterically. "I was madly in love with him; still am. That's how it was so easy for you. . . . I fell for a cheap carbon copy of Johnny!"

Abruptly she stopped sobbing, and he flinched at the hate in her voice. "Get out! No, don't touch me! You make me feel unclean!" she hissed.

In the hall, she caught his arm, and pulled him round. He was amazed at the strength in her slight form. "Promise me he'll never know. Not for myself; it's for his son's sake I'm asking."

He mistook the eagerness in her tone for a spasm of weakness on her part. "I'm never likely to meet him. I promise. But why end it like this, Lori? Can't we still be friends?"

Her hands clenched and her knuckles showed white. "Friends? With you? You can't understand!" she spat. "We're through! It would never have began. But Johnny never mentioned your

last name. I took it for granted it was the same as his, Davis."
She added, in a softer tone: "He used to call you Ted, isn't that
right?"

He nodded. "Yes. It's my first name; my middle one's Shern.
Why?"

She tossed her head and he thought how childlike was the movement. "Perhaps it won't mean anything to you, but he talked
a great deal about the grand fellow his brother Ted was. . . ."
Again that bitter laugh. ". . . Almost amounted to hero-worship.
You see, that's another reason why he must never learn what we
did."

He turned the door handle and before he went, he said quietly:
"Lori, it took two of us to forget Johnny. You were his wife.
I knew nothing. . . ."

"Get out!" she screamed. "How low can you be?"

His hand, he observed with detachment, was still trembling after
he had downed the third large whisky in the little pub near King's.
Cross. He would leave with the first train in the morning, he
decided. No use spending what was left of his leave in London.
He looked at his wrist, and for the first time realised that his watch
was missing.

20

DOUGLAS was drunk. Drunker, he judged, than he had ever been before. He stabbed the door-bell of the flat, swaying, and his shoulder brushed against the doorway.

Terry opened the door, and in the failing light he caught a blur of the surprised shocked expression which crossed her face.

"I'm all in . . . just want to sleep . . . had a helluva journey . . . !"

His head spun sickeningly as it sank into the pillow, and then utter oblivion enveloped his restless mind.

Two hours after Terry had put Douglas to bed, Kiwi and Sue came in. The New Zealander noticed Douglas's suitcase.

"So he came, after all?" he commented.

Terry looked at him curiously. "You said that as if you hadn't expected him to come back!"

Kiwi became flustered, and cursed Douglas for his unpredictable ways. He had told him clearly that he would not be back for at least five days.

"Not at all, Terry," he mumbled. "He said he'd be straight back and . . ."

Sue, hearing him falter, asked quickly: "Where is he?"

Terry nodded towards the bedroom. "He's dead out! Seems he's been on a one-man binge! Really looks ghastly. Do you think I should call a doctor?"

"Don't do that; he'd go bats," Kiwi answered firmly. He picked up Douglas's tunic from a chair. "Gee, what a mess! Was he rolled or something?"

Sue shrugged indifferently. "Looks as if he slept in it!" she said contemptuously.

Kiwi looked at Terry. "Well, it proves you were wrong in your suspicions. There were no strings attached to that trip."

"I never said there were."

"Oh yes," Kiwi replied softly; "and it showed in your face

too." He laughed and patted her shoulder. "It'll be all right now."

It was after lunch next day before Douglas awoke. Kiwi brought him a cup of black coffee and watched his hand shake as he drank it.

He noticed it again as his friend was shaving. "You look bloody awful, Shern!" he said.

Douglas dried his face, and applied a septic stick to a deep cut on his chin.

"I can see that," he said tersely. "Get me a drink. That'll help."

"Wait until you've had something to eat. The girls left some pies in the oven."

Douglas put down the towel. "I don't feel like eating. Just a drink. Please, I need it! You don't know how bad!"

Kiwi slipped into the living-room, and brought out one of the bottles of Scotch he had taken from the mess. He tipped it up to the light, and saw it was half full.

He poured out a treble and splashed it with water. Douglas was behaving like that flask-carrying skipper who had died in the wreck of P—Peter, he thought.

Handing him the drink, he said: "Look, Shern, that's all you get. Tell me what's wrong. You look like a whipped cur!" When no answer came, he prompted. "Get it off your mind."

"No, Kiwi! I couldn't! You see, I reached a new low this time!" Douglas wandered into the living-room and sank down in the armchair. He saw that his uniform had been neatly sponged and pressed. It was draped over the back of a chair.

Pointing to it, he asked: "Who cleaned it up?"

"Terry did, after you had gone to bed," Kiwi said quietly.

A fit of depression came over him. He'd lied and cheated to her too. He had never bothered to think about himself much until he had opened that Pandora's box, lying on the deep rose-coloured eiderdown on Loraine's bed—the quilt which somehow was always on the floor when they awoke in the morning.

He did not think he had ever loved Loraine. The attraction was mostly physical, but what made it worse, he still wanted her after he knew that she was Johnny's wife.

What was that about Lack of Moral Fibre? Christ, that was funny. The Air Force thought he had so much of it, they had commissioned him! He burst out laughing, and stopped abruptly as Kiwi eyed him curiously

"You all right, Shern?"

Douglas smiled bleakly "Let's drink to the best bloody bomb-aimers in 186!"

"Get a hold of yourself, Shern, for God's sake," Kiwi rasped.

Douglas rose unsteadily and bleakly eyed the clock on the mantelpiece.

"I can take a taxi back to the mess and buy my own, if that's how you want it!"

"Be sensible, Shern! Groupie would have you thrown out in an hour. He's in no mood for the prima donna stuff. Maybe you don't know, but seventy-three went down the other night on a Berlin raid—four of them from the squadron . . . !"

"I know, I know; I can read! We'll get it some night, so why harp on it?" Douglas retorted irritably.

The New Zealander sighed deeply, heaved himself from his chair, and crossed to the window. Behind the heavy curtain nearest the door, he bent down and came back with the bottle.

An hour later, he put Douglas to bed. He was still sleeping when Sue and Terry arrived home.

Terry slipped into the bedroom and her eyes flashed with anger when she came out. "He's been at it again! He smells like a brewery!" she said scornfully.

"Take it easy," Kiwi said wearily. "He was going to the mess unless I gave him some."

"Did you have to give him the bottle?" she demanded angrily.

Sue moved towards the fire. A perplexed look crossed her face.

"What's wrong with him?" she asked.

Kiwi shook his head. "I don't know. It's something pretty bad. But he won't talk about it."

The next morning Terry drew aside the New Zealander before she left for work.

"Does Lori and Johnny mean anything to you?"

When he shook his head, she went on: "He was rambling in his sleep. Kept muttering about Lori and how sorry he was for

Johnny. Then I heard snatches of L.M.F., the name Davis, and something about a new low. Does it make sense to you?"

"No," Kiwi said, "it doesn't."

"L.M.F.," she urged, and he noticed she hesitated slightly; "that's what they call flyers' who throw it up, isn't it?"

Kiwi nodded gloomily.

Sue came out of the bathroom. He kissed her lightly and later waved to her as she hurried down the street, with Terry, to catch their bus.

Douglas joined them at tea, and for the first time since he'd come back the dullness had slipped from his eyes. His manner was so repentant that Terry decided not to mention the ramblings of the night before.

"I don't think he's noticed it!" Sue said suddenly to Terry.

Terry laughed and said: "No; he's not very observant."

Taking Sue's hand she turned it slowly. Douglas caught the sparkle of the tiny blue points of light glinting from the engagement ring.

He reached over, lifted her hand, and felt Terry's press on his as she released her grip. For a moment he looked at the blue sapphire, set in the splinters of diamonds, and looking across at Kiwi, said: "Well, why didn't you tell me?"

Kiwi flushed. "Got it today, Shern, when you were sleeping. Wanted you to come with me, but I guess you were . . ."

"I'm sorry, Kiwi, deeply sorry! I've messed up a lot of things," Douglas interrupted. He broke off suddenly, before going on brightly: "Look, you'll have a little engagement dinner on me? I'll get a taxi and we can go out to that little place at Tinnet. We have to be back tomorrow, so we might as well make a night of it!"

Terry caught his arm. "Not too much of a night."

Douglas bowed mockingly. "I'll be on my very best behaviour."

They had finished their meal and were sitting in the low-roofed bar of the country hotel when the sound came to them. First it was low and muffled. Swiftly it rode on the air currents and rose to a thundering crescendo of ear-shattering pulses.

The cane table they were seated round quivered. The thin wine glasses resting on it vibrated in a quick jerky dance. At the bar a few heads instinctively looked up at the oak beams, then down at the stained varnished floor.

Terry searched Douglas's face as the bombers roared over. His face was calm, but the cigarette in his hand wavered. That tremor could be the back-wash of that London journey; on the other hand . . . she dismissed the thought.

Kiwi blinked. "Sure missed something this week, Shern. Practically every other night they've been going out and all Maximum Effort do's by the sound!"

Sue stiffened and Douglas saw her hand tighten on the New Zealander's arm. He smiled nervously at her. "They're keeping the cushy ones for us," he said.

"We could do with a few, Shern," Kiwi replied.

Later that night, as he prepared for bed, Terry slipped her arms round Douglas's neck and, looking straight into his eyes, said: "Shern, who are Lori and Johnny?"

His fingers tightened on her waist and quickly went limp.

"*Who?*" he demanded.

"You were rambling in your sleep last night. You kept calling for them, darling."

He kissed her lightly. "I must have been raving. I don't know any people with such names. There's lots of Johnnys on the station, but no one called Lori." Before she could press him further, he tilted up her chin. "Terry, how much does a good ring cost? I mean, a bigger one than Sue's. You see, I know now just how much I love you."

She clung to him tightly. "Oh, Shern, you'll never know how much I wanted you to say that! All this last while I've been tortured with doubts. It was silly, but I love you so much."

Her long silky hair brushed lightly across his face and his senses reeled before a passion that scorched his whole body.

21

THE target was Nuremburg—deep and seemingly safe—in the South-East tail of Germany. Eight hundred Lancasters and Halifaxes of Bomber Command were to attack and saturate the city, rip out its industrial heart. There would be no large scale diversions because of bad weather over the North Sea.

Dorton briefed them and with the aid of a weather chart explained why the diversions they had come to expect could not be laid on. Tapping his thigh with his light cane he told them: "However, a force of fifty Halifaxes will make a 'gardening' operation in the Heligoland Bight. That we hope will help to fox them. Met reports are fairly encouraging. They anticipate cloud cover to Nuremburg, with probably a fair amount of it on the way back. But the gunners had better keep a sharp look-out. There will be a half moon. . . ."

He broke off and smiled sympathetically as he heard them groan. Personally, he didn't like the look of the Flight Plan tonight. A small force laying mines in the Bight. The main force coming in over Belgium. Too big a difference in the blips, the enemy radar screens would pick up. Too startling a gap in the span between the two forces. If the enemy controller decided to ignore the mine-laying force and sent his Ruhr night fighter force airborne, the bomber stream coming from the Belgium coast could well run into them.

Glad of the cloud cover forecast in the Met reports he continued with the briefing. Later he drove down to the Flights and watched them take-off. Twenty-three Halifaxes and their take-offs were, on the whole, smooth. His fears were probably groundless, nothing really to account for them. It was a big raid. Big as any they had mounted on Berlin, he reflected. Something in the region of 2,400 tons of H.E. and incendiaries would hurtle down on Nuremburg.

In the mess he had a large gin and again he wondered how the enemy controller would react   At Command, men with more detailed data before them, pondered on the same question.

And the Hun controller, carefully filtering through his latest radar reports, came to the same conclusion as Dorton.   Before him was information as studiously compiled as that which had earlier, much earlier been scrutinised by the architects of the raid.   But it was more recent, and being more recent it was more accurate. Disregarding the reports of a force, since identified as small, as having no material menace to Keil or Berlin, he classified the Heligoland radar sightings as of little consequence.   A feint too crude to hoodwink him into believing the main attack would be in the East.

Deciding thus, he concentrated his night fighter force over Bonn and Frankfurt.   Everything pointed to a target in the South-East. Even so, he held back until the first bomber wave crossed the coast and swung inwards on a course of 140 magnetic.   All the latest Met reports backed his reasoning.   Of course 'latest' that was the key.   They banked, obviously, on cloud cover.

He hesitated no longer.   He would meet the British bombers coming in.   The sky was clear from the coast inwards and his fighter pilots could rely on visual identification from the light of a half moon.   He gave his orders and watched critically as his plotters traced the course of the enemy bomber force.   He saw it wheel by Aachen and move relentlessly South-East.   Tonight it would be different, he mused.

Douglas saw the cloud disperse when they were still some way from the enemy coast and he cursed the failings of the weather men.   As they skirted clear of Aachen he searched the sky.   It was unusually bright, brighter than he had seen it for a long time. But, of course, there was half-moonlight.

Christ, things didn't look so good.   Almost naked in that pale shimmering light.   Titch, in the mid-upper turret, first saw the tracer.   Over the intercom his voice sounded fretful and hurt . . . "Combat.   Port Quarter!"

"Okay, I see it," Carson retorted.

Masters picked up his dividers, spanned the track to go.   They had 240 miles yet and a fighter in the main stream already.

It would not help his navigating if they started weaving so early.

Douglas slipped from the H2S set, and scrambled into the nose. Ahead he saw a ball of fire splash against the night sky. Bomber disintegrating. Tracer rippled across the starboard beam quarter. Nothing, as far as he could see, was coming up from the ground. What did it matter, he thought. The fighters were more deadly. He switched on his intercom.

"Skipper. Bomb-aimer here. Staying put in the nose."

He slapped a drum of ammunition on the free Vicker's gun, peeping through the nose, and cocked the firing button to Fire. Scare gun though it was, the action gave him more confidence.

"Good idea, Shern," Carson replied crisply.

To Sergeant Green, who had taken over from Pastone, as engineer, Carson said: "Don't keep reporting combats. But watch and keep an eye on the gauges." Stocky, red-haired and with small excited eyes, Carson reflected, that he did not have much confidence in the new man. For one thing Green was too talkative, for another he invariably talked at the wrong times.

They flew on and Carson marvelled at the combats he saw. Bombers were blowing up, right, left and centre. He considered jettisoning the load the next time the engineer shouted 'Fighter', but promptly dismissed the urge. The attack must come. They couldn't always be as lucky as they had been. God, what a night and so far to go . . . then they had to come back.

The flak coming up from the target seemed a secondary worry to the gauntlet they had run with the JUs and the FWs. Carson wondered, as he made the corrections on the bombing run, how many combats Douglas had seen. "Left . . . Steady now . . . Steady. Bombs Gone. Jettison bars across . . . Close bomb doors and let's get the Hell out of here!"

Never before had he heard the bomb-aimer slur so fast through his drill. He saw two more bombers burst into flames as he banked the Halifax on course for the coast. The half moon was bewildering bright. He could make out the shapes of two Lancasters with a Halifax above and slightly ahead of him.

A second later tracer spewed in four fantastically moving lines from the Halifax ahead of them. Violently he flung over the control column and pushed it forward. To hell with the Flight

Plan, he was going to loose height. The fighters were following them out. Anywhere, he decided, in that vast turbulent sky, was safer than in the mid-stream of the bomber force. Every fighter in the area must be among them. From the direction of the tracer and cannon fire Carson was certain the night fighters were flying to and fro across the force. And with each flight a bomber exploded or plunged earthwards, crippled and on fire.

Callaghan saw the FW 190 streaking down on them as he peered over the barrels of his four Brownings. His red-rimmed eyes, glazed with horror at the rings of fire, twinkling wickedly from the leading edges of the fighter's wings.

The tracer was whipping past at an acute angle when he screamed to Carson to corkscrew starboard. For a split-second he wondered if he had given the correct evasive action. It was on his port but his back was to Carson. Yes, it was right enough. Elevating the Brownings, Callaghan stabbed the firing button. The night fighter must have corrected his sighting angle, with a touch of rudder, for its second burst thundered along the fuselage behind him.

At that precise second his own burst sprayed the FW's tail. Most of it, he saw, went under. Before he could correct his fire angle the night fighter flashed over. There was no fire from the mid-upper turret, he realised. Either Titch was hit or he was looking somewhere else and could not get his turret round in time.

Carson rolled S—Sugar from the corkscrew. His gyro-compass was spinning crazily and his artificial horizon had toppled with the dive. They heard him breathing heavily as he gulped in the oxygen.

"See anything, gunners?" Carson's tone was crisp, apprehensive.

"Rear-gunner to Skipper. Think we've lost him."

Carson caughed into his mask and the sound rasped in their earphones.

"First, who fired?" he demanded.

"Me, skipper."

"Who in the hell's me? Keep to the drill."

"Callaghan, Skipper. Saw him come in out of the corner of my eye. Was searching my starboard quarter and had just swung round the turret."

"Did you get him?"

"Doubt it. Maybe his tail."

"All right, Jock. Keep looking while I call the others," Carson said.

"Mid-upper and the engineer's all right. I've just had them on so let's hear from you, navigator."

"I'm all right and so is Shern," Masters replied.

Carson flicked his eyes from the altimeter across to the A.S.I. and then glanced through his clear vision panel. They were hit, he could tell that from the feel of the controls and hit bad. The rudder, the starboard rudder, was not responding.

"Rear-gunner . . . Skipper here. . . . See anything wrong with the starboard rudder?"

Callaghan's voice crackled in his ears. "Hard to tell, can't get a good look."

God, he had forgotten to call the Wireless Operator. Probably he was listening in to his set and had not heard him call for the crew to report.

"Wireless Operator. You Okay?" He called again, but only their deep breathing came over the intercom.

"Shern," he said, "slip through and see what's up with Ted. Probably his plug has come loose," Carson added as an after-thought.

Douglas rose from beside Masters, and edged his way into the Wireless compartment. Morphy was slumped over his table. His forehead bounced gently against the radio set, with the movement of the aircraft. The back of his head was blown off.

Douglas's eyes alighted on the set. Pieces of blood soaked scalp, with tiny bits of bone sticking to them were splattered across the dials. A vivid red scarf was clotted round his neck and congealing fast. A riverlet of crimson trickled down from the lobe of the wireless operator's right ear.

He leaned forward and lifted Morphy's wrist. Hurriedly he dropped the limp, cold hand and wondered why he ever expected to feel a pulse beat. Masters came into the compartment. Douglas looked up and saw his face was a sickly white. Switching on his intercom he called Carson.

The reply shocked and awed came to him. "Are you sure? Have you . . ."

"Quite sure," Douglas said, anticipating Carson's question. He rolled the Wireless Operator back into his seat. The eyes were bright and staring. He thought they had the look of a small boy's when opening a Christmas parcel.

"Weave, Skipper. For Christ sake, weave. Two combats above and an 88s' flashed below." Callaghan's Glasgow accent was sharp, imperative in its eagerness. Carson flung the bomber on to its port wing-tip. God, would this night never end. He called Masters.

"How far to the coast?"

"Forty minutes," Masters said. Forty minutes when forty seconds could be a long lifetime. In the nose Douglas carried out his own inspection. There was a foot-wide slash where the transparent covering joined the fuselage and six neat perforations in the plastic. As he scrambled back into the navigation hatch the Halifax lurched and he nearly fell across Masters.

There was a dull thud and the curtain screening the compartment from the glass house was ripped from its hanging. Douglas paled as he saw the dead wireless operator's foot sticking through. The sudden lurch had toppled him from his seat. With the engineer's help he carried Morphy into the fuselage and laid him face upwards on the long seat. He looked better that way, Douglas decided. It hid the hole in his head.

They crossed the enemy coast low, and ten degrees starboard of the Flight Plan. They were too tired, too indifferent to heed the light flak coming up on their port. The fury they had faced had long since drained away the effects of the Pep pills. Their systems reacted against the chemical charges. They trembled and shuddered.

Now they faced a landing with a right rudder which was practically useless. Even so, Carson displaying a skill which astounded himself brought the Halifax down to a heavy but safe landing.

Next day Dorton drove down to the S bay, inspected the bomber, and put Carson in for an immediate award of the D.F.C. He found only two bullet holes in the tiny wireless hatch and reflected gravely that a nod of the operator's head might have meant the difference between him living and dying.

At lunchtime the mess was unusually quiet as the one o'clock news came over the radio. The losses had come through a few hours earlier to the Intelligence Room and the number was 104, but that included the known 'ditchings' in the North Sea. The aircraft which had crashed in the sea after sending out 'Mayday' signals would not be included in the number. The Command knew where they were and knowing reasoned they were not 'missing'.

". . . Ninety-four of our Bombers are missing. . . ." A gasp went round the Sergeants' Mess drowning the rest of the announcement. It was all true and not a nightmare, stark in its reality of a night that never was.

Some one in a detached, unemotional voice had broadcast it to the world.

Morphy's death shocked the crew of S—sugar, yet at the same time they marvelled at their own good luck in getting the crippled bomber home. And as the days slipped by, the crazy hunch their mid-upper gunner had had, that fighters could be vectored on to H2S aircraft, was proved to be fact. The order came through that the radar sets must not be switched on until they approached the enemy coast.

"We now have reason to believe," the senior intelligence officer told them, reading from a signal flashed from Group, "that the enemy are able to pick up transmissions from the H2S sets when they are switched on shortly after you are airborne."

He went on to say: "Further, we think that the JU 88's have been fitted with a special device which enables them to 'home' on to radar aircraft. The attacks are invariably made from underneath."

Douglas was pondering over the Intelligence Officer's warnings when the mess orderly handed him a registered letter. Signing for it, he noticed that the writing on the envelope was small and neat, and he knew it had come from his sister-in-law. By the feel, he guessed it contained his watch.

Ripping the envelope open, he took out a single sheet of delicately perfumed notepaper. It carried no superscription other than 'London, Thursday'.

There was no greeting and the words he read brought a flush to his face.

"Enclosed is your watch, which I came across while cleaning the flat. What we did was wicked but your part was vile, for even after knowing I was your brother's wife you wanted to go on. I am not excusing my own wickedness, but when I learned Johnny was your brother I was appalled at what we did. Yet, out of this evil has come a flicker of good. I know now how much I love him."

A mess orderly came over and told him he was wanted on the telephone. Hurriedly, he thrust the letter into his pocket and strapped on his watch. On the phone was the mid-upper, urging him to come to the Sergeants' Mess dance which had been arranged for the following night.

"This weather doesn't look like clearing for a couple of days, so we should be all right," Titch informed him.

He said he would come, and the gunner asked quietly: "Let's have a quid, Shern. I'll pay you back on Friday."

"I knew there was a catch!" he said jokingly.

Terry kicked off her shoes then tried to rise from the armchair into which she had sunk. The effort, after the drink she had, was too much and she fell unsteadily back.

"Whee! It was some party! Those sergeants certainly know how to celebrate!" she said.

Douglas closed his eyes, then opened them quickly, as the gas-fire in her bedroom spinned dizzily before his eyes.

"Lord, I feel tight," he said.

"Give me a cigarette, darling," she purred.

He fumbled in his pocket and pulled out a battered packet with one cigarette in it.

"Dammit! I've only got one."

"You shouldn't chain-smoke. But you have it. I'm going to bed," she said.

"I need one for the morning," he muttered. Systematically he went through his pockets, turning them out as he searched for a loose cigarette end which would see him through.

Terry switched off the bed-light and called softly: "Put the fire out."

He tossed his tunic over a chair, and heard it fall to the ground. He groped his way to the fire and knocked up the switch.

* * * * * *

His head was aching when Terry shook him.

"Come along, darling," she said; "you've only fifteen minutes if you're to get the bus. Kiwi's waiting on you."

"To the devil with it!" He turned over and buried his face in the pillow.

Someone pulled him roughly round by the shoulder, and he saw it was the New Zealander.

"Cobber," he said, "you've only yourself to blame if you feel as you look. Damned stupid trying to out-drink the S.W.O. That fellow's got a paunch that will hold gallons! Now come on, get dressed quickly."

Slowly Douglas got up, hauled on his uniform and, unwashed and unshaven, stumbled out of the flat.

Kiwi was at the bus stop when he caught up with him. "God, you look bloody, Shern! Just as well you don't celebrate engagements every night."

"Celebrate what?"

The New Zealander shook his head. "Don't tell me you can't remember? You announced to the whole mess that you and Terry were 'engaged as from now'. They're your own words I'm quoting. It was around midnight and, boy! were you high."

"Yes," Douglas said evenly; "I recall something like that, but I hadn't meant to make it that public. Did I make Terry seem a fool?"

Kiwi laughed. "No, it went over quite well. By that time, nearly everyone was well pickled."

22

HE sensed by her tone over the telephone that something was wrong. When he asked what it was, she said icily: "You dropped a letter. I found it crumpled round a cigarette packet."

Mechanically his hand swept to his tunic pocket, crushing the rough cloth of the battle-dress. No, it had been in his walking-out dress. He had dropped the letter from Loraine when searching for the cigarettes. No doubt about it!

"How could you be so rotten? I've been sick all morning at the thought of it!"

She sobbed softly into the mouthpiece and her voice trembled as she said: "No wonder you went to pieces when you came back! Your own brother's wife! God, how . . ."

"Listen, Terry," he interrupted earnestly; "don't say any more. I know how it must look, but I can explain everything. You've only got a fragment of what happened and it's distorted the entire picture. It's not nearly as bad as you think. . . ."

"For God's sake, stop lying!" she screamed. "Not even an accomplished liar like you can get out of this. It's all true, isn't it?"

"No, Terry! No, I swear it!"

"Don't make it worse," she interjected heatedly.

He kicked the door of the telephone kiosk open. The sweat was cold on his forehead and the cigarette between his fingers made his eyes smart.

She was slipping from him, he knew—and this time the diabolical thing was that he was really in love, even crazy about her.

"Darling, please listen," he cried frantically. "It was before I met you!"

"Oh, you liar! You hadn't got the watch when you came back. Remember you told me it was being repaired? I should have listened to Sue. She said at the beginning you were no good!" The voice was heavy with anguish.

He knew it was all over even before he heard the metallic click of the replaced receiver.

In a daze, he walked from the kiosk and wandered into the mess. Kiwi saw he was shaking as he recounted what Terry had said. But the initial shock had gone and the version he gave the New Zealander was carefully phrased.

"You can fix it, Kiwi. You and Sue. You know the truth and you must help!"

Kiwi eyed him coldly. "Are you on the level, Shern? Honestly in love with her?"

"I swear it, Kiwi!" The tone was frantic in its eagerness.

"Somehow I believe you," Kiwi said after a moment. "I'll see what I can do; but I don't hold out much hope."

It was Masters and Carson who helped Douglas from the mess that night. They carried him to his quarters and put him to bed.

Carson switched out the light, closed Douglas's room door and said to Masters: "Something's on his mind. I wish I knew what it was! Never seen him that bad!" "Could it be a woman?" he added as an after thought.

Masters grunted. "That's one thing it couldn't be. That bastard's too much in love with himself to spare any love for someone else."

Douglas was downing his third cup of black coffee in the mess the following morning when Kiwi eased himself on to the chair beside him.

"It's no good, Shern. I saw them both last night. Terry is through with you, and she means it this time. It's no good trying to make out otherwise. Incidentally, her version varies quite a bit from the one you told me, and frankly, hers rings of truth!"

Douglas ignored the thrust. "How did she look? I mean, was she hysterical or anything like that?"

Kiwi shook his head. "No, Shern. If she'd blown her top I wouldn't have been surprised. Instead—you won't like me putting it like this—she acted as if she had some sort of premonition things would turn out as they did. Very calm, and something very decisive about her."

Douglas chewed his inner lip. "Did she pack up my things?"

"No."

"Who did, then?"

"I did."

Douglas rose from the table. "I'm going to see her tonight," he announced firmly.

Kiwi pushed back his chair. "I wouldn't do that, Shern." There was a sharp crack in his voice.

"Hell, I'm not going to allow her to believe what some neurotic wench wrote!"

"You're fogetting, Shern, that the wench, as you call her, did *not* write to her."

"If I could get ten minutes with her, Kiwi, I could explain it all, smooth everything over."

The New Zealander said impatiently: "NO! You've shot the lot and lost. Better face it."

"Why are you so damned sure?"

"All right; I was going to spare you the details. But you've asked for it. She wouldn't pack your things; said touching them made her feel unclean. If you'd heard the scorn in her voice you'd have no doubt about how she felt."

"I suppose Sue helped her to make up her mind. She never liked me!" said Douglas angrily.

"Don't bring Sue into this!" Kiwi retorted heatedly. "Any doubt Terry might have had vanished when she remembered that you told her your watch was being repaired when you came back from London on that last leave.

"There's also the envelope and the postmark. Seems, too, you talk a bit in your sleep?"

Douglas said limply: "What do you think I should do?"

"It doesn't matter what I think!"

"So you believe it, too?"

Kiwi picked up his gloves, thrust them into his pocket and said roughly: "What do you think?"

Douglas watched him walk away, and a great feeling of loneliness came over him.

The next evening Wing Commander Strange, who had now replaced the missing Carter, took Carson aside and bluntly informed him he did not consider his bomb-aimer any asset to the Officers' Mess.

He told Carson: "I'm giving you the chance to pull him together.

If you can't manage it, I will personally deal with him. I will not tolerate him getting drunk again in the mess."

Strange turned on his heel, hesitated and swung round. "You had an engineer who went L.M.F., hadn't you?"

"Yes, sir; but I'm sure it's not the case with Douglas."

Strange grunted and moved away.

Carson sought out Masters, and told him what the Wing Commander had said.

"It may well be that he is cracking up," Masters said.

"I don't think it's that," Carson replied thoughtfully. "I think we'd better have a word with Kiwi. They're pretty close, and he might be able to shed some light on what's troubling Douglas?"

Masters shrugged his shoulders. He had been studying the New Zealander carefully lately. He wondered how many more had detected the nervous flickering of the eyelids he noticed in the New Zealander when the latter became agitated.

For that matter, he had been quietly observing the older crews on the squadron. Not so many of them left now. But quite a few, an alarming number, in fact, had acquired some small, almost imperceptible sign of nerve strain. One had to look for it, but it was there. Some, Masters discovered, picked the soft skin round their nails, until with constant pressure the skin became hard and brittle. Others shot furtive glances round the mess and nibbled at their nails. Then there were those who chewed the soft flesh inside their cheeks.

It was an interesting study, Masters mused. Every other day he minutely inspected his own features for signs of nerves. But he had long since trained himself to control his emotions. He had been ice cool, even on that leave from navigation school, when he had come home unexpectedly and found Rita in bed with the Naval Lieutenant. Long before that, he had known their marriage could never last. Still, he reflected, the Lieutenant came from a wealthy family and the costs he would get from the divorce court should be generous.

Masters nudged Carson, knowingly, as Douglas came into the mess and made towards the bar.

"Now's as good a time as any to tell him to stop acting like a candidate for a psychiatric class!"

They intercepted their bomb-aimer and for a full half-hour Carson talked to him quietly but sternly, pulling no punches.

Douglas listened equally quietly. After they had finished, he said: "Sorry I've drawn you into this. I'll make myself scarce around here."

After he had gone, Carson said to Masters: "That was what I was afraid of. He'll stop drinking in the mess, but it will be the village pubs from now on. We'd better watch him. If he doesn't snap out of it, I'll see the Medical Officer."

"Good idea," Masters agreed, "that would be better than approaching Strange. Douglas sure hates the new Wingco's guts."

Carson smiled ruefully. "Reckon that cuts both ways. The Wingco seems to have taken an equal dislike to him. Must be something, after all, in this chemical reaction stuff!"

23

APRIL came, and the month brought a new threat to the Yorkshire and Lincolnshire bases of Bomber Command. Not entirely an unexpected threat but the intensification of one that had always been there.

The shadow of the intruder flitted ghostily but never silently through the broken cloud layers above the home aerodromes of the Halifaxes and Lancasters. It waited for them and attacked them as they orbited the friendly, re-assuring flare-paths beckoning them down at the end of a raid.

The Luftwaffe, powerless to break the ever-increasing strength of Harris's saturation raids, moved special intruder squadrons to new air strips on the coast. From these airfields they took off to join the main force bombers on the last leg across the North Sea.

The home coast ahead, and the grey waters of the North Sea below, lulled the men in the bombers into a false sense of security.

So the funereal pyres of the Lancasters and Halifaxes glowed brightly in the Lincolnshire wealds and the Yorkshire dales in the early hours before the dawn. But the losses were never included in the lists of aircraft missing.

As Flight Lieutenant Martin expounded to his crew in A Flight hut: "You can't list an aircraft as missing when you know where its charred fuselage is!"

Davis looked thoughtfully at his skipper. "Waal, it's sure tough getting it over your own 'drome. Should be a warning to those gol' damned gunners to stay awake."

His Flying Officer rank had recently come through. It had been circulated in the same orders promoting Martin to Flight Lieutenant.

"Anyway," Martin went on, "we should be able to pick up any intruders on 'Fish Pond'* provided the H2S is on."

Davis frowned. "There's no way, Marty, of identifying the blasted 'blips'?"

"No," Martin replied; "but say there are four 'blips' on the W.O.P.'s screen. Three of them are moving more or less orthodox but the fourth is coming nearer and nearer towards us. Then it's fair to reckon that's the intruder."

Sergeant Best butted in. "Anything I see which hasn't got four engines gets my four barrels!"

"Might be a Mosquito!" Kiwi pointed out.

"Just too bad," Best snapped, "he's no damned right prowling around bombers, especially at night."

Martin scratched the lobe of his right ear. "Think, then, we've got this intruder drill fairly well taped?"

They nodded and, winking at Davis, Martin said: "We don't want any slips, now that Kiwi is almost married. Say, when are you going to legalise it?"

Kiwi reddened. "Soon as we finish this tour."

"Jeez," Martin laughed, "we're practically finished! Only three more trips to do. You've no need to worry. Daddy here will see you through."

"Who's worrying," Kiwi asked sharply.

Martin smiled. "You must be, or you'd marry the girl and take us all to your wedding!"

The seed was sown, an idea reaped, as Kiwi thought about it that night. By morning he had decided to get married as soon as the necessary papers could be arranged.

A week later, he married Susan with a special marriage licence. Group Captain Dorton granted a forty-eight hour pass to the crew of F—Freddie.

As he shook hands with Pilot Officer Leonard Kiwi MacArthur he smiled warmly.

"MacArthur, you are not properly dressed!" he said gravely.

Moving to his desk, Dorton thumbed through some papers and,

---

* FISH POND. Radar device worked from H2S master unit by wireless operator. It enabled him to pick up aircraft as 'blips' on small radar screen in his compartment.

taking out a foolscape page, which had come from Group an hour earlier, he said: "Glance at that."

He watched the startled look come over the New Zealander's face, and heard him stutter: "D.F.C., sir?"

"Yes, I put you in for it some time back. After all, you *are* my best bomb-aimer. Better get it up for the wedding picture!"

Coming round from his desk, he patted the New Zealander affectionately on the shoulder. "You'll come through this tour all right. That's one thing I am quite certain of. In the meantime, the very best of luck."

Martin was stitching the ribbon of the D.F.C. on his bomb-aimer's tunic when Douglas entered the mess.

"Just heard the news," he said. "I want to congratulate you."

Kiwi eyed him sheepishly. "There'll be one coming up for you one of these days."

He paused and, looking uncomfortable, added: "Shern," there was a catch in the voice, "I'm sorry you couldn't come along as best man, but you understand how awkward it would be since Terry's bridesmaid?"

Douglas laid his hand on the New Zealander's arm. "That's all right. Don't give it another thought. . . ."

"Attention . . . Attention . . ." The broadcast system drowned the rest of his words . . . "All Captains, Navigators and Bomb-aimers report for navigation briefing at 1400 hours . . . Attention . . . Attention . . ."

Martin laughed deeply. Looking at Douglas, he said: "Think of us, boy, when they're throwing the dirt up at you tonight! Come to think of it, maybe the chopper is waiting for you this time! You're the next crew after us to be screened, huh?"

"Carson's take-offs long ago innoculated us against choppers," Douglas said.

"Wouldn't bank on that," Martin retorted airily, "innoculations wear off. Carter got it on his last trip!"

Douglas smiled cynically, and left the mess. But Martin's remarks niggled uncomfortably in his mind.

After he had gone, Martin said: "The Wingco's gunning for him. Heard he and one of his fitters started a brawl in the Swan last night. Dead drunk they were!"

* * * * *

The Intelligence Officer droned on monotonously . . . "This is one of the most heavily used, if not the most over-worked, marshalling yard in South-East Germany. . . ."

Masters sighed wearily, nudged Douglas and whispered: "Why must they give us the bloody history of the target? Next they'll be telling us whether the architecture is Gothic or not!"

As they worked over their charts, Masters stroked his chin pensively. It had become a habit with him lately, Douglas noticed, almost as conspicuous as Kiwi's blinking.

Masters said, a trifle too casually, he thought: "Karlsruhe; we've never been there before! Wonder if its going to be sticky? Too bad you bust up with that piece in town; otherwise you'd have been at Kiwi's wedding and we'd have been on pass!"

Douglas scowled and his eyes swept down to the Mercator chart. Karlsruhe, he saw, was roughly thirty miles south of Mannheim and about the same distance north-east of Stuttgart, two particularly dicey targets. But what made him uneasy was the knowledge that it was only a hundred and twenty-five miles south-west of Nuremburg. About eighteen minutes flying time, by a Focke-Wulf 190. Good chance as well of the Ruhr's night fighters intercepting them on the flight in. If not, they would probably be waiting for them on the way back.

With this in mind, he said: "It could be sticky, Larry. But half the force are going to Munich tonight, so it will be a question of which raid they select."

Masters grimaced and his eyes swept over the big room. Odd how it reminded him of his geography class at secondary school. The quarter-inch maps of Europe covering the green painted wall; the coloured posters showing bombing angles and bombing drill; the bare wooden forms and the ink-stained tables. Only the boys were a bit bigger and science had given them more costly toys to play with. Apart from that, things had not changed much, he ruminated. There was the same roll call and the absent faces. Only they did not require a sick note to cover their absence. The R.A.F. took care of that, and sent out telegrams. Come to think of it, Y—Yorker's skipper, navigator and bomb-aimer were not at the briefing. Turning to Carson, Masters asked: "Yorker on tonight?"

Carson looked up from the Flight Plan he was working on.

"Skipper's got a bad cold and their bomb-aimer's going to Kiwi's wedding."

Douglas, listening to Master's query, laid aside his dividers, picked up his air computor and mentally cursed Hogarth. This was the first time he had heard about Hogarth going to the wedding. Probably he was escorting Terry. He knew Kiwi had introduced them.

Well, they were going out tonight, and that put them further ahead of Y—Yorker on the Ops board. And Y—Yorker and her blasted bomb-aimer would have to make up for this night. They had merely borrowed time.

Sergeant Green, S—Sugar's engineer, scanning the sky below them from the astro-drome, saw the red target indicators spluttering against the blackness. Yellow fires, mere pin-points to him at the height they were flying, at, winked amongst the reds.

Green's voice came over the intercom. "Shern, I think we're well past the target."

Carson banked the Halifax, and Green, looking down the flaming exhausts of the port wing, shouted sharply: "That's the target without a doubt!"

Carson peered critically at the fires, then levelled out the Halifax. "Looks," he said, "as if we're well off course and well behind E.T.A., Larry. Are you sure of that last course?"

Douglas, sitting beside the navigator, heard the engineer's remarks and Carson's query. Rising, he shuffled into the nose.

Plugging in his intercom, in the socket alongside the bomb-sight, he heard Masters say: "Thought I was dead on. I make it three minutes to go before the T.I.s are due to go down."

"Well, they're bombing! No bloody question about it!" This time it was the mid-upper gunner speaking.

"Watch the mucking sky!—Not the mucking target!" Callaghan snarled from the rear-turret.

Masters cut in: "The winds have been spot on since we crossed the coast. Can't understand it. But I'm not going to argue with the Pathfinders. We'd better turn on!"

Douglas watched sceptically as the red target indicators burned among the yellow fires. There was something he didn't like about it. Something was out of place. A stick of bombs burst across the indicators. Then a second and a third stick.

He flicked on the graticle sight and glanced along the drift counter. Yet the T.I.s were not burning with their accustomed vividness. They were dull, sloppy and lifeless. Even the fires had an anaemic look about them.

He called Masters. "What heading are we on?"

"168 magnetic!" Masters replied.

That was the heading he'd drawn on the target map for the run in. Yet the indicators were burning too far port of them on a heading of 135 degrees. They were different tonight. Nothing like their usual brightness.

"Hold it, Skipper," he called. "It's a phoney! They've lit up a dummy target, and a poor one at that! Keep on Larry's original course and ignore those stupid bastards who are bombing. They've probably never seen a target before."

"Are you sure? More are bombing now!" Carson's voice was doubtful.

"Quite sure," he replied.

Fifteen seconds later, the trade-marks of the Pathfinders stained the night sky, the vividness of their reds and greens dazzling the eye.

Carson saw them, and said: "Good show, Shern! This heading brings us dead on to them."

Ahead, he could see aircraft bombing the indicators, and dark red flames, streaked with yellow, rising from the marshalling yards at Karlsruhe.

Kneeling over the bomb-sight Douglas watched the indicators curl lazily along the sword-sight, clear and naked in the light of the bursting camera flares.

God, that was good bombing. Someone had put a stick straight across the yard, wiping out part of a cluster of reds.

Douglas let all his bomb stations go except the incendiaries in his starboard wing racks. Smoke from the gutted engine sheds crept along the sight. He plunged the jettison bars over, releasing the fire-bombs in the wing. They should burst in the streets behind the marshalling yards . . . his own contribution.

"Close bomb doors," he snapped.

For the first time, he became aware of the flak and the big round drifting balls of smoke it left in the sky. A Halifax skidded above, its exhausts glowing dangerously near to them.

"Hell! That was close," the engineer said.

The flames from the target laughed uproariously. They reared from the red-ringed aiming point to taunt the pallid flickers from the dummy target lighted by the city's defence to divert the fury from the night sky above.

24

THE half cottage was small, compact, with two doll-sized windows breaking up the monotonous outline of white-washed wall. The low ceilings in the living-room and bedroom emphasised the cramped floor space, but the gay chintz coverings and the solid well-used furniture gave the cottage a warm friendly atmosphere.

As warm, Sue thought, as its buxom, rosy-cheeked owner. She felt she liked the place from the moment Kiwi lifted the heavy brass knocker and let it fall on the solid weather-beaten door.

The thatched roof was old, but it had been recently trimmed.

"It's not much of a bathroom, but the geyser does work."

She turned to the plump woman in the red cardigan and green skirt. "Why, it's charming, Mrs. Harrison. It's even better than Mr. Hart said."

"We'll take it, then," Kiwi said.

He'd known they would, for the Ostler's landlord had told him it was the best accommodation they could get in the village. He felt the warm pressure of Sue's hand on his arm. "I'll pay in advance. Monthly or weekly?"

"It's entirely up to you."

Mrs. Harrison had taken an instant liking to the tall, slim New Zealander and his petite blonde wife. He couldn't, she considered, be much older than her own son, who was out there in the Burmese jungles. It was the third time she had let the rooms to young, newly married officers from the squadron. They had all been nice couples. All very much in love with each other. Twice she had heard those girl-wives sob quietly as they packed their cases and few belongings to leave the cottage for the last time, their husbands in some unmarked grave.

This, she assured herself, would be the last time she would let the rooms. Now she found herself suffering a little of what these wives went through every night the big black bombers went out, wearily climbing for height, always reminding her of elderly coal men staggering up steep flights of stairs with heavy loads on their backs.

She stopped herself from putting her arm round the girl and telling her she had nothing to worry about. Instead, she murmured:

"Monthly!"

As she watched the New Zealander write out a cheque, she was inwardly glad she had said that. It showed more confidence in her expectations of the airman's life. It sounded better than 'weekly'. The slip of a girl beside her would have immediately read her fears.

"I'm afraid we haven't much with us. In fact, very little!"

She turned to the girl, and said gently: "Neither had I when I was first married. Anything you want, just ask for it."

After she had gone, Sue said: "She's such a dear, darling. I'll have to thank Mr. Hart."

Kiwi slipped an arm round his wife's shoulders. "You'll have the chance, sweetheart. He's giving us lunch."

They took a long time over the lunch. There was no hurry, for the little pub was always empty at noon. After they had eaten, Sue scraped back her chair, and smiled sweetly at the big burly landlord.

"That," she said, "was the tastiest chicken I've had for a long time. What with telling us about the cottage and giving us this meal as a . . ."

Hart interrupted, brushing her protest aside. "It's been a real pleasure, Mrs. MacArthur."

She excused herself, and after she had gone Kiwi followed Hart downstairs to the tap-room. Hart, kneeling under the counter, brought out a bottle of champagne. Laying it on the bar, he brushed the dust from his hamlike hands. Carefully he brought three champagne glasses from the cupboard behind him.

Motioning to the New Zealander to be quiet, he said: "You didn't think this place could produce the bubbly stuff, eh? Little surprise for the bride!"

Kiwi shook his head. "There's one thing I'll miss when I leave the squadron."

"What's that?"

"Landlords like Freddie Hart!"

Hart's big shoulders rocked with laughter. But when he spoke, the laughter was gone and his normal placid eyes were grave. "Whose aircraft caught it last night? I heard the gun-fire. When I got out of bed I could see the blaze from the window. Transport driver from the station passed a couple of hours ago, but he wasn't sure."

"God! Did they attack the 'drome?"

Hart looked up, and the puzzled expression slipped from his face.

"I'd forgotten," he said, "you wouldn't have known." He broke off as he saw Sue come down the stairs. Kiwi followed his gaze, and noticed the sparkle in his wife's eyes as they rested on the champagne bottle.

"Oh, darling, you shouldn't have?" she said softly, slipping her arm through his.

"Blame me!" Hart said. "Just part of the wedding lunch."

Impulsively Sue leaned over the counter and kissed him lightly on the brow. Kiwi grinned broadly as Hart's ruddy face changed to a deep red.

They were finishing the bottle when Old Charlie came in. Kiwi's face softened as he watched the old farm-hand make his way to the bar. He had always known him as Charlie, though some day he would find out his real name. Bent double, like an aged dwarf, his gnarled bony hand leaning heavily on his black hawthorn stick, he beat a steady tattoo on the wooden floor as he hobbled towards them.

The old man smoothed back a grey, flimsy lock of hair from his crinkled brow, tapping the floor impatiently with his stick.

Hart greeted him and pulled a pint of bitter, setting it on the counter.

Old Charlie took a long draught, wiped his mouth with the frayed cuff of his coat, cocked a bright eye at the New Zealander, and raised his pint pot.

For a moment his eyes took in the girl, then swept past her to the window. Placing the pint on the bar, he croaked impishly: "Hee! He's found your lair at last! Took a long time, but old Jerry's no fool. Hear he nearly blew you off the map!"

Hart said sternly: "Enough of that, you old rumour-monger. The airfield's not touched."

The old man cackled deep in his hoary throat. "Wasn't it, by gum? Ask the officer; he'll be telling you different!"

Kiwi looked into his rheumy eyes, and said quietly: "I was on leave, Charlie. Seems I picked a good time!"

"Aye, you did at that, son. Lots of plain coffins have been going past here this morning. Phillips and Mellor have been doing well."

He grunted, before taking another pull at his pint. "War's good for like's of undertakers!"

Sue glanced anxiously at the old man and then at Hart, who was hastily polishing a glass he had nervously picked up. The landlord saw the concern in her face.

"Charlie here is talking nonsense. There was no bombing attack. Seems a night fighter was waiting for the bombers when they returned. Don't have all the details, but one of the transport boys came past this morning. . . ." Hart paused and put down the glass he was polishing. "According to him, the German pilot shot down two, and scurried back." Turning to the New Zealander, Hart went on: "You might know the transport fellow. A Corporal Summers. Said they lost two, apart from what was lost over Karlsruhe."

"You don't happen to know what aircraft they were?" Kiwi's voice was casual, but Sue detected an underlying note of anxiety in it.

Hart frowned. "'Fraid I don't! He wasn't sure, and you know how things get messed up second-hand!" He picked up the glass and frantically started polishing again.

"What did he say?" Kiwi demanded.

"Well, he thought one of the crashed aircraft was your friend's . . . S—Sugar."

Sue, her eyes carefully observing her husband's face, saw him glance down at the three empty champagne glasses. They were giving off thin stabs of blue light as they reflected the sun's rays from the low narrow window behind them.

Kiwi watched the flashing pin-points of light. They looked, he reflected, like miniature searchlights in an inverted crystal bowl. They should be probing upwards, he thought. So Douglas had got it over his own airfield, if the story was true.

He felt Sue's fingers bite deeply into his forearm.

"There's nothing definite about it." Hart added hurriedly. "As I said, this fellow isn't at all sure. He'd heard Carson had a bet he would be first back. The two aircraft which went down were the first and second to arrive over the field."

Kiwi, who had listened in silence, asked softly: "Can I use your phone?"

Hart nodded and raised the flap of the counter, stepping aside.

Five minutes later, the New Zealander came out of the back room, and they knew by his face S—Sugar had got down safely.

"Set them up, Freddie! Douglas and Co. lobbed down okay. Don't know the full story; but the Adjutant tells me they had to feather an engine on the way back. Got down among the last aircraft."

Hart mopped his brow with a handkerchief. "Certainly relieved to know that. He's a damned fine fellow, that Shern."

Sue caught the affection in the landlord's voice and glanced at her husband.

Kiwi nodded.

A heavy vehicle crunched on the gravel outside. Sue turned towards the window.

"Darling, it's our bus," Sue said quickly.

Hart saw them to the door. He walked slowly back into the bar, and smiled at the old farm-hand. After a while, he said: "It's a queer war, Charlie. Tonight that young fellow may be over Berlin. I wonder if he ever thinks about it."

"Thinks about what?" the old man urged.

"Nothing, Charlie. I was only thinking aloud."

The old man grunted and eyed him strangely.

Kiwi and Sue spent the afternoon packing their belongings from the flat. As Kiwi placed the suitcases in the tiny hall, Sue glanced at her wrist-watch and said: "I'll make the tea. Terry will be home any minute."

"Sorry you're leaving?" Kiwi asked, pointedly.

Her eyes met his, clear and frank. "No: but there is a little ache in leaving Terry. We've been almost like sisters. She's going to feel very lonely."

He pulled her to him and gently stroked her hair. It had been the luckiest day of his life when he had met her, he thought.

"Len," she murmured . . . Funny, she never called him Kiwi any more, always Len. . . . "I'm glad it was you I met."

He held her tighter and mentally recalled their first meeting in the Atlantic Hotel.

"No! No!" She shook her head vigorously. "It's not what you're thinking. Shern didn't attract me in the slightest."

"He's good-looking," he said teasingly.

"Yes," Sue said slowly; "like a flashy piece of rolled gold. Scratch it, and the glitter comes off to reveal base metal beneath."

Kiwi shook his head gravely.

"Don't be too hard on Shern. There's a lot like him flying. Men who have built up a fine steel barrier to hide their real feelings. They retreat, Sue, behind this barrier, and allow a completely false self to take over. Sometimes the automatic curtain splitting the true personality from the false becomes stuck. Then you only see the pseudo-character. With Douglas, it's the easy-living, well-paid aerial axeman with a contract written in borrowed time. That's what he actually told me he felt he was when he first came to the squadron."

"But you're not like that, Len? For the life of me, I can never understand the common denominator which brought you two into a friendship."

Kiwi laughed lightly. "I'll be indebted to him for one thing."

Sue tilted her head. "What's that?"

"He brought us together. You know, darling, I'd never had had the nerve to walk up to you like he did that night."

She laughed softly. "He's brash, if that's what you mean . . ." Her eyes looked earnestly into his. "Tell me, Len, that London affair. It was all true, wasn't it?"

"Yes," he said evenly, "it was all true. Why do you ask?"

"Because even then, even after Terry knew, there was still a thin thread between them. He snapped that by persistently lying right to the end. It was that which made her really sick. Terry loved him deeply. But he cut that last slender fibre himself."

A key rasped in the door, and they broke away as the sound of high heels clicked along the hall.

* * * * *

They had finished their meal when Terry said casually: "I heard at work today that Greman night fighters were waiting for the squadron when they got back last night. They say five were shot down."

"They have it twisted as usual," Kiwi replied. "Two were lost over the target, or on the way, and two were shot down over the 'drome by one night fighter."

"Anyone . . ." She bit her lip. "Anyone you knew?"

Kiwi searched her face and detected a troubled look in her usually serene eyes.

"Yes, I knew most of them." He paused expectantly but the reply he had hoped for did not come. A moment later he said quietly: "S—Sugar got down safely."

An uneasy, tense silence fell over the room. Terry scraped back her chair and her taut nerves relaxed.

Rising quickly from the table she stared out of the window with an air of concentration.

When she spoke her voice was low and toneless. "That's horrible, and over their own base."

Before they left Sue took Terry aside. She gazed compassionately at her strained perplexed expression and said confidentially: "Terry, there's something which nearly slipped my mind. There's a big dance on Friday in the mess. You must come along."

Terry tossed her head and her eyes misted. "No, Sue. I'd rather not!"

Sue smiled wistfully and taking Terry's arm shook her gently.

"You're being a silly girl, and I know why. I wouldn't have asked you if he was to be there. Len tells me he's blotted his copy book in the mess. Now he keeps well away except for meals."

She looked reflectively at her friend. "Besides, Jack Hogarth is very anxious to see you again. Len says he is . . ."

"Please!" Terry interrupted testily. "Whether he will be there or not doesn't interest me. It's just that I'm not keen. Jack seems a nice fellow, but at the moment I hate all men."

But before Sue joined her husband in the hallway she successfully overcame Terry's objections and extracted from her a firm promise that she would think again about coming to the dance.

·   ·   ·   ·   ·   ·

Kiwi heard the snarl of a motor-cycle engine being revved up outside the cottage door, as he stretched out on the sofa, while Sue unpacked.

A few minutes later the engine spluttered, stopped and there was a pounding on the door.

Sue called from the kitchen: "Oh, darling! We're having our first visitor."

Kiwi went to the door and threw it open and his mouth loosened in surprise when he saw Douglas. "Who is it, Len?" Sue cried expectantly.

"Shern," he called evenly, but there was no response to his reply. Douglas winked knowingly and beckoned with his thumb towards the farm-labourer standing beside the machine and grinned.

"If you're still interested in a motor bike, this one should do. Lad here is going into the Army and wants a quick sale."

Douglas rested his hands lightly on his hips and half-turned round. "I've tested it out. Nothing to brag about, but it's good enough to take you to and from the station."

Kiwi ran his eyes over the mud-splattered machine and then looked at the young farm-hand. "Don't know," he said, "if it's worth while. I'll soon be finished here!"

"Hell," Douglas said, "you can always take it with you, or you could even sell it to some of the 'bods' on the station."

Kiwi walked over to the motor-cycle, started it and rode it down to the village. When he came back he shook his head.

"Clutch is slipping," he said, "and the brakes aren't so hot. Give you twelve pounds for it."

"Crikey," the youth said, "I wanted at least twenty!"

Kiwi laughed. "You'll never get twenty or anything like it for that heap of scrap-iron, not if petrol was de-rationed tomorrow!"

Douglas interjected: "Better take it, son. If it wasn't that he wanted it for getting back to the station, he'd never consider a wreck like that. As it is, I know another fellow who has a better bike than that and who'd sell for less."

The youth scratched his tousled head, while he thought the matter over for a couple of minutes. "All right," he said at last: "make it thirteen pounds in cash. No cheques and it's a deal."

Kiwi went back into the cottage and the youth, turning to

Douglas, said: "Dunno if I should have let it go for that. If it was overhauled and cleaned up, I could get a lot more for it."

Douglas grinned and said: "If you'd the cash to pay a garage. And remember, you owe me five pounds from that 'crap' game in the back room of the Swan!"

"I'll pay you after I get the money, but I'll never play dice again," the youth said.

"Tell me," Douglas asked, "how come you had all that cash on you? You must have had about ten quid that night!" The farm-hand smirked sheepishly, and Douglas added: "Hear there's a lot of black-market bacon deals going on round here. You the van-boy or something?"

The youth flushed and shuffled uncomfortably.

Before Douglas could question him further, Kiwi came out with Sue.

The New Zealander handed the notes to the farm-hand and Sue said cuttingly: "I don't think that cycle's worth ten pounds."

Nodding curtly to Douglas, she went back into the cottage.

"Don't think Sue's too happy about the deal," Douglas said lightly.

"Oh! Sue doesn't really mind! She knows I've been after a bike for some time. Must have one to get back to the station. These damned push-bikes are no use..." He paused. "Care to come in for a few moments?"

"No," Douglas said. "Thanks all the same, but I've a little business to attend to."

The farm-hand nodded reluctantly and together they walked down the street.

25

DOUGLAS noted how Kiwi fidgeted impatiently as Wing Commander Strange went through the briefing; how the New Zealander's body tensed when he learned that Brunswick was the target. Brunswick was flanked thirty miles to the east by Hanover, a hundred and twenty miles to the west by Berlin, with Magdeburg almost half-way between. It was an area ringed by heavy-calibre guns and fast-winged night fighters.

This was to be F—Freddie's last operation, the 29th trip to hell and back. . . . God, Douglas mused, let us have an easier one than this when our last raid comes up.

His eyes strayed from the Wing Commander's stocky, broad-shouldered frame to his chubby face and sand-coloured hair; hair that never quite hid the bald patch at the back.

Strange's grey eyes swept over the rows of battle-dress clad air-crews. They were deliberate, orderly and very astute eyes.

German night fighter pilots, Douglas decided, probably had eyes like that when they scanned the burning cities below and climbed still higher towards the bomber stream, their gloved hands itching on the firing buttons, of their 88's and 190's.

". . . so the H2S aircraft will take-off immediately before the rest of the squadron and join force A. And to make certain this is an entirely radar attack, the bulbs in the graticle sights have been removed."

Strange nodded towards the Met Officer and went on: "Forecasts show there will be ten-tenths cloud over the city. That gives us ideal conditions for testing the accuracy of H2S in a full-scale attack. The non-radar aircraft will rendezvous with the main force bombers here"—the Wing Commander tapped a red blob on the map which peeped from the North Sea—"and carry on to the secondary target."

He passed his billiard cue to the bombing leader, smiling faintly as he faced the crowded room.

"It is possible," he said, "that Fritz will take one of these attacks as a diversionary raid. He has never shown remarkable imagination and it is unlikely he will expect two major attacks on two targets so widely apart. Once again, remember radar sets must not be switched on until the enemy coast is neared."

Strange motioned to the bombing leader to take over, and demanded crisply: "Any questions?"

Douglas half-rose, hesitated and promptly sat down. He wanted to ask the Wing Commander why they could not have carried the graticle bulbs in their pockets in case the sets broke down. But he decided against it. He didn't like the Wingco and he knew from past encounters with him that Strange wasn't crazy about him.

As they waited for the trucks to take them to their respective bays, Douglas strolled up to Kiwi.

"Lucky boy, Kiwi!" he said. "Tomorrow it'll all be behind you."

The New Zealander smiled ruefully. This, Douglas thought, must be the worst trip in the long tour. Memories of all the other nights, the near misses, the skirmishes with death, would all be flooding back into Kiwi's mind.

"You'll be all right, Kiwi," he said sincerely; "I've a strong hunch about it."

God, he hoped so. Things they said had improved since Dorton had taken over. Hell, they must have been bad before. But one crew had managed to cheat the reaper, to touch down, only a few nights earlier, on the black concrete with a full tour behind them.

Reflecting on this, Douglas regretted he had had so much to drink in the Ostler the night before. Still, it was on the money he had taken from the youth who had sold Kiwi the cycle.

He chuckled to himself as he recalled the forlorn look on the lad's face as he had paid his debt. That was one who would think twice about playing dice with him again . . . especially his, the loaded way! Better be careful about it. If word got to Strange's ears he was playing dice in the village there would be hell to pay.

The New Zealander mumbled something as he climbed into the truck. He couldn't quite catch the words. Lighting a cigarette, he watched Kiwi and the crew of F—Freddie wave mechanically as their truck headed for the Flights.

Douglas relaxed as Carson opened the throttles of S—Sugar wide and called 'Lock'. That peculiar smell which reeked from aircraft came to him, that mixture of oil, petrol and the warm air from the heaters which didn't help his aching head.

He felt better after Carson lifted the Halifax from the concrete. He remembered the other, earlier take-offs, which now belonged to another era, as if someone else had experienced and sweated through those living nightmares.

The airfield's flare-path twinkled below, tiny blue ghostly needles of light, rapidly vanishing as the wispy, swirling cloud base embraced the Halifax. When they broke out of the blanket of grey vapour, Carson said: "Take her over, Shern. I'll claim her before the coast comes up."

Five hundred feet above them Flight Lieutenant Martin snapped on his intercom, watched the luminous altimeter needle creep past the twelve thousand feet mark, then called his crew.

"We're treating this as a first Op. With all the drill and all the trimmings. Cut out all joking and general messing about. Right, we start now!"

Systematically and with an odd curtness in his voice Martin called them up. Tersely he said to Davis: "I'm going to weave as soon as we cross the coast. It will give the gunners a better chance of seeing what's beneath us."

"Aw, Christ Marty," Davis drawled, "you'll muck up my whole plot!"

"That's too bad," Martin snapped, "and from now on don't talk unless you've something important to say."

"You feeling all right?" Davis retorted sharply.

Martin fought back an impulse to scream at his navigator. God, but he was edgy tonight. It was cool in the cockpit yet his fingers were hot and sticky in his gloves. That was the way his hands were when he held the control column on the bombing run. No use in fooling himself, tonight he was experiencing real fear.

The knowledge chilled him and he glanced hurriedly over his shoulder and saw that the engineer was engrossed in watching his gauges. Martin lowered his head and quietly prayed. The last time he remembered praying in an aircraft was on his first raid, shortly before they reached the target.

The old dread he had of being trapped in a burning aircraft suddenly swept over him. Someone coughed sharply into a mask and the sound jarred in his ears. He switched on his intercom and the panic left him as he snarled:

"Someone's got their bloody mike on?"

There was a faint click and the buzzing sound which came over the intercom when a microphone was left on died abruptly.

A little later, Best asked permission to test his guns. Martin said sternly: "Skipper to rear-gunner—Go Ahead!"

A sharp tremor of invisible hammers beat along the Halifax's fuselage as Sergeant Best thumbed out a half-second burst.

He reported to Martin. "Rear turret guns okay."

"Mid-upper to Skipper . . . permission to fire?"

"Shoot away!"

The four Brownings chattered angrily and the thick, sickly smell of cordite wafted into the cockpit.

"Mid-upper to Skipper . . . Guns working."

"Roger!" Martin snapped.

He eased the control column back and watched the altimeter needle quiver on the 20,000 mark. He levelled out and moved the throttles a fraction forward, and trimmed the Halifax.

Kiwi called from the nose to say the coast was coming up. A light barrage of flak snaked well port of them. He estimated it was hundreds of feet below.

He watched the clouds glowing in a ghostly way as the searchlights played idly along their base, scurrying like luminous rats as they scampered here and there for an escape hole into the clear sky above.

F—Freddie's four radial engines beat steadily and monotonously through the night sky. Only the occasional pitch of the bomber as she hit the slip-stream of some aircraft ahead upset the smoothness of their flight.

"Ten minutes to target . . . first radar check mark coming up in six minutes!" Davis announced.

Kiwi screwed the red knob above the bearing counter a couple of notches higher and the brilliance of the radar screen increased.

He jerked his eyes away, hurriedly shut them for a few seconds, blinked and daubed his right eye gently with his silk-covered hand.

Continuous staring at the outlines on the cathode ray tube made his eyes smart.

"Remember," Davis urged, "when you get the final fix, I start calling out backwards the time count."

The bombers, they had been told at briefing, would fly past Brunswick, then wheel in a slow deliberate formation and start the time run from east of the city. On the approach, the bomb-aimers would pick up on the H2S the huge factory owned, according to Intelligence, by Reich Air Marshal Herman Goering. From the factory, they would begin the bomb run on Brunswick.

As Martin turned the Halifax on to the approach heading, Davis checked the Air Speed, Height and Course on his duplicate panel and pulled out his stop-watch. An extra length of cable had been attached to the bomb-tit to cover the stretch from the nose to the bomb-aimer's position beside the H2S set.

Kiwi eased himself round from the Mark 14. bomb-sight head, knelt down beside the bombing computor box and checked that the pre-flight settings had been correctly fed in. He set on a new wind-speed and a new wind direction which Davis had given him a few minutes earlier.

He switched on the Bombing Master Switch, selected and fused the bombs. Then he set the 'Mickey Mouse'* device. The New Zealander rose and gazed speculatively through the perspex of the nose. What he saw sent his limbs jerking convulsively.

Brunswick's concerto of murderous fire hosed through the cloud. layer below to leave a closely interwoven pattern of grimy pock marks in the clear sky ahead—a sky brilliantly illuminated in the bursting camera flares and exploding shells. The frantic, feverish race by the German ground-gunners to fill the aerial box ahead of the bombers and keep it filled with H.E. was on. And he knew they must fly through that box barrage. No point in weaving, even if they could take evasive action.

More than likely they would corkscrew into a burst. Pure luck from now on. Skill didn't come into it any more, Kiwi reflected. A faulty fuse setting by a German gunner could be just as effective as a carefully predicted shell. Christ, how he hated the run in on

---

*Mickey Mouse: Device for automatically releasing the cans of incendiaries carried in the wings with correct time lag.

a target with the bomb-doors wide open, revealing the unprotected bomb-racks.

Kiwi turned away and stumbled into the navigation hatch, bitter in the knowledge that they could have been given an easier target for their last trip. Hurriedly he scrawled a note on a piece of paper and passed it to Davis. On it he had written: "Here's your chance to let them go. Press when I shout 'Now'."

Davis read the note and nodded curtly. The New Zealander caught the flash of enthusiasm in his navigator's eyes. He had for a long time promised Davis that on one trip he'd let him release the bombs.

"Herman coming up. . . ." Kiwi recognised the tension in his own voice as it came back to him over the intercom.

"Left! Left! . . . Steady! . . . Right! . . . Steady now! . . . Steady! . . ." His tone was sharp, imperative . . . "Hold it!"

The tiny blob of light was creeping up the dimmed screen.

"Bomb doors open! Marker coming up!" he said.

"On Marker!" he corrected.

As his bomb-aimer said "On Marker!" Davis stabbed the button of his stop-watch and began to count "—Nine—eight—seven—six —five——"

To Best in the rear-turret the seconds seemed long, desperately drawn-out hours. God, this was worse than straight, visual bombing, he decided.

And for what? he wondered. Probably their load would only make craters in some farmer's field. They could see nothing. The set was their eyes, impartial, remote and unfeeling.

" . . . Four—three—two—one." Davis's voice was toneless.

Kiwi saw the longer, jagged blip that was the city beneath them crawl over the bearing ring, and shouted, "Now!"

The bone in his navigator's right thumb gleamed white, then pink. The Halifax reared and her lethal load spewed earthwards.

Kiwi slipped through the black-out curtain and shoved the jettison bars over. Through the perspex nose his mind photographed a fragment of the night sky—a night splashed and sprayed with the bright marigold flashes of heavy A.A. shells.

Pieces of spent shrapnel tip-tapped along the black belly of the bomber, like skeletons dancing jerkily on an empty oil drum.

Always the sound made him shudder. A dull red glow was

spreading in a great infectious rash through the white vapour beneath them. Brunswick was burning.

Sergeant Best, cold and uncomfortable in the rear-turret, stole a quick glance at the clouds. Long dull streaks of red were spreading through the grey canopy above Brunswick, reflections of the fires which were sweeping the city.

It looked, he thought, as if they had pulverised Brunswick. The blood drained from his face and his ears sang insanely as Martin flung the Halifax into a terrifying corkscrew to starboard. As the bomber came out of her power dive and the blood gushed back into his face, Best peered over his Brownings. He fancied he saw a long burst of tracer above and to his port.

He heard the mid-upper say: "Couple of combats two o'clock port quarter!"

Best felt the Halifax skid viciously to starboard as Martin shouted: "Engineer, watch those combats! Mid-upper, keep looking . . . you all right, Charlie?"

"Fine, Skipper," he said.

Martin looked at his altimeter. Saw it was hovering on the 10,000 feet mark. A bit lower than he'd intended. The starlight was bright, too bright, for it gave the clouds a snowy, glaring whiteness he didn't like.

Bracing himself against the seat, he cursed into his mask. The shadow of the Halifax was racing across them, hedge-hopping over the wispy peaks, a sitting target for any fighter, an unmistakable etching of black on white. He pushed forward the control column and his airspeed needle moved sharply up the scale as he nosed into the safety of the cloud cover.

Davis came on, his tone that of a hurt, exasperated man. "For Christ's sake, Marty, get back on course! You're ten degrees off . . . Better turn on quick. Coast is coming up and we are well port of track."

"Turning on. Roger!" Lord, ten degrees off. So many things to watch, and that was the elementary check. How'd he missed that? His eyes swept over the panel and he checked the glowing dials again.

Blast it! He wouldn't cross the coast in cloud. For one thing, he couldn't be sure how dense it was. If searchlights were concentrated on the cloud base, they would magnify and distort the

Halifax into a gigantic porpoise, making it easier for the ground gunners to direct their fire against the bomber. Yet to shed the protective layer, and probe the starlight above, would mean a loss of speed, when he needed every knot to hurtle over the coastal defences.

"How far from the coast, navigator?"

"Should be coming up in ten and a half minutes," Davis said.

The swirling vapour was perceptively thinner. The white coating of ice crystals which had covered the leading edges of the Halifax's wings was now changing from snow-white to a murky grey.

It was as he feared, the cloud cover was breaking.

The coastal guns acknowledged the bombers ahead with yellow and orange-red flashes. He noted abstractedly that they were bursting some thousands of feet above him.

"Three minutes to coast!" Davis called.

Martin pushed the control column forward, and at the same time sent the Halifax into a gentle, undulating corkscrew coming out of it two degrees starboard of track. He saw the light flak curl slowly upwards, to whip past them in lightening-fast streams, uncomfortably near their port wing-tip. For a frightening moment, he thought the guns were vectored on him.

A faint streak of red unfolded from the apex of the tracer cone. Swiftly it blossomed into a dark red box of flickering flame.

"Lancaster's copped it," he heard the engineer call, as he pushed the throttles wide open and corkscrewed to starboard. He levelled out five thousand feet above the sea. Hard on that Lancaster, he reflected, but thanks to it having attracted the fire from the light guns, he had slipped through.

"Rear-gunner to Skipper. That Lanc's going down fast."

"To hell with him! Didn't I warn you to watch for fighters?"

The snarl in Martin's voice jolted Kiwi from his thoughts about his forthcoming leave with Sue. Long looks at flaming bombers, cart-wheeling earthwards, left the watchers open to any sneak attack. Martin was right, and Kiwi was glad he was taking no chances, especially tonight.

They were now over the North Sea. Very soon the red beacon light flashing out their squadron identification letters would blink encouragingly from the blackness far below.

Kiwi recalled his first trip. How different it had been then! There was none of this nerve-twisting anxiety about getting home safely, although they had wanted to get back just as eagerly. The difference was, their minds had been attuned to the odds that some night in the unspecified future the fighter or the flak would get them.

There would be no more such nights, at least not for a while. And the war might well be over before their second tour was due to begin.

Then they'd been too busy going through the routine on the first operational trip to know what it was all about. Over-confidence became the greatest danger.

Leaning against the Vickers gun, he tapped it affectionately.

He had never had to fire it once in anger. They never attacked from head on. Looking back, he considered again how very lucky he had been. Still, he admitted, they were an efficient crew. Apart from tonight, there had never been any of this 'Skipper to Rear-gunner' routine. 'Marty to Tony. Tony to Reg'. That had always been the way with them. After tonight they would split up. Days would slip into weeks and months. Years would pass, but they would always remember the crew of which they had been an integral part.

Martin was calling base. It was almost over. He slipped into the glass-house. Five aircraft were in the circuit orbiting at the stepped-up heights given by control when Kiwi spotted the two long dashes from the beacon at Nissindon. He thought it had never looked more friendly than it did tonight.

He heard the controller's voice come over the R.T., calling on S—Sugar to pancake. So Carson and Douglas had got ahead of them. Good luck to them, for when they landed they would lengthen the odds against S—Sugar or Y—Yorker coming through a tour . . . for these were now the oldest crews on the squadron.

Kiwi experienced a feeling of deep, unfathomable sadness as Martin taxied the Halifax to the dispersal ramp. He should have felt relief, but now they were safely on the aerodrome, an anti-climax had set in.

Martin cut the throttles. Kiwi noticed his shoulders sag. For a long moment Martin caressed the control column wheel with his gloved hand, wrapped, he was sure, in his own sacred thoughts.

Tonight he was saying good-bye to F—Freddie. Some other crew would take her over. They would be awed at the long lines of stencilled bombs on her fuselage. He hoped it would give them confidence for the ordeal which lay ahead of them.

Perhaps they would be a little afraid, afraid the reaper would call her in, tired at last of the long drawn out game she had played with seven men and an aircraft letter F.

26

THE telephone shrilled sharply. Dorton slammed the steel filing cabinet shut, strode to his desk and picked up the receiver.

The Waaf operator's voice purred in his ear. "Please hold the line, sir. Air Commodore Cartingham to speak to you."

"Dorton?" Cartingham's tone was crisp, precise and eager.

"Yes, sir."

The Air Commodore cleared his throat. "Group did a damned fine job on Brunswick last night. Recco pictures show seventy-five per cent of city devastated by fire. That's much more than we ever expected, especially with ten-tenths cloud. . . ."

Cartingham coughed. "Command is chortling about it. Wish we had H2S on a large scale a year ago. By the way, you can feel particularly pleased. Your radar aircraft had exceptionally good results. Clear A.P.'s Sending you six new H2S aircraft."

"Glad to hear that, sir. Knew we had good aiming points, but never thought it was general throughout the Command. This is becoming a crack squadron, you know, sir!"

Cartingham chuckled softly, and Dorton doubted if he had ever before heard the Air Commodore in such good humour.

Cartingham talked on, but before he rang off Dorton asked: "Excuse me for bringing this up, but the squadron have been working very hard lately and the Officers' Mess are planning a buffet dance."

"The Sergeants have already had theirs. . . ."

"Well, what's stopping them? Can't remember them having one since you came."

Dorton smiled. Cartingham was in an even better mood than he had imagined.

"They have provisionally fixed it for Friday night, but there is no way of knowing whether they will be . . ."

"I know, I know," Cartingham interrupted; "they want to find out if they can be put on a stand-down!"

Cartingham paused and his tone was serious. "Wish I could do it. Even Harris himself wouldn't be able to look that far ahead. All depends on the weather, for one thing, target, number required. Look here! I'll see what I can do, but make it clear to them that if a 'Maximum Effort' comes along, they will be expected to meet it. Hold the line."

For fifteen minutes Dorton leaned back in his chair, with the telephone receiver resting lightly against his ear. He was about to flash the operator and inquire if he had been cut off when Cartingham came through again. "Unless something very special comes along, you can take it there will be a stand-down; at least a partial one. I've arranged for your new aircraft to arrive Friday morning. You can get the air tests and training started that afternoon. That's the only way I can arrange it."

The Air Commodore grunted into the receiver. "By the way, I'll try and get over myself. Though don't bank on it, as I'm pretty well chained here."

He rang off and Dorton gently replaced the receiver.

Unless something very special came up, then, their stand-down was assured. Cartingham knew the value of a full-scale mess party as a fillip to morale. Not, Dorton mused, that 186's morale was low any more; yet an 'At Home' was overdue.

The new radar aircraft, plus the H2S Halifaxes he already had, would now tip the scales, giving the squadron a slight majority of all radar bombers. He sank back in his chair.

He felt good and he felt he had a good squadron.

"Damn it all," he said aloud, "one of the best!"

Kiwi, leaning against the rough-hewn garden fence at the back of the cottage, saw the new Halifaxes, their black, bulbous bellies glinting in the early sunlight, sweep low over the aerodrome. He watched until the last one touched down.

He knew the bombers were coming in that morning but the expected stand-down had not come through. From the telephone kiosk in the village he rang the station and asked for the Officers' Mess.

He whistled jauntily. The stand-down must have come; otherwise his call would not have been accepted.

Douglas was not in the mess but Carson took his call. Some of the gayness left him when Sugar's skipper informed him there was only a partial stand-down. Met reports, Carson told him, were undecisive but there was a fifty-fifty chance of a sea fog coming in around midnight, which would blot out the coastal 'dromes until around five in the morning.

Group, he gathered, were holding back for later weather forecasts. They expected to know definitely by mid-afternoon.

"That's too bad, but you're not a stand-by crew, surely?" he said.

Carson, he thought, sounded a trifle disappointed.

"We were not originally. But a couple in the stand-by crews have suddenly gone ill. Friend Douglas has kind of messed things up. On his own initiative, he button-holed the Wingco and volunteered the services of Sugar and Co!" Kiwi heard Carson breathe deeply into the mouthpiece. "Said we couldn't care less about the party. When Strange tackled me about it, he put it in such a way that I could hardly back out. Personally, I don't mind very much, but the N.C.O.s are hopping mad. Evidently the Sergeants' Mess have made a snap decision to hold a dance as well."

Kiwi felt his grip on the receiver tighten. "That was high-handed. He isn't the skipper . . ."

"Don't worry about that," Carson interjected firmly; "the crew made that clear to him."

"You know, Lew, I've known Shern a long time, but that was a bastard thing to do. He promised me faithfully he'd turn up for this party. It was to be a sort of farewell one to me. Sue and I leave here on Monday?"

"Yes," Carson said, "Martin told me you were being posted to an O.T.U. in Oxfordshire."

Kiwi rang off and cursed Douglas long and hard as he retraced his steps to the cottage. He had discreetly arranged for Sue to bring Terry along, assuring her that Douglas would not be there.

And Douglas had messed the whole plan up. It was his last chance to meet Terry and he had thrown it away. He had promised too he would take his call to the mess. Yet he hadn't even bothered to be there.

S—Sugar's mid-upper gunner laid down the glass of lemonade he had been sipping and grimaced. Enviously he watched the stand-down crews drinking at the bar, warming up for the party.

It made him bitter and bad-tempered. .

Turning to the rear-gunner, he said: "Jock, I have long since come to the conclusion that we have a rotten, stinking bastard for our bomb-aimer."

"Personally," said Sergeant Mooney, their new wireless operator, "Douglas strikes me as a bomb-happy case."

Callaghan snapped a light to his cigarette and inhaled slowly. "There's such a thing as tempting the fates. If we get the chop tonight, it will be through him upsetting everybody!"

Titch downed his drink. "Shern has been a different person since he came back from London with that Pilot Officer's ring," he said pointedly.

In the end it was the Met forecasters who gave 186 Squadron the full stand-down they had been hoping for. Their latest reports were unanimous. Not only could the coastal airfields expect dense fog, but also all aerodromes in Yorkshire and Lincolnshire.

The general stand-down came over the broadcast system at 1615. Douglas heard it as he was lathering his face.

He had the room to himself, now that Kiwi had gone to live in the village. It was larger and slightly more comfortable than the one he had had as a Flight Sergeant. He wondered who his new room-mate would be. Hell, he thought, it didn't matter a great deal. A few more trips and he would be finished, one way or the other.

And he didn't care much who did the packing, himself or the sergeant from the Orderly Room, who was long practised in the business. There was nothing in his personal belongings of any value and he'd long since torn up all letters. He had watched them smoulder and burst into flames, to become crisp black ashes of once amorous affairs.

As he burned them, he had wished again he had done the same with the letter from Loraine. The letter, he recalled bitterly, had lost him the only woman he had ever really cared for. Still, it didn't mean anything any more. Lighting a cigarette, he stared for a long time out of the window. His forehead puckered in a puzzled frown.

Strange, it had taken him so long to realise just what Terry had meant to him. By Monday Kiwi and Sue, his only links with her, would be gone. Perhaps if she was coming to the dance tonight, there might be a chance of talking to her.

He dismissed the thought as pointless, just as hopeless as thinking a week ahead. There were two things he could do tonight, he decided. Kill time in the Ostler or drop in to the Sergeants' Mess. A new crowd of Canadians had arrived on the squadron and there was bound to be a dice game in the backroom. With his loaded dice there was always a chance of picking up easy money.

He took down his battle-dress and felt in the top left-hand pocket for his dice. After twenty minutes of diligent searching panic swept over him. The dice had gone! He might have lost them or he might have misplaced them absently. If they were found . . . He shuddered at the thought. Those he had played with would recognise the yellow streaks in the ivory . . . not everyone, for most of the old, regular school of dice players were now listed in the 'Missing' columns, but the chances were that someone would spot them.

He sat for a time concentrating, trying to recall when he had had them last. He remembered vaguely juggling with them when talking to the Wing Commander outside A Flight office. Yet he was certain he had put them back into his pocket.

Then he thought: if they were found by someone who recognised them he could always deny they were his. But he'd have to get another set, a straight set, to prove his had never been lost. Toast them over a fire and the whiteness would turn to musty yellow, the colour of the dice usually used by the school.

Dressing rapidly, he looked at his watch and decided to get the bus into town. The shops would still be open and he could get a pair without much searching.

It was close on nine when he arrived back on the station. Coming from the main gate, he met the Station Warrant Officer and accepted the latter's invitation to a drink in the mess.

He knew there was something behind the S.W.O.'s smile, and it came to him when two buses pulled up outside the entrance to the mess. The N.C.O.s had been busy. They had quietly collared most of the prettiest girls in the town and brought them to the mess in private coaches paid out of the mess funds.

Slipping away from the S.W.O., he looked into the small billiard room at the rear of the mess. Fifteen players were bent over the big table. Through the haze of tobacco smoke came the sharp click of the dice.

His hand closed on the new pair he had purchased and he swore softly. To play with them would be to play with luck. With his old pair, how different it would have been. Reluctantly, he closed the half-open door and went back to the bar. As he edged round the packed door leading to the dining-room, now transformed into a dance floor, he noted the fact that the Sergeants had indeed secured the cream of the local women.

There was a surprising number of pretty girls, but they were all partnered. A pert red-head with a provocative smile and a willowy figure glided past in the arms of a Flight Sergeant. As they swung away from the doorway, he caught her eye. She smiled back invitingly. He waited impatiently for her to come round again, hoping the music would continue, for otherwise he would never find her in this mass of dancing couples.

He rose on his toes when he saw her come round again, and pointed to himself. She nodded over the Flight Sergeant's shoulder. He met her as she squeezed through the group of Sergeants round the doorway, and he was aware of one or two hostile looks that were directed at him. She was not at all sure, she told him, if it would be quite the thing to leave the Sergeants' dance. In the end she agreed, he thought, rather readily.

In the Officers' Mess he found her a table near the buffet bar.

He was coming from the bar with fresh drinks, when he saw Terry dance past with Jack Hogarth. She looked lovelier than he had ever seen her. The low-cut white evening gown, which flared from her waist, vividly accentuated the long dark hair which was hanging in soft waves on her shoulders.

He wondered how Kiwi had persuaded her to come. God, he should have waited in the mess for that phone call the New Zealander said he was to make. Now he was saddled with another girl, and he couldn't be sure whether Terry had seen them or not.

He slipped through the couples crowding the bar and made his way to his own table. Putting down the glasses, he excused himself from the red-head.

The steady beat of a rhumba came to him as he neared the floor.

Carson, he saw, was dancing with Terry. Side-stepping two couples, he tapped him on the shoulder. His skipper smiled broadly and stepped aside.

But there was no smile on the girl's face. He caught her hand quickly as she turned to walk away and, drawing her firmly to him, glided her towards the middle of the floor, away from the searching eyes of any onlookers.

"Terry, I must talk to you! There is . . ."

"Please," she interrupted; "I don't want to hear or see any more of you. I wouldn't have come had I known you were to be here. I understood from Kiwi that . . ."

"Don't hate like that," he cut in. "Please, darling, just let me . . ."

"Don't call me that." The voice was cold and cutting. "Keep that for the girl you came here with!"

"I didn't bring any one here, Terry. Just someone I met. How did I know you were . . . ?"

Before he could complete his sentence, she wrenched herself away and stalked off the floor, her gown flaring behind her. He felt his neck burn and the blood flood to his face. Wing Commander Strange danced by with a blonde woman and he saw the angry look which flashed over the Wingco's face. A few couples near him glanced curiously in his direction, plainly perplexed; and then he realised he was standing alone on the floor.

He pushed through the dancers and walked to the bar. An Australian Flight Lieutenant was sitting beside the girl he had brought from the Sergeants' Mess. Neither of them noticed him, as he slipped out of the room. The fog was swirling in from the sea as he walked back to his sleeping quarters on the far side of the perimeter tract.

It was nearly one in the morning when Susan, her evening dress pinned above her calves, slipped on her heavy coat and mounted the pillion seat behind her husband.

Kiwi kicked the starter and the motor-cycle back-fired and spluttered as he swung out of the station on the three-mile journey to the village.

The fog was getting thicker and the feeble beam from the cycle's headlamp was swallowed in the whirling, ice-cold mists sweeping over them. It reminded him of his days at elementary flying school when he had flown as a pupil pilot in the open cockpit of a Tiger Moth.

He opened the throttle wider. That was the only thing he liked at E.F.T.S., the cold bracing wind whipping past his face, singing mournfully in the struts. Slowly it cleared the alcohol from his brain.

He shouted something to Susan, but the words were carried away by the wind. He felt her hands tighten round his waist as he flashed low round a corner. His hand eased back on the throttle. The humped stone bridge of the village should be coming up soon. He felt the cycle rear. That must have been it, he thought. Suddenly he caught a glimpse of a pin-point of red flickering light in the greyness ahead and slightly below him.

His feet crunched viciously on the brake and his hand wrenched round the clutch grip.

The rear of the bus loomed terrifyingly in front of him. The brakes! . . . the gol' damn brakes! . . . he had forgotten to fix them! . . .

Two white, startled faces, transfixed in horror, peered out at him from the rear window of the bus.

A great jarring pain shot through his forehead and he felt himself floating.

"It was tragic. I just can't understand how ..." Dorton broke off, and his tired grey eyes swept from the Senior Medical Officer to Martin's white, taut face. "Both dead! Yet only a few hours ago they ..."

The Group Captain's voice trailed away and his eyes settled on the big white clock over the mess bar. He slowly turned over his wrist and saw that the clock was exactly right. His watch showed it was almost 0330 hours. They watched him leave the mess. Martin turned to the S.M.O. "Can I see them?"

The grey-haired Medical Officer shook his head firmly.

"Better leave it until the morning."

They buried Pilot Officer Leonard Kiwi MacArthur, D.F.C., and his young bride in the village churchyard on a warm bright morning in April. That evening a brooding atmosphere hung over the mess. The sombre tension in the great hall reached an agonising climax when the crew of F—Freddie marched stiffly to the bar.

Martin ordered seven large whiskies and his eyes were hard as he watched the white-coated barman lay them on the oak counter. Then, with a deliberate measured movement, all six simultaneously raised their tumblers to the solitary glass left on the long bar and drank in silence.

With the same slow motion they laid their glasses on the bar, turned on their heels and walked out to the waiting transport that was to take them, for the last time, from Nissindon.

Douglas sat alone in his room and moodily contemplated the half empty bottle of Scotch in his right hand. With an effort he willed away the mocking images tormenting his mind with memories of the past. The sequence of events revolved in dizzy circles in his brain.

He smiled again, in grim irony at the tragic fate of Kiwi and Sue. He raised the bottle slowly to his lips and took another long pull in an endeavour to stupefy his confused and troubled thoughts.

27

THE battle was on to paralyse the German railway network for the coming invasion of Europe. Again the heavies of Air Chief Marshal Sir Arthur Harris were to be the aerial sledgehammer with which the Western Wall was to be smashed, and thus softened up for the infantry.

The mass saturation raids on the great cities of Hitler's Reich were temporarily halted and the bombs screamed down on vital transportation centres in France and Belgium. With the switch from strategic targets to tactical assaults, the Squadron and the Command's losses were correspondingly lower, and Dorton was to experience nights he had never before known—nights when he sent out twenty-two aircraft, and looked on a loss of two as heavy.

And as the life of the men who flew the bombers took on a new span of time, a gayness came to Nissindon, a truculent devil-may-care atmosphere pervading the Messes. The older crews, those of S—Sugar and Y—Yorker in particular, never quite caught the new spirit. Amid the new faces, they felt like strangers in their own messes. More and more they withdrew into themselves, avoiding new friendships as they remembered the old, acutely aware how the new crews were jokingly laying odds as to which of them would finish first, which would go down.

In the mauling of the big raids, they alone were left of those crews who had known the fury of the Ruhr, Berlin, Nuremburg, Leipzig, Brunswick and the other hell-spots deep in Germany.

F—Freddie, flown by a new crew, went on the attack on Aulnoye. Later, her crew likened it to a practice bombing trip, but Douglas, in the nose of S—Sugar, took two dummy-runs before he released his bombs.

On the first run, he was about to press the bomb-tit when he remembered he had forgotten to select and fuse the bombs. On the second, he completely misjudged the drift on the sighting angle.

After they had landed, he went straight from the briefing to his hut, telling Carson he had no appetite for the flying supper. And two hours later his skipper found him in an uneasy sleep, an empty half bottle of whisky lying beside his bed.

Carson sought out Masters, who was emphatic that they should have a quiet chat with the S.M.O. Carson thought for a long time before shaking his head.

"No, Larry," he said. "I don't think it's the ops that are worrying him. No doubt they have a bearing on his condition, but Kiwi's death has jolted him badly and twisted his whole outlook. You see, he blames himself for that accident. Told me it was he who got the bike for him!"

"He's even crazier than I thought, then," Masters said: "for Kiwi had been asking everyone to look out for a cheap second-hand cycle to get him to the village."

"I know," Carson replied, "but he believes he's a Jonah. Raved to me after the funeral that he brings evil to everyone he comes in contact with. He's got some cock-eyed notion that for a long time he's absorbed the hoodoo they said was on the S Bay."

Masters laughed. "He's bloody balmy! Obviously, it's the first symptoms of the D.T.s The point is, though, what are we to do about him? This way, he's a liability to us!"

"I don't know, Larry," Carson said anxiously. "We'll have to watch him very carefully. It would be hard if he cracked up with only a few more to do. That's the devil of it!"

"It would be equally hard," Masters replied, "if we should go down some night because of Douglas not being able to bomb without a dummy-run."

Carson shrugged and together they walked towards the Flights, each wrapped in his thoughts.

Two days later, S—Sugar found they were among three crews on stand-down. Douglas, morose and edgy, refused to be persuaded by Carson to come into town with them.

He was lounging in the mess when Strange entered. The Wing Commander looked round the big room with the air of a man who had lost something. Seeing Douglas, he walked over to him.

Douglas waited until Strange nodded to him, before rising to his feet.

"Still feel in a volunteering mood?" The words were faintly mocking, and a thin smile played along the corners of the Wing Commander's lips.

"Not particularly, sir."

Strange frowned. "Pity, that, for I may have to send some S.P. into town to collect your crew."

Douglas started, and Strange noticed the flash of surprise which came over his face.

"R—Robert's bomb-aimer has had an accident. Came round B Flight hanger with his eyes shut and crashed his bicycle into an M.T. lorry. Luckily, the lorry was going slow, but he's broken his right arm. Unfortunately, we haven't a spare bomb-aimer, so it means pulling out R tonight, unless we get a replacement."

The Wing Commander glanced round the mess. "Any idea where your crew have gone?"

Douglas ignored the question, and asked: "What's the target?"

Strange's left eyebrow arched. "You know I can't tell you that unless you agree to fill in. However, I can say this, you've been on far stickier ones."

Douglas thought rapidly. Warrant Officer Tanson, a burly black-haired Canadian, was the pilot of R—Robert. He was a good pilot; in fact, could have been a Flight Commander long ago but had steadfastly refused to be commissioned.

"All right, put me down! Now, what's the target?" His tone was indifferent.

"Acheres!"

"Never heard of it, sir."

"It's a big marshalling yard on the outskirts of Paris, and you'd better be damned careful, bombing tonight. We don't want any loads going wide and landing in Paris. Get along to the navigation briefing. They'll give you all the details," he said airily.

Paris. They had never been there before. The Command had struck a few nights earlier at Villeneuve St. Georges, a railway centre just south of the French capital.

From what he had heard, the flak had been moderate, but the Hun would have got over the initial shock and switched nigh fighters to the city's defence.

Take-off was at 2125 and the whole trip was estimated to take less than five hours.

Tanson, he recalled, had a good navigator in Flying Officer Ron Hobson and an alert rear-gunner in Phil Tyson, reputed to be about the best on the squadron, with a FW 190 to his credit.

Lot worse crews he could have got. Anyway, Tanson had done about fifteen operations and was as crafty and as skilful as they came.

He had the feeling Strange was about to say something more to him in the mess. He had been acutely aware that he had been watching him lately. Caught his sly looks at odd moments. There were, too, the obscure remarks he had passed about gambling on the station.

He thought of the dice again, and wondered.

28

OVER France the stars shone big and bright above the main
force from a slow moving endless conveyor belt of black
velvet. Scanning the vast panorama of needle-sharp pointers
Douglas found Vega and Altair. High on his starboard Polaris
burned above Dubhe.

He stretched himself leisurely along the bombing mat and
watched the flak snake round the bombers ahead. He watched it
with detachment, for there was nothing he could do about it.
It was fascinating to glimpse the varied hues of the light flak, fear
chilling, when he remembered the lethal powers of the garish arcs
of fast moving light.

The glaring white flashes of the camera flares burst ahead and
around them, illuminating for seconds the black trails left by the
heavier shells. Listlessly they floated past, mute reminders to him
of their once deadly bursts.

"Sentinel One to Reapers! Bomb the Greens! . . . Sentinel
One to Reapers! . . . Ignore that cluster of Reds. They are off
the aiming point! . . . Bomb the Greens!!"

Clear, crisp and unruffled the voice of the Master Bomber came
over the R.T. from somewhere far below them, down amongst
that fiery volcano of light and heavy flak.

"Sentinel One to Reapers! . . . Undershoot that last cluster of
Greens by two seconds! . . . Do not bomb the Reds on any
account! . . . Sentinel One to Reapers, rep——" The voice
broke off abruptly.

Lurching, reeling, tilting and rolling in the slip-stream of the
bombers ahead, the greens staggered up the sword sight of
R—Robert. Douglas extended the drift handle, allowing it to
spring back into position, satisfied with his run-up.

"Steady, Skipper! . . . Steady! . . . Left now! . . . Hold it!"

The indicators were coming up nicely, and the Halifax was steady on her run.

"Sentinel Two calling Reapers! . . . Sentinel Two calling Reapers! . . . Concentrate on the Greens! Ignore all Reds! Sentinel Two to Reapers. . . . Let 'em go on the Greens!"

So they had got the Master Bomber, wheeling round the target thousands of feet below them—an aerial policeman directing the jammed traffic above, making sure that their loads went where they were intended, cutting to the minimum the risk of bombs bursting in Paris.

Douglas wondered if they would get his deputy. He had seen two fighter flares on the run-in. The FWs and the JUs were airborne.

"Steady now! . . . Stea——"

The heavy calibre shell exploded below them in a jagged, blinding flash. It bathed the nose of the Halifax in a dazzling shower of ice blue light, then suddenly plunged it in darkness.

Simultaneously with the explosion came the screech of steel ripping through flimsy metal. The blast lifted the bomber and flung it violently on to its starboard wing, where it hung precariously for a split second, before plummeting in a fast sickening dive into the technicoloured arcs of the flak. A nauseating smell of cordite filled the nose.

Douglas, partially stunned by a glancing blow from the butt of the swinging Vickers gun above him, stumbled groggily to his feet. He fell back and felt the bomb-tit tear free from its cable.

The pull of gravity as the loaded Halifax dived out of control glued him to the floor as a fly paper holds a fly. Twisting round, he gripped the bomb panel with his right hand and hauled himself slowly to his feet. Tightly clutching the spar above the computor box, he staggered into the navigation hatch. The navigator was rising shakily to his knees as he clambered into the glass-house. Tanson was slumped over the controls, his head lolling effortlessly, his hands swinging limply at his sides, as the stricken bomber hurtled down on Paris.

The engineer, blood seeping through a ragged tear in the left shoulder of his battle-dress blouse, was bent over the pilot, pulling and half dragging him from his seat.

Douglas reeled dizzily against the petrol gauges, brushed a hand across his mouth, then realised his oxygen mask was loose and the tube unconnected with the supply.

Hastily, he plugged into the cockpit's main supply cock and helped the engineer to lift Tanson from the pilot's seat. Frantically he hauled the Warrant Officer out and clambered into the seat. As he pulled back on the control column, he glanced at the instrument panel. The altimeter needle was falling through the 13,000 feet mark. They had begun the bomb run at 18,000 feet. The Halifax was dropping with the speed of a concrete pillar. . . . Then he remembered the bombs. They were still on the racks!

Plugging in his intercom, he fought with the controls. Slowly he got the Halifax out of the dive. Quickly he neutralised the rudder, eased back on the throttles and trimmed the bomber to level flight.

His head felt light and the silence was uncanny. Suddenly a babble of voices flooded through his earphones in high-pitched excited tones.

"Listen," he heard himself shout; "this is the bomb-aimer. I've got her under control. Our height is now 10,000 feet. I can hold her like this so there will be ample time to bale out. First, I'm making a check, though at a rough guess I don't reckon anything vital has been hit."

He gulped in a mouthful of oxygen and the sound of his heavy breathing came to him over his ear-phones. "If this is so, I can fly her back. You can bale out over England."

His eyes flicked over the instrument panel. "First, I'll tell you what's happened. Shrapnel from a near miss ploughed through the floor of the cockpit. Your skipper's been hit—I don't know how bad yet. The engineer is wounded but he is taking him back along the fuselage. Now give me your reports. To avoid confusion, say who you are . . .

"You O.K., rear-gunner?"

Tyson said breathlessly: "I'm okay, but bloody shaken!"

"We all are, but we're going to be all right." Douglas wondered at his own confidence. It was a lie, he knew, but he had to make them feel at ease.

Calling the mid-upper, he asked if he was hurt.

"Feel all right, except for a bump the size of a cricket ball that's hatching on my head," came the reply.

"Navigator?"

Hobson's voice was calm. "Apart from a flesh wound in the left leg, I'm fine. The W.O.P.'s fixing it for me!"

"Okay," Douglas snapped, "as soon as the W.O.P.'s through, get him to go back and help the engineer. Do what you can for Tanson. I'll steer a rough course on Polaris until you give me one for base. Remember, I want it quick, for we still have the bombs on."

"Christ!" Hobson shouted. "I thought they'd gone! Can't you let them go?"

Douglas reached for the jettison toggle, then remembered the bomb-doors were closed.

"No," he said, "they might land on some French village."

"Okay! I'll get a fix as soon as I can," the navigator retorted.

Douglas had got the Halifax to 13,000 feet, when Hobson said: "Engineer's shoulder is in bad shape. I've patched it up as well as I can and the bleeding has stopped. Skipper is seriously hurt. Shrapnel wounds in the left thigh and an ugly wound on the forehead. He started groaning, so I've given him a shot of morphia from the kit. Trouble is, it's so damned cold in the fuselage and, apart from the gunners, no one has a flying jacket."

Douglas moved the trimmer forward a couple of degrees, and watched his air-speed creep up as the nose went down. "Do you think he'll come round?" he asked.

Hobson interrupted: "If you're banking on him coming round in time to land this kite, forget it. Personally, I think he's got concussion. He's lost a lot of blood as well!"

Douglas thought rapidly for a few seconds. "All right, then; come back and set a course for home. Tell me when I can jettison this load safely."

He swung the bomber on to course 350 magnetic. The last wind they had was from the west and its strength was 35 m.p.h. If his rough calculations were correct, they should pass to starboard of Amiens. The flak from there would confirm the course he was flying.

Calling the engineer, he said: "How's the tanks? Have a look at the gauges, and then slip back and keep an eye on the skipper."

"Sure," the engineer replied. "But the tanks are fine. I changed them before we went into the target. They should be okay until I switch on to landing tanks."

The word 'landing' jarred through Douglas's brain. Christ, they talked as if they expected him to land the Halifax! Often he had toyed with the idea as he had followed Carson through on his landings. Sitting safely beside Carson, secure in his skill, it had been easy to lull himself into the belief that he too could bring the bomber down. Landing a light, single-engined Harvard was a whole lot different from a four-engined bomber . . . But what of Tanson? . . .

Static line . . . that was it! They could drop Tanson over base and the parachute would open when the line was taut. With a bit of luck, he shouldn't drift far . . .

Parachute! That was what had been niggling at his mind. No, he couldn't! Yet! . . .

The navigator's voice interrupted his thoughts. "Course for coast is 338 true. That will take us slightly starboard of Dieppe. Keep on it and we cross the home coast port of Dungeness. I'll give you a straight course from there to base, skirting clear of the London A.A. defences. Remember to switch on your I.F.F.* Anyway, I'll remind you later."

Douglas yanked the Halifax on to the new course, then levelled out. As a double check he set the course on his pilot's compass. Flying on his repeater compass, he noted, he was a couple degrees off course. His Air Speed Indicator was steady at 185.

They were ignoring the Flight Plan, but the navigator's course took them away from the known flak belts. They should cross the enemy coast at a sparsely protected area.

They flew in silence until Hobson called: "Okay, Shern, you can jettison the load. The enemy coast is fifteen miles behind us and from the silence of the gunners, they're either asleep or haven't seen anything!"

Someone, he couldn't recognise the voice, chuckled hoarsely into the intercom.

He opened the bomb-doors, glanced at the light on the panel which showed they were open, and pulled the toggle. The control column kicked against his hand and he knew they had gone.

---

* I.F.F. Identification Friend or Foe device to warn radar system in England that aircraft approaching was friendly.

Trimming the aircraft, for unloaded flight, his eyes scanned the flickering luminous dials on the instrument panel.

Hobson said: "What do you intend to do when we reach base?" The navigator's voice was matter of fact, confident they would reach their own aerodrome. It heartened him and he breathed heavily into his mask.

"Call them up, let them know our condition. Then make a timed run for you people to bale out and . . ."

"What about the skipper?" The voice, which cut in, he recognised as Tyson's, the rear-gunner.

"Put him out on a static line!"

There was a pause, and Hobson said: "We'll have to put him out fairly low, otherwise he'll drift. The wind's from the west and strong enough to take him out to sea." He cleared his throat, and added: "Even with a low drop he might come down in some outlandish place. There's the jolt of landing as well. Frankly, I don't think he could stand that in the condition he's in. The way I see it, he's got to be rushed to hospital right away!" The tone was stark in its earnestness.

Again a thoughtful pause, and the navigator went on: "Shern, they tell me you practically finished a pilot's course and have done a lot of flying in a 'Hali'—at least a fair amount at the controls. Do you think you could put her down?"

Douglas found himself shifting uncomfortably in his seat. He had been afraid the navigator was leading up to this question. Now, he had bluntly put the matter to him, a coldness came over him.

Fighting back the panic which swept over him, he remembered his main fear. "It might be a bit on the rough side, but I think I can. All rests on a good approach, and I've plenty of juice to try a few dummy approaches."

He managed to make his voice seem confident enough.

He swallowed hard. "I'd only need two. One in the rear turret to keep the tail down. The other to operate the throttles."

There was a long silence and then Hobson said curtly: "I'll operate the throttles."

This time it was the engineer who interrupted. "No, you won't! That's my job and I've no hankering for a caterpillar badge."

Tyson in the rear-turret said: "The same goes for me!"

Douglas thought quickly. "Then it's settled. The mid-upper, the navigator and the W.O.P. go. Better check over your 'chutes in case they've been holed."

"I'm staying put!" Hobson replied huskily.

"Mid-upper here. Don't take it bad, Shern, but I always wanted to have a golden 'cat' on my tie. This way I can get it easy. I'll hit the silk if it's all right?"

There was an uneasy silence for a few moments.

"I'll come with you." Douglas identified the voice as the wireless operator's.

Their decision to jump worried him. Yet in his heart he could not blame them. They would be crazy to stay.

He reached for the button to snap his intercom on, hesitated, and his hand dropped back to the control column.

Changing his mind again, he switched on the intercom. "That's sensible. Once again, I don't want those staying behind to under-estimate the risk."

They protested again, said they were staying, and he marvelled at their guts. In their minds must be a clearly etched picture of what awaited them if he misjudged the landing. His eyes swept over the instrument panel. In their position his own decision would have been clear enough—to bale out.

But without them he would be finished. With no one to work the throttles and keep the tail down, he could never land the bomber.

Hobson's voice grated over the intercom. "Switch on your I.F.F. and alter course in four minutes to 358°!"

Douglas swung the Halifax on to the new course. He thrust back on the throttles and began the descent.

As they crossed the Wash, he peered at his watch. The luminous hands pointed to exactly 0120. He braced himself in his seat. Fourteen hours earlier he had stood at the open grave in Nissindon churchyard as the coffins of Kiwi and Sue had been lowered into the freshly dug earth. The soft breeze had lifted the veil from Terry's pale, beautiful face, as she stood on the steps of the village church. He had tried to catch her eye but she looked past him . . . That had been in another lifetime.

Either it never happened or he was dreaming it all

Thank God, they had cleared the London defences. He had the ugly feeling that, despite the I.F.F. being switched on, a night fighter might have been sent up to intercept them, suspicious of a lone bomber, so well off the laid down Flight Plan. The navigator's voice scattered his reflections.

"Fly on course 010° for twelve minutes. Then we'll make the approach from the sea. That way we can't miss the beacon."

He called the engineer. "Don't forget about switching to the landing tanks."

"No chance of that," came the reply; "but I want to empty the tanks we are on first. We may need every drop."

"I don't think so," he heard himself say; "anyway, don't cut it too fine!"

As he realised the subtleness of the engineer's reply, he cursed softly. He was thinking ahead. The less petrol on board, the better if they had to crash land.

His admiration for Tanson's crew increased.

"Now . . . quiet, everyone. I'm going to call base!"

From the glass-enclosed top storey of the control tower, the runway cut through the aerodrome in a wide, long ribbon of black concrete, its edges sharply defined by the glacier blue lights, evenly spaced along the grass.

Dorton watched the last Halifax land and taxi along the perimeter track. On hearing R—Robert's emergency call, he had driven straight to Control with Strange.

The atmosphere in the tower was electric. Five men were to be left in the bomber circling above them. They would either be eating a flying supper in half an hour's time, or their broken, twisted bodies would be cremated in the petrol seared wreckage of the bomber.

It was as simple as that, Dorton reflected grimly. Douglas either landed the Halifax or crashed in the attempt. He turned from the long window, walked to the controller's desk, hesitated and moved back to the window.

Little groups of people, ground crews and crews who had just landed, were spacing themselves at vantage points beneath the control tower, expectantly waiting for the Halifax's first attempt to come in.

Dorton again paced the floor but this time he spoke in a slow, measured voice. "Apart from the wireless operator and the mid-upper, the rest have decided to stay. I've warned them once more of the risk they are taking. R—Robert is now at 5,000 feet heading inland on a timed run. On the way back, the W.O.P. and the mid-upper will jump . . ."

Dorton's mouth twitched and he gazed at the controller thoughtfully. "Get on to the searchlight battery again and tell them to pick her up. But warn them not to dazzle the pilot. Stress they must concentrate two beams on each side of her."

The controller nodded, and picked up the receiver. Strange listened for a moment, stubbed out his cigarette, then hastily lit another.

"They should all abandon the aircraft after putting Tanson out on a static line," he suggested.

His tone was decisive, almost curt.

Dorton spun round and there was a trace of irritancy in his voice.

"I have already impressed that on them; but they don't know for certain how badly wounded Tanson is."

Glancing from the Wing Commander his eyes settled on the white-faced Waaf sitting beside the controller. "Douglas is to make two approaches. If he is satisfied with them—more important, if we are—he will bring her down on the third. He's a capable man, and personally I think if his approaches are good, he can do it."

His eyes swept back to Strange. "He has had two hundred hours, you know, as a pilot and has a fair amount of time at a Halifax's controls," he said caustically.

Strange retorted tersely: "Landing a Halifax is different, sir!"

"It's been done before," Dorton snapped, "by a crew member with less experience than he has. No doubt before this war is over it will be done again!"

Selecting a cigarette from the packet on the controller's desk, Dorton tapped it on his thumb and, looking calmly across at the Wing Commander, said quietly: "He can do it, with our help. By that I mean, we are going to bring him down. At least, you will . . . you've had more experience on Halifaxes than I've had!"

"Go through the landing drill with him and get him to check

each move. Make him feel you are up there with him—his instructor, checking his approach. That will give him confidence!"

Flicking a match to his cigarette, Dorton inhaled deeply and strode back to the long window.

Four searchlights formed the long edge of a box which was slowly toppling towards the airfield. Clearly illuminated in the centre was the Halifax.

The R.T. set crackled. "Roland Robert to Mary Miss. Starting run. W.O.P baling out on count of five . . ." The voice was unnatural in its anxiety. The little group in the control room instinctively started, as the voice said ". . . Five—four—three—two—one NOW!"

There was a long pause and the set crackled again . . . "Roland Robert to Mary Miss. One W.O.P. gone . . . Mid-upper coming, same count!"

The voice was counting, evenly, and curiously calm ". . . Three—two—one NOW!" A longer pause and Douglas said: "Mid-upper gone!"

Dorton saw the parachutes billow open and swing gently against the broad beams of the searchlights.

Two searchlights swung from the Halifax, to form a triangle over the floating canopies.

Turning from the window, Dorton walked crisply to the controller's desk, and picked up the microphone. "Mary Miss to Roland Robert! Group Captain here! Listen carefully! That was a damned fine run. Both 'chutes are floating down nicely. Wing Commander Strange is going to talk you down. Try to imagine that he is sitting with you, watching and correcting your approach. Follow his instructions implicitly, and you'll find landing a Halifax isn't that difficult. Remember it's heavy, and that makes it easier to bring in . . . a lot easier than landing a Harvard . . ."

God, he had to lie, but the man at the controls of the bomber had to be put in a confident frame of mind. If he suddenly lost confidence and panicked . . . !

He dismissed the thought and said evenly: "On both approaches the Wing Commander will call out the drill. Go through each movement and repeat it. When he tells you to correct your air-speed, height or angle of approach, do so. But do it easily and unhurriedly. Above all, keep relaxed and don't hesitate to open your throttles and go round again.

"One thing more! Halifaxes have been landed by bomb-aimers before." Lying again: there was only one case he knew of, but it must be made to sound easy. . . . "So take your time about it. I'm handing you over to the Wing Commander. Is all that clear?"

The R.T. spluttered and the voice, apprehensive, almost inaudible said: "Yes, sir. I think so?"

Dorton handed the microphone to Strange, and said gently: "Get him to relax. He sounds all tensed up . . ." Turning to the controller, he snapped: "You have already alerted the crash tenders and the ambulances?"

An anxious pair of hazel eyes looked up at him. "Yes, sir: they're standing by at the end of the runway. Each end, sir."

Dorton crushed out his half-smoked cigarette and strolled to the window, his hands deep in his trouser pockets.

R—Robert's port navigation light flickered above the Drem lighting, marking the circumference of the airfield. Strange was speaking into the microphone in a thoughtful, calculated tone.

"What height are you at?" he heard him ask.

Over the R.T., Douglas's voice seemed anxious . . . "Five thousand feet."

"Good!" he heard Strange say. "Keep the airfield's boundary lights in view and make a wide circuit. Start losing height until your altimeter reads one thousand feet. Keep about one mile and a half from the main runway. By the way, you have changed the tanks to landing?"

"Yes, sir. We're on tanks one and three!"

The light on the glide path indicator glowed red. Still too high. God, no, he was too low! His hands trembled as he pulled the stick back, his eyes instinctively flicking over the Air Speed Indicator.

One hundred and twenty knots. Even his air speed was a little high. Douglas glanced at the engineer sitting beside him. Saw the tensed haggard face relax into a forced smile.

No room for error. The engineer must be experiencing what he had gone through with Carson on his first wild take-offs. But it must be a thousand times worse now. His mind ran over the indicator colours. He should have known. He had sat many times beside Carson, coolly, critically watching those lights, judging the angle of approach.

Red—Approach low. Green O.K. Amber too high. Flaps . . . yes, he had done that. . . . Maximum lift-quarter flap. . . . Carson always said thirty degrees. . . . Hell, he wasn't sure. . . . All messed up. . . . Keep calm. . . . Relax. . . . Go round again.

He swallowed twice, and from his throat something croaked over the R.T. Couldn't be his voice. . . . "Roland Robert to Mary Miss. Going round again."

His ear-phones crackled and Strange's voice purred in his ears. "What went wrong? You seemed to be coming in smoothly enough."

Smoothly enough? May have looked that way from the control tower but he was approaching low and fast. From their visual lookouts they'd have spotted it eventually. Then it would have been too late. No: he was on his own. The knowledge lanced through him. And with it came fear. There would be a distinct time-lag between any mistake he made and its correction from the watchers below. And the time-lag could be fatal. He shot a side-look at the engineer, noted the expectancy in his eyes, and licked his lips, before nodding.

Smoothly the throttle handles were pushed forward. The Halifax roared over the runway, climbing for another circuit.

"Under-cart up!"

"Under-cart up," the engineer said.

"Flaps up!"

"Flaps up." The engineer smiled, but his face was wan, in the dim blue light of the glass-house.

As his right hand dropped to the trimmer wheel, Strange's voice came over.

"You're doing fine. Get back to one thou'; you look a bit high from here. Start your bank. Easy! Not too steep! Level out now. . . . Fine! You're down wind. . . . Ease back on the throttles and get your air speed down to 150!"

Douglas, his eyes scanning the panel in front of him, his hands resting lightly but firmly on the control wheel, repeated the check.

"Get your Revs up!" The engineer was already carrying out

234

the Wing Commander's order as he banked the Halifax into the funnel.

The runway lay ahead, a shaded matchbox glimmering on both sides with ice-blue pin-points of light.

"Radiators closed." The engineer was good, amazingly good. "Wheels." The voice was crisp, efficient. Douglas glanced from the altimeter. All right for height. The A.S.I. showed 115 knots. He saw the lights come on the panel and knew the undercarriage was locked.

The runway was slightly larger now. About the size of a half-crown stamp, he reckoned.

Strange's voice was throbbing through his ear-phones, tense and anxious. "Do you hear me, Douglas? Repeat A.S.I., reading, height and colour on indicator?"

His eyes swept ahead. Half amber and half green were glowing on the glide path indicator. Gently he moved the control column and slapped on full flap. He swallowed nervously and repeated the check over the R.T.

"Fine. Just get your air speed down to 104. Keep that angle ... use the throttles, not the stick." Strange urged.

The indicator was steady on green and the pale blue lights were leaping to meet him. The blurred outline of the boundary hedge whipped under the Halifax's nose. The lights boxed him in.

"Cut!" he shouted. The engineer closed the throttles. As he did so the Wingco's voice echoed Douglas's command. The start of the runway whisked beneath. He felt the bomber float and his feet threaded lightly on the rudder bars.

Something warm and sticky trickled down the sides of his face. . . . "Ease back! ... Keep that nose up! ... Stick right back! ... Hard now! ..." Strange's order, tense and rasping, jarred in his ear-phones.

The Halifax's great undercarriage slapped heavily on the black concrete, then bounced. The wheels touched heavily again, and settled. With an effort he stopped the control column from kicking forward. The blue lights were hurtling past and the rudder was heavy, when with his right hand, he knocked up the ignition switches.

The lights were coming slower now, the controls sluggish and sloppy. Christ, they were down and lumbering to a stop. The black ice ahead was clearer, more sharply defined, and was taking longer to flow into the yawning belly of the bomber.

His feet juggled on the rudder pedals. Keep her straight! Cautiously Douglas felt for the brakes, and tapped on the pressure. R—Robert rolled to a stop, and a great weight lifted from his shoulders. He slumped forward and the Sutton harness dug deep into his shoulders. A hysterical torrent of words flooded over the R.T., but his bruised and tension-racked brain refused to decipher them.

Hobson and the others found him like that when they clambered back from their crash positions in the fuselage. Beside him in the co-pilot's seat, breathing heavily, fresh trickles of blood seeping through the thick wool of his battle-dress, the engineer grinned weakly at them.

Inhaling deeply from the cigarette the navigator thrust into his mouth, Douglas undid the Sutton harness, looked through the windscreen at the dimmed head-lamps of the vehicles racing towards the Halifax, and said: "God! You people have guts!"

Hobson's shoulders jerked. A weary smile creased his drawn lips.

"Better get the skipper out," he whispered.

As they left the briefing room, Strange took Douglas aside and guided him to his car.

When they pulled up outside the darkened huts of C Flight, Douglas knew beyond all doubt that Strange had known all along. Knew he had forgotten to take his parachute with him in the rush to stand-in for R—Robert's bomb-aimer.

The tension he experienced during the approach flooded back, but this time with it came an overwhelming tiredness. It seeped in waves through his body, sapping what strength he had left. Now they would all know and, knowing, would understand the whole truth of why he had had to land the Halifax.

All his life it had been like this. Empty triumphs, hollow victories which turned out so different from the way he had planned. He turned slowly, and his eyes met the steady stare of the Wing Commander. For a moment he looked into Strange's grey eyes, then his gaze swept to the blacked-out huts in front of him.

"You'd better pick up your parachute!" Strange's tone held no hardness; it was softer than he ever thought it could be. Yet it bit into him with the force of a whip-lash. . . . "Or had you forgotten?"

"No," Douglas said heavily; "I realised it when I first thought of baling out." His voice sounded flat, dead and hopeless.

"Better check it in then, and forget about it. At the same time, get rid of these!" Strange said warmly.

Something rattled in the Wing Commander's hand and he felt two cold cubes being thrust into his hand as he stepped out of the car.

His hand groped for the switch. The three naked bulbs in the long room glared in a hard harsh light. He walked to the dust-covered bench running alongside the far wall of the hut, and picked up the dirty brown pack that was his parachute. Stumbling dazedly towards the door, he switched out the light.

For a little while he stood on the steps, breathing the clear cold air of the night. Then he flung back his left hand and, in a wide swinging arc, the two ivory cubes curved over the grass verge. The rough surface of the field would probably counteract the delicate balance of the dice. For once they would fall over for a straight, unloaded throw, he mused.

The red glow of the Wing Commander's cigarette burned from the darkened interior of the car. He strolled over and laid the 'chute on the back seat.

He wanted to tell Strange many things, how he could never have got the bomber down without his help, how his voice, crackling over the R.T., had kept him anchored to the pilot's seat when panic swept over him as the lights of the runway rose to meet him.

But Strange knew it all, and a great deal more besides.

The Wing Commander let in the clutch. They were almost at the Officers' Mess when Douglas spoke . . . "It's no use saying how much I appreciate what you've done. I mean, coming from a person like myself it would be . . ."

"I told you to forget it!" Strange interrupted. "You'll get an immediate award for this."

"Does the Group Captain know about the 'chute?"

"He does not!" Strange interjected sharply. "It's better that he doesn't. You see, he thinks quite a lot of you! For some reason or other he looks on the S Bay as his own particular one. Can't think why. Can you?"

"No," Douglas said miserably. "I can't."

29

FOR the rest of that week Douglas sipped the heady wine of a man who had chanced all and come through. Yet his triumph was bitter sweet. One man had known about the parachute and that man had also known about the dice.

There was no doubt but that he had dropped them when talking to Strange. The Wing Commander had picked them up, probably played idly with them, and in doing so, must have been struck at how they always rolled to a stop with seven uppermost.

He had been wrong about the Wing Commander. Wrong about a lot of things and a lot of people since he had come to Nissindon.

May came and was on the wane when the last bomb of their tour was stencilled on the nose of S—Sugar. It represented Aachen, German marshalling yard, where Hitler's armoured divisions were streaming through to reinforce the defence of the Western Wall against the coming invasion.

Carson brought them back with his quiet confidence and his implacable strength. Scanning the developed aiming point pictures in the Intelligence Room later that morning, Douglas shook his head. His voice was distant, incredulous. Masters looked at him steadily, unbelievingly. "Call it what you like," he said. "We got our A.P. and our tour is over!"

Douglas stared hard at the picture, smeared with A.A. and air-to-air tracer streaks. "Our plate should have been blank."

Carson leaned over his shoulder, tapping the picture with his right hand. "How come?" he asked.

"I judged it roughly. I'd forgotten to switch on the graticle sight. Realised it when the T.I.s were coming along the sight, but I would have died of heart failure if we had to go round again!"

Carson laughed softly. "I'd have jettisoned the load if you had called for a dummy-run." They laughed with him and filed out of the room, leaving Carson alone with his bomb-aimer.

Carson waited until Douglas turned from the board, and asked: "Now that our tour's over, have you any plans? I mean, you could get another chance at a pilot's course if you wanted. Would be a lot easier, too, now that you're commissioned and with the record you have."

Douglas smiled wanly. "Once I'd have jumped at the chance, Lew. It doesn't matter any more." A doleful expression clouded his eyes and he shook his head gravely. "No, Lew, it wasn't meant that way. Besides, I'm too tired to begin it all again."

Carson glanced at the floor. "Larry and I are putting in for the Pathfinders. Don't think instructing is up our street. If you'd care to come along with us, we'd like to have you."

"God! Haven't you two had enough?" Douglas asked sharply.

Carson chuckled, and ran a hand through his unruly hair. "Things will never be quite as bad as they were. The next tour, being a second, will be shorter. On the whole, a lot easier . . ." Carson tapped his bomb-aimer's left tunic pocket . . . "Pathfinder wings would look good there . . . You could tear up that address book and start another!"

Douglas frowned. "I tore it up some time back. I'm a phoney, Lew! Even this ribbon they've given me was got under false pretences. You may look surprised, but you'll be a damned sight more shocked when I tell you I had to land R—Robert. There was nothing else I could do. . . ."

"Get a hold of yourself, Shern. It's merely the anti-climax. It comes to most who have just finished a tour. You could always have baled out, but I bet you never even gave it a thought!"

"With what?" Douglas rasped.

"God, you don't mean you . . . ?"

"I mean that exactly! Strange knew it. He found my pack after I'd gone."

"That doesn't alter one iota of what you did," Carson said.

"Not if I had told them in the first place. Made it clear to them. I didn't because I was terrified they would have all elected to jump. Then I could never have got her down."

"What matters," Carson said firmly, "is that you did. You had the confidence to bring her in and there was no need to alarm them. Anyway, Tanson might not have lived had he gone out on a static line. That's the way I look at it. I'm certain that's the view the Wingco took. There's no need ever to mention this again."

"You really believe that?"

"Every word of it!"

Douglas looked searchingly at his skipper. "You make me feel a whole lot better, Lew," he said at last. "Better than I've felt for a long time. It might surprise you, but I've hated this last while on the squadron. Loathed every minute of it. Not so much the flying, but the mess I'd got into. You had no idea about . . ."

"Forget that too, Shern," Carson interjected. "I happen to know more than you think. You see, we were getting worried about you. I had a talk with Kiwi. He straightened a lot of things out. He was a great guy, that. A man I was proud to know . . ." Carson broke off, as if embarrassed by his display of sentiment. Quickly he said: "Come on, I'll buy you a drink. It's been a long time."

"He was all that, and a great deal more," Douglas said. "It was his last night and I never saw him. . . ."

Carson took him gently by the arm and moved towards the door.

"Come on; it's been a long time since I've got tight. Let's get stinking and shock them all!"

Douglas eyed his skipper critically. "Drink for drink and no kinds barred?"

"No kinds barred!" Carson said quietly.

Douglas grinned, and in silence they walked towards the mess.

Sergeant Watson carefully laid the oak leaf of his mention in despatches along the top seam of his left tunic pocket. The needle pricked the horny skin of his thumb. He cursed lightly.

Curly looked up, with an air of mock surprise, from the cigarette he was rolling. "Pity you ain't got a ribbon there, Tubby! It would show it up better. Can hardly see it from here."

"To hell with you," Watson snapped.

Curly chuckled deep in his throat, licked the gummed paper and struck a match. "Wonder what the new crew are going to be like? Funny, but when I clapped eyes on Carson and Co. I never thought we would see them screened!"

Watson pulled the thread tight, deftly knotted it and cut it with his teeth.

"They were scruffy all right," he agreed. "Made me ill to look at 'em. The engineer was the only one who looked at all promising. Strange to look back and see how wrong we were! Often wonder what that engineer is doing?"

"Cleaning out latrines somewhere!" Curly answered. "By the way, do you think we'll get a forty-eight? I mean, there's no sense in keeping us around the station since we're crewless."

Watson fondled his right ear before replying, "Should do. New crew aren't due until Monday."

His armourer scratched his chin thoughtfully. "Wonder how Carson and Masters will get on? They're going on Pathfinders, the gunners tell me. Tried to get the rest of the crew to go with them."

Watson shook his head. "Trouble with you, Curly, is that you're always wondering about something. Since you've asked, I'll tell you. They'll do fine. That fellow Carson is going to end up as a Wingco or in the 'Missing' columns of *Flight*. Same goes for his navigator. Both are set on permanent commissions and the more 'gongs' they collect, the better."

Curly looked pensively at the spanner in his right hand. "Tell me, Tubby, what's the attraction. The only sane two in that crew are the W.O.P. and the engineer. The rest are plain crazy. Titch is slap-happy. Callaghan is a bundle of nerves, has been ever since his brother crashed. Douglas is a psycho case. Asked me last night if I believed that the S Bay was evil . . ." The armourer hesitated as he saw the look which had come into Watson's eyes. "Evil, that's what he said!"

Watson slipped on his tunic, and slowly buttoned it.

"You mean, Curly, that you asked him if he thought the hoodoo was still on the bay? Don't interrupt! I know damned fine you planted the idea in his head. Know, too, how you both got so bloody drunk one night that the two of you took on all comers in the village pub!"

Curly flushed and his lips parted to reply when Watson rasped: "For Christ's sake, don't interrupt! The truth is, that Douglas looked on himself as a Jonah. You're every bit as superstitious, as crazy as he is. Together, the two of you kept harping on the so-called bad luck of this bay so often, that both of you came to believe he'd absorbed the spell!" Watson paused before adding: "I don't know what's been troubling Douglas this last while, but he's been acting like . . . God! Stop trying to psycho-analyse the whole crew and . . ."

"Acting like who, Tubby. . . . Pastone?"

"You've no right to say that, Curly. Just because he smelled of drink on that last trip . . . Hell, here's the old man! Get weaving on that bloody turret!"

Dorton pulled up under the port engines of the Halifax, and leaned out over the driving seat window.

Watson saluted sharply and walked towards the car. The Group Captain waved lightly. "Well, Watson, you and your team can feel particularly proud today. You have taken a crew through a tour of operations against some of the heaviest defended targets in Europe. Never once had they to turn back through engine trouble."

Turning in the direction of the armourer, Dorton beckoned him over. "For that matter, Watson, never once did their guns jam. And I can't recall them ever having a bomb hang-up on them!"

"No, sir," Curly said, "they never brought one back. Too mean a bomb-aimer for that."

"Mean?" Dorton repeated absently. "Oh, the bombs! Yes, he was mean about them. Keen on his aiming points! Fine type! That's how it should be. No good you fellows sweating to load them if the bomb-aimer is careless where he puts them."

He chatted easily with them for a few minutes. Abruptly, he let the clutch in and they watched him drive down the perimeter track. "He's made this squadron! He's damned well made it himself!" Watson said, speaking his thoughts aloud.

"He and Carter!" Curly said proudly.

Dorton parked his car outside the main block, housing the administration building, and walked up the two concrete steps to the long corridor. Idly, he flicked through his In-tray. He signed the leave and posting drafts of S—Sugar's crew. The I.O. had been responsible for the D.F.M. going to the engineer. That was a mistake. They had all earned a ribbon, but the quota was not elastic. Callaghan should have had it. Too late now. He should have stopped that one. But then, he was away that day and Strange had counter-signed it. Nothing he could do now. Strange should have known that the engineer and the wireless operator were comparative newcomers to the crew. Their first wireless operator had been killed, while their original engineer had gone L.M.F. He was certain he had acquainted the Wing Commander with the cases. Probably it had slipped his mind. Things were better now. And they would never get that bad again. The wheel had turned. Carter and himself, he reflected, had helped to instil a new feeling into these men. At least he liked to think that. The thought nevertheless gnawed in his mind that they had merely managed to give the wheel a slight jolt. Squadrons had had runs of bad luck and heavy losses before. Suddenly, without any reason, their luck had changed. A new atmosphere came over them as the wheel rolled a notch, its lethal scythe hovering over some other airfields.

Group would undoubtedly take a different view. To them, he would be the Commanding Officer who had put 186 back into the air again. Blithely they would forget that even during its darkest days the squadron had never failed to operate, had never been grounded in its entirety. Yet it had time and again failed to meet "Maximum Efforts", the supreme attestation demanded by Group, Command, or for that matter the Air Council.

It was mostly a matter of approach, understanding their difficulties and, in understanding, mapping out the formula on which they could rise above adversity.

Carter's resolute courage and his utter contempt for danger had blazed the way for them. He himself had merely guided them, making things easier when they were on the ground by cutting out unnecessary restrictions.

Their heaviest loss of any night in the last month had been three aircraft. This last ten days they had lost none. True, the targets were less heavily defended—marshalling yards in France and the Low Countries. They were now the top priorities, and the flights over enemy territory were correspondingly shorter. Soon the invasion would come and the odds would become better still.

He picked up the three forms, neatly pinned together from the In-tray on his desk, noted it was a request for marriage leave from the pilot of the new C—Charlie.

Dorton smiled and his eyes settled lightly on the wall calender. May 30th. It would be a June wedding, then, for the Waaf Corporal in the Adjutant's office. He leaned back in his chair.

That was the girl Farley had tried to get posted to Group. He needn't bother any more. She'd get a different type of posting now. Better that way. Marriages. . . . First there was Carter's then MacArthur's. Both brought him numerous anxious moments. Neither of them knew it, with the possible exception of the Wing Commander, would never know now how much worry their marriages had caused him. Carter's, because it had been broken; MacArthur's, because it was beginning.

His thoughts wandered on. Thank God, S—Sugar had come through. Y—Yorker was the last of the original crews left since he had come to Nissindon. Two more trips and Y—Yorker, with some luck, should also be screened.

They were going out again tonight. The Belgium military base of Bourg Leopold was the target, a base, according to Intelligence, which had been crammed two nights previously with crack detachments of German infantry.

Corporal Diston squatted on an empty oil drum and nibbled nervously on the nail of his right thumb. From the Y bay he could see the long lights of the flare-path twinkling ghostily. Twenty-two Halifaxes had gone out that night and twenty-one had so far landed. Y—Yorker was the twenty-second and she had called control while still some way from base to say she was approaching on three engines.

Diston crushed out his cigarette and shuffled wearily to his feet. His armourer cocked his head expectantly and motioned him to be silent. The drone from the homing bomber started low and gradually stepped up to an impatient growl. A few moments later they heard it roar overhead.

"That's Yorker all right," Diston said confidently.

His companion grunted as the sound of the Halifax's engines faded away as it swept inland, losing height before turning to begin the landing approach. He was about to reply to the corporal when a strange new note reached his ears. The high-pitched scream of a low flying, fast moving aircraft. Diston looked up sharply.

"Twin engine job! Sounds like a Mosquito," he added casually The muted roar from the Halifax's radial engines drowned the sound of the newcomer as Y—Yorker banked gracefully into the funnel of the flare-path.

Suddenly the angry rattle of machine gun-fire, intermingled with the harsh staccato cough of cannon fire, drifted to them from the black, star spangled canopy above. The airfield's air attack sirens wailed. A stream of light A.A. shells from the ground Bofor guns hosed in a fiery pyramid of criss-crossing arcs of white, yellow and red light.

The long lights of the flare-path were plunged into darkness and abruptly the guns ceased firing. Above the syncopatic beat of Y—Yorker's engines rose the deeper, full-throated whine of the intruder.

Diston caught a glimpse of the hurtling shape above him, saw for a fraction of a second, the huge white crosses on the under surface of the black wings. Saw the long lines of the tracer dart wickedly from the leading edges of the wings to lick along the Halifax's bulbous fuselage.

Flames flashed back from the wing petrol tanks. Y—Yorker lingered uncertainly in her flight. Then her nose dipped and she over-shot the runway to fall lazily below the cliff line. Seconds later a muffled boom rolled up from the sea.

Diston swallowed and shouted to his armourer but his words were smothered as the ground defences opened up again. Then the firing stopped. The high pitched snarl of the intruder faded softly on the still night air, died quickly, as the German night fighter headed further out to sea on a course for the Dutch airfields.

The Corporal walked unsteadily to the oil drum and sat down heavily. His armourer came over and he saw him fumble in his tunic pocket and bring out a ball of cotton wool. Slowly he unwrapped the wool and extracted a tiny leather covered box. Snapping back the lid, he flashed on his torch. Diston leaned over. Blue and yellow rays glinted from white satin. Gently he took the box from the L.A.C. and glanced at it for a few moments before handing it back.

"That the ring?" he said bitterly. The L.A.C. nodded and Diston rubbed his chin reflectively.

"He was going to ask her tomorrow night. Shern's girl, wasn't she?"

"Yes," his armourer replied softly. "Jack was crazy about her."

Strange met them as they walked towards the briefing room.

"It was Yorker . . . there couldn't have been any . . ."

The Wing Commander shook his head grimly. "No, Corporal. It was Yorker. We tried to warn them that an intruder had attacked two aircraft over an inland 'drome but we got the alert too late."

"You'd better have this then, sir. Their bomb-aimer—Jack Hogarth—left it with me," the armourer said limply.

He eyed the Wing Commander doubtfully. "Had, I think a sorta feeling something like this would happen. I never took it seriously, though, for they all have funny ideas when they're nearing the end of a tour. Told me he had bought it this morning."

Strange frowned, took the grimy ball of cotton wool, felt the box inside. He looked puzzledly at the L.A.C.

"It's a ring, sir. He was going to get engaged tomorrow," the L.A.C. smiled thinly. "Was to have been a surprise. Only he wasn't sure how she would take it. Hadn't known her long and . . ." The voice tailed off.

"Local girl?"

"Yes, sir."

"Know her?"

"Only slightly, sir. She was at the Officers' Mess, the night of the accident." The L.A.C. paused. "Understand Pilot Officer Douglas knows her."

Strange ran his tongue over his lips. "Very good. I'll see she gets it." Distractedly he added: "No point in sending it to his relatives. They probably know nothing of this girl and it might only upset them, if he hadn't mentioned it to them."

DOUGLAS laid his suitcases on the wet, glistening surface of Platform II and waited for the night connection to York. In his pocket was his leave pass, travel voucher and the order posting him as a bombing instructor to an O.T.U. in Oxfordshire.

He checked his watch with the big white blur of the station clock. The clock, he noted, was five minutes fast. In another fifteen minutes the train would be in. The man on the barrier had said it was running on time.

Barely a dozen people were on the platform. The gentle June drizzle had stopped. The light from the evening sun glinted and gleamed on the wet concrete. From his stance he could cover everyone entering the station through the arched doorway below the barrier.

His crew had left Nissindon five days earlier, Carson and Masters, on leave, pending a posting to a Pathfinder Squadron. They'd be going out again. The others had gone to various units as instructors. It was unlikely, even extremely remote, that their paths would ever cross again. It was better that way. They had long since learned of each other's strengths—more important, each other's weaknesses.

He sighed as he thought of Terry—now he was leaving her for ever. He had spent five days aimlessly wandering about the town in the hope of meeting her. Strange had thought him churlish for his refusal to take the ring to her: but he had not felt inclined to tell him of his affair with the girl.

The bars in town had been conspicuously empty of Air Force men all day. For this was the Day. . . . D-Day . . . yet he had to learn it from the B.B.C. news while waiting in the lounge bar of the Atlantic.

He'd have given a lot to have been on the raid. Not with the assault forces going up the beaches, but with the mighty air armada pounding the gun emplacements and the concrete defences the ground forces had to get through.

He had heard the bombers come home around 0439. Maybe they were standing by again tonight . . . He looked at the clock impatiently. There was not much time now, and yet he still hoped. He had watched the youngster deliver the note and he had seen her open the door and take it.

The girl in the white tight-waisted raincoat and the yellow beret gazed into the spluttering embers of the fire in the grate.

Two hours ago it had been bright, its red glow warming the sudden coolness of the June evening. It was then she had read the note from him and, on her first impulse, had gone into the hall to put on the raincoat and beret.

The soft light from a dying sun filtered through the window, casting pale shadows through the room. It showed up the frayed ends of the carpet, and the cigarette burns where it fringed the hearth.

The monotonous ticking of the clock on the mantelpiece grew louder, almost deafening in her ears. A long sliver of sunlight splintered on the tiny diamond, set among the pin-points of emerald, which peeped from the white lining of the box, on the table beside her.

She saw by the clock it was fourteen minutes past eight. Slowly she tore up the note, dropped the fragments into the grate and rose to her feet.

Deliberately and methodically she unfastened the belt of her coat, and slipped it off, tossing it over the chair. The beret she let listlessly fall to the floor.

Limply she sank into the armchair and ran her long slim fingers through her hair.

Suddenly her body heaved and she began to sob.

A long white stream of compressed steam shot from the wheel

base of the engine. Jerkingly, then smoothly, the connection for York pulled out from Platform II.

Douglas glanced at his watch. It was twenty-five minutes past eight.

Still watching the platform, he flicked up the leather strap. The window rattled into the heavy door of his compartment.

There were two figures on the platform. The tall, gaunt ticket collector with the white hair and the plumb red-faced woman with the wicker basket over her arm.

He pulled hard on the leather strap, and slipped the bottom notch over the brass stud on the carriage door.

He sat wondering for a while, and a thin smile creased his lips. Well, they were two people among a few million more for whom things hadn't worked out as they had intended. But they might have had. He had had the chance and had thrown it away through his own wrongheadedness.

He thought of Johnny and Loraine: Kiwi: Sue; Carter and Carson. A lot of lives had ended. A lot of lives were changed. The battle for a finger-hold on the beaches of Normandy would transform many more.

In the distance he heard the steady roar of the bombers, coming nearer. Rapidly the noise rose in pitch. He let down the window, and the pulsing drone of the Lancasters and Halifaxes battered against his ear-drums in stunning waves of sound.

He leaned further out of the window, twisting his head skywards. Everywhere, as far as his eye could see, they were tiers upon tiers of four-engined bombers flying steadily towards their target. This time they were not heading seawards, on course for the great industrial centres and cities of the Third Reich but on an arrow-straight flight for Southern England—Beachy Head and a Channel littered with ships.

He closed the window, lit a cigarette and noted that his hands were trembling. He put down to excitement the tingling sensation which was flooding through his body.

The carriage was empty. He rested his feet lightly on the seat opposite and gazed pensively at the smoke curling in wide, loose eddies from the end of his cigarette.

He recalled Hogarth and a slight shudder rippled up his back to twitch the muscles of his shoulders. His thoughts switched to the girl in the drab grey-bricked house in the little street which ended in a cul-de-sac, and a spasm of deep sorrow came over him.

It would have been better if he had been up there with the bomber stream. No time, then, to think and dream of what had been. Better now, after all, if he had gone with Carson and Masters.

THE END

SS PANZER BATTALION
LEO KESSLER

JANUARY 1940 . . . the coldest winter within living memory and the phoney war still paralyses the Western front. But at the Adolf Hitler Kaserne, a new battalion of SS troops trains for a mission so secret that it is known only by its WEHRMACHT code name, ZERO.

THE VULTURE — Major Horst Geier — is the only man who knows that the objective is the key Belgian fortress guarding the junction of the River Meuse and the Albert Canal — the most impregnable fort in Europe, which must be taken regardless of the cost in human lives if Hitler's hand-picked SS Panzer troops are to turn the flank of the Maginot Line.

SS PANZER BATTALION is the first novel in a new series about ASSAULT REGIMENT WOTAN, a crack unit in the Waffen SS.

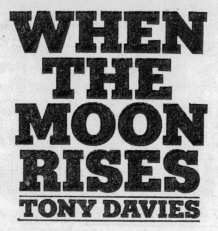

WHEN THE MOON RISES

TONY DAVIES

A trainload of British prisoners of war steams
slowly through the Italian mountains.
Suddenly there is a screeching of brakes and
the sound of shots from the guards. Two
British officers have made the leap for
freedom . . .

Tony Davies's first escape bid ends in
recapture and transfer to a new camp in the
north. When he escapes again he and his
companions are faced with a 700 mile walk
along the spine of the Appenines to the Allied
beach-head at Salerno. The journey begins as
a schoolboy adventure : it ends as a terrifying
and deadly game of hide-and-seek where
the Germans hunt down the fugitives like
animals and courageous Italian peasants risk
their own lives to save them.

ESCAPE FROM THE RISING SUN
IAN SKIDMORE

'The oily dust fell everywhere, on hungry stragglers searching for their units, on armed deserters who roamed the streets searching for loot, on . . . fear-crazed men fighting their way at the point of a gun or bayonet, pushing women and children aside . . . The dead lay in the streets . . . but no one collected the corpses now.'

Singapore had fallen. The British Army, retreating in disorder before the onslaught of the Japanese shock-troops, had been told to surrender. One man was convinced he could escape.

Geoffrey Rowley-Conwy seized a junk and sailed for Padang. There he joined a group of fellow officers for a desperate escape-bid in a dilapidated sailing boat across the Indian Ocean to Ceylon. 1,500 miles of open sea swept by the fury of the monsoon and patrolled by Japanese fighter planes on the lookout for British survivors.

'One of the best and liveliest escape stories of the Second World War . . . enthralling.'
Times Literary Supplement